Th   s

K
Hall
&Co.

The Holiday Murders

MARSHA LANDRETH

G.K. Hall & Co. • Thorndike, Maine

Published in 1999 by arrangement with Walker Publishing Company.

G.K. Hall Large Print Paperback Series.

The text of this Large Print edition is unabridged.
Other aspects of the book may vary from the original edition.

Set in 16 pt. Plantin by Minnie B. Raven.

Printed in the United States on permanent paper.

Library of Congress Cataloging-in-Publication Data

Landreth, Marsha.
     The holiday murders / Marsha Landreth.
         p. cm.
     ISBN 0-7838-8827-9 (lg. print : sc : alk. paper)
     1. Turner, Samantha (Fictitious character) — Fiction.   2. Women
physicians — Wyoming — Fiction.   3. Wyoming — Fiction.
4. Large type books.   I. Title.
PS3562.A4774 H65   1999
     813′.54—dc21   99-047888

For Knute Landreth, M.D.,
who made Brant, Ross, and Sam possible.

Prologue

"You can't go in there, Dr. Turner. Mr. Talbot —"

Sam pushed through the county attorney's door before his secretary could bar the way. "Goddammit, Jeffrey! This is the last straw."

"What's this?" Jeffrey picked up the speeding citation the coroner slapped onto his desk.

"It's a goddamn present from the Easter Bunny!"

The attorney ran his fingers nervously through his thinning blond hair as he weighed his options. His option, actually. Sam had no appreciation of subjectivity and viewed the world through clinical eyes. Perhaps after another couple of years Sam would get used to their ways. Though he wouldn't hold his breath.

"Mr. and Mrs. Kowaski, would you mind waiting in the outside office for a moment? Apparently, Dr. Turner needs to speak with me."

His secretary, having followed Sam in, ushered out the complacent middle-aged couple. "Would either of you care for a cup of coffee?"

When the door closed, Jeffrey waved the citation. "You bring it on yourself, Sam. You can't drive like you're still on a California speedway. This is Wyoming. Slow down."

"Goddammit, Jeffrey, do you know where I got that sucker?"

He read the citation. "Lewis and Clarendon."

"Ha, ha." Sam pounded on his desk, tumbling a stack of briefs. "A half a block from where the rest of our illustrious police force was so diligently trampling all over my evidence. By the time I got there the body'd moved from the floor to the bed, for chrissakes!"

The ticket fell from Jeffrey's hand. He slumped in his chair, his eyes unfocused. "Another woman?"

Sam backed off and plopped down in the chair Mr. Kowaski had warmed. "You didn't know? That's two now. And I'm willing to stake my reputation it's the same man."

"Both of our reputations couldn't get us elected dogcatcher in Sheridan. Not now."

Sam took in a deep breath, then pushed up out of the chair. "So. You'll fix the ticket?"

Jeffrey shook his head. "Tell you what." He reached into his gray suit for his wallet. "I'll pay it."

"Goddammit, Jeffrey! I want you to fix it! They see this one and they'll take my license."

He took out a twenty and paper-clipped it to the ticket. "Wyoming's not going to take your license away . . . you're a doctor."

Sam smiled. "Really?" The smile vanished as quickly as it had come. "It's obvious *you've* never gotten one. The last one cost me fifty-five."

Jeffrey slipped the twenty out from under the paper clip. "I'll fix it."

8

"That's what I love best about you." Sam headed for the door.

And Jeffrey was looking at what he loved best — the way her skirt swished as she walked.

1

Sam woke with a start. Last night's fireworks display exploded in her mind's eye as she fumbled for the alarm. She gradually became aware that the room was light, but not with the summer brightness that usually woke her before the shrieking alarm. She collapsed on the pillow, her head butting against the journal she had been reading before she fell asleep. Her glasses bit into her left shoulder, but she didn't care. She wanted only to recapture the dream. John and she were sailing on their catamaran. No, it was too large to be their catamaran; more likely a schooner.

The blaring came again. She flung an instinctive hand to the alarm and banged the top. It didn't help. She was awake enough to recognize the blasting as a horn when it erupted a third time.

"Sam," came a voice over a loudspeaker, "are you awake?"

She stumbled out of bed, tripping over Boomer halfway to the window. He had already surveyed the situation and decided it had nothing to do with him. She scrambled to open the window.

"Doc Turner, can you hear —"

"What do you want, Hank?"

The sheriff continued to speak into his

handset, his voice booming out of the speaker mounted between the red swirling lights on top of his brown Bronco. He had no fear of waking the neighbors. Guy Walker's ranch was a good mile down the road, and he was the nearest. Besides, Guy was old and most likely didn't wear his hearing aid to bed. Jake, Sam's Indian ranch hand, wouldn't have counted in Hank's mind. "Jeff Talbot called and asked me to fetch you to town. Said he didn't want you turning your outfit over in the barrow ditch. Almost hit a deer myself on —"

"Goddammit, Hank! Just tell me what's happened."

"What's happened? Wasn't yesterday the Fourth of July? A holiday —"

Another murder. Sam slammed down the window and turned to struggle into faded jeans as she looked around the room for her boots and socks. The boots were on the patio. She'd gotten them muddy tramping through the tangle of vines down by the creek after Boomer's Frisbee overshot. Boomer had hidden the socks. No doubt behind the stack of magazines downstairs in the library. He was big on stashing things there. Too bad a hundred-pound yellow Lab isn't tall enough to drop dirty clothes in a washer. She tucked her nightshirt into her pants and then tore it out when she couldn't zip up. She took a fresh pair of socks out of a drawer and ran down the stairs.

She had to get there before the city's police

11

chief and his good ol' boys went through the place like bulls in a glass factory. Jeffrey was there; maybe he was fending them off. She grabbed her mud-caked boots and hurried through the kitchen, down the hall. She stepped into an early-morning mist and gingerly started across the sharp red shale drive. Enough pain. She plopped down on the wet grass. The lawn needed mowing, she realized as the blades sprang up around her. "Where'd it happen, Hank?" she asked, brushing shards of shale from her feet.

He put his lips to the mike. "Colony South."

She pulled on a sock. "My hearing's tops, Hank," she shouted over the roar of the creek. "You don't need the loudspeaker now."

A vermilion tint climbed to his beige Stetson. With lanky clumsiness he reached a brown sleeve through the window, stretching his jacket tight across his broad belly, and racked the mike. His stoop shoulders and thrust jaw contributed to the general notion that he was a simpleton. A pity he didn't wear his height better. He was smart enough to take advice, something she couldn't say for the moronic police chief.

She tugged at a boot. "Know the address?"

"Wrote it down." He leaned back through the window. Behind him to the west a spidery strato-cumulus cloud heralded the inevitability of more unseasonable rain.

"Never mind." Colony South was a small housing development on the south hill at the edge of town. She should be able to see the bustle of excitement from the road. She got up and raced by Hank.

"Hey, hey, hey," he said, jerking her back. "Jeff said I was to fetch you in."

She thumbed toward her red Jeep Cherokee. "Got to get my bag."

He let go.

Sam dashed to her Jeep and jumped in. She was halfway down the drive before he was able to turn around and follow. The red lights were flashing and the siren blaring by the time she pulled onto the blacktop.

"You're supposed to ride with me," he called over the loudspeaker.

She stuck her hand out the window and motioned him ahead. As he finally passed on the straightaway, she yelled out the window. "Need my car, Hank." She was happy to hear the siren die, and didn't mind the red lights going off, but when he slowed to fifty-five, she swung around him. The lights and siren started up again, and he chased her that way for most of the ten miles. Every so often he'd reprimand her over the loudspeaker. When a pickup merged onto the two-lane highway, signaling the start of morning traffic, Hank zoomed around and gave her a red-flashing escort.

No-Chin Skip was leaning against his patrol car talking to Jeffrey. She was uneasy that the chief was nowhere in sight. Bill was probably in the house playing detective.

13

The shrimp from the newspaper was beside her before she started up the walk.

She had no use for him or the worthless newspaper he worked for.

"What is your opinion on this third holiday murder?"

"Sherman, I haven't been here half a second yet. What am I supposed to know about any of this?"

"Can I take some pictures inside?" he asked as he blinded her with the flash of his god-awful camera.

"When pigs fly." She felt Jeffrey's fingers tighten at her elbow. He slipped the black bag she always kept in the Jeep out of her hand and whisked her up the brick steps.

"Why do you always do that to him?" Jeffrey whispered.

"Because he asks stupid questions. And he can't write for beans. Where's Bill?"

"Out of town."

She lifted her eyes to the clouding sky. "Thank you, Lord."

Sam stepped into the gold-flecked marble foyer and then onto the mauve carpet in the living room. The house smelled of fresh paint. A plastic tarp covered the living-room couch, but she could see enough of it to know that it was mostly pink, like everything else in the room. "Pretty gaudy, don't you think?"

Jeffrey shrugged diplomatically.

The house, perched on the side of the hill, had

14

a commanding view of the Holiday Inn out by I-90. A meadowlark chirped and pecked at the moist dirt around the pink roses. "Who lives here?"

"I sent the sheriff after you. Why didn't you come with him?"

She was actually touched by the gesture. In some company Jeffrey would be considered quite the catch. With his baby blues and fair hair he looked more like a hunk tennis pro at a swank country club than a county attorney in a dinky cow town of 15,000. But he, like every other man she had met since John's death, inspired nothing more than friendship. "Seems Sherman's not the only person around here asking stupid questions. I might want to get home sometime. Where is she?"

He nodded down the hall as he picked a hair off his red sweater and inspected it.

Sam plucked the hair from his fingertips and started down the hall. "You're not going bald, Jeffrey. You're just paranoid."

"Bald."

"Paranoid," she called over her shoulder.

"I can see my scalp."

"And vain." She whirled around and pulled at her T-shirt. "Look at all this hair."

"That's dog hair."

"Boomer's not bald either," Sam said, stopping dead as she stepped into the bedroom.

The legs of an attractive brunette were straddling the mahogany bedpost on the bottom right

15

side. She was naked, save the nylon stocking around her neck. "That's strange."

"What?" Jeffrey stayed as close to the door as possible. He didn't have the stomach for this kind of thing. Most people didn't.

"She has fair pubic hair." He didn't comment. "Who is she?"

"Lisa Henderson. New owner of the travel agency."

"New in town?" Sam knelt beside a satin-sheen pink flowered nightgown. It was ripped, but not bloodstained.

"Six, seven months, according to a neighbor."

Sam leaned over the body to have a better look at the bulging eyes. "Family here?"

"Don't think so."

Sam wandered over to the woman's kidney-shaped make-up table. Lisa Henderson had expensive taste. There was one blue case of Christian Dior lipstick after another lined up at the base of a three-way mirror. She picked up the nearest tube and uncapped it. The pink stick was worn almost to its plastic casing. She picked up a pyramid-shaped bottle of perfume. Two and a half ounces of perfume, not cologne. "Fred Hayman Beverly Hills 273," she read. "Fancy." She dabbed some on her wrist as she walked over to Jeffrey. "Take a whiff." She held her wrist up to Jeffrey.

"Nice." He leaned back against the doorjamb.

"Expensive, wouldn't you say?"

He nodded.

She put it back in the space between two French brands she'd recognized. "Wonder why she'd move here. Has the look of a model or actress."

"Someone might wonder the same about you."

Sam took the rape kit out of her bag. "Who found her? Kind of early in the morning to be paying a visit."

"The next-door neighbor. She thought she heard some commotion over here. Sent her husband over when he got home . . . after the bars closed."

"Did she see anyone?"

"No. Heard a scream or two. A door slam. Her dog barked." He took a rape case out of the pocket of his ski jacket. "Guess you don't need this one."

Her cheeks were inflamed. She felt the prelude to a lecture. "Guess not."

"You always carry a rape kit in your bag?"

"Not always."

"Why this time?"

"Did they get pictures yet?" she asked, shrugging off the question.

He nodded and looked down the hall. "What is it, Skip?"

"Thaddeus is here to pick up the body." The funeral director was Johnny-on-the-spot, as usual. Skip came in and leaned over Sam's shoulder to gawk at the body. He was so close Sam could smell coffee on his breath.

She sniffed the head, smelling a strong scent of

chemicals. She ran a comb through the hair; the victim had had something done to it recently. She would put a strand under the microscope and see if the woman had enough melanin to be a brunette, but she doubted it. "She's a natural blonde, I'm almost certain."

"That seems backwards," Jeffrey said from the door. "A blonde dying her hair brown."

"Maybe she didn't want folks to know she was a dumb blonde." A bit of a southern twang crept into Skip's voice. He hadn't always lived in Wyoming. He reached a finger out to touch her hair.

Sam slapped his hand away. "You fool. Go stand beside the sentry until I've finished. Or better yet, in the middle of the street."

He moved to the door. "Jeff, you'll like this one. There's a hundred-dollar bill on the table. There's a smart blonde at one corner, a dumb one at another, the Easter bunny at the third, and Santa Claus at the fourth. Which one's going to get the hundred-dollar bill?"

"The smart blonde?"

"No," Skip slapped Jeffrey on the back, "the dumb blonde. The others don't exist."

Jeffrey and Sam locked eyes. "Dr. Turner has taken offense, Skip."

"Oh, sorry, Dr. Turner. I didn't mean blondes like you."

"How's that, Skip?" She tried to keep her voice smooth.

"You know. I mean, you don't even wear lipstick. I meant —"

18

Jeffrey cleared his throat. "Why don't you go outside and tell Thaddeus we'll call him in as soon as Dr. Turner finishes."

"Yes, sir."

When he was gone, Jeffrey walked over to her. She felt him gather up her hair and run his fingers through it, down her back. "Other women need to give nature a hand. You're a knockout the way you are."

Sam sighed. "Think she was hiding from someone?"

"Looks like our boy. Same M.O."

Sam nodded. "I'd stake my career on it. I meant . . . I don't know what I meant."

"I think she's just another random victim."

"Me too. But it's strange. And look at the cutis anserina on her appendages. You don't see that every day." She took his hand. "Here, feel." She stroked the goose bumps on the victim's arm.

"Don't." Jeffrey pulled away.

"It's of no diagnostic significance, but I always find it an interesting postmortem occurrence. Don't you?" She turned to see Jeffrey pressed against the wall.

"Really, Sam. Here's a beautiful young woman who's had her life snatched away, and all you care about is gooseflesh. Isn't anything sacred to you?"

"Jesus Christ, Jeffrey! Give me a break." She turned back to her work. She wanted to be gone before Thaddeus came waltzing in. He reeked of years of formaldehyde. Not to mention he still harbored ill feelings over losing the election to her. Most of the coroners in Wyoming were undertakers.

Maybe she should think of the victims more as the living people they'd been. No, then she'd go crazy. That three-year-old girl sacrificed by devil worshipers still crept into her dreams every now and again. And John, of course. She should have been able to save him.

2

A gust of fall rustled the pages of the Pentagon logbook as Natalie wrote *Derek Turner, visitor.* He held the corner down for her. The civilian security guard nudged him through the metal detector. Natalie had put on fifty pounds since he'd seen her last. She wasn't slim then either, not like the days at West Point. How he'd envied his roommate. She was a brunette in those days; now she was well on her way to being gray. She wasn't forty yet, but Tom's three-year lost battle with cancer had taken its toll on her as well.

"Must be lunch hour." He gestured toward the uniformed and civilian personnel hurrying toward the tunnel that led to the parking lot. "You look good," he said, giving her a hug.

"You always were a liar."

He hugged her all the harder.

She squirmed free. "You can't imagine my surprise when I heard your voice," she said as they started down the basement hall. "What brings you to Washington?"

A very mysterious summons. "Just wanted to see you."

"Don't believe that for a moment. Read your article on Algeria not too long ago. Don't you ever get tired of traveling?"

"What? Tire of the romantic life of a foreign

21

correspondent? Banging one out from the trenches to the soothing sound of clacking keys?"

"Don't give me that! I followed Tom from camp to camp all over the world. I know better."

He slipped an arm around her well-padded shoulders. "So how are the kids?"

"Tommy's at West Point now."

"You're kidding!"

She sighed. "We're getting old, Derek. Of course, you hide it better than I. You don't look much different than you did twenty years ago. Tall, lean, military bearing, and your Grecian-god good looks."

"You're making me blush, my dear."

"Who would know with that tan?" He maneuvered her out of the way of an Army colonel she nearly ran into. "I could forgive you all that. What I can't forgive is the thick dark hair that shows no signs of graying."

"Your eyesight's deteriorated anyway."

She laughed in the merry way she had when they were fresh and their futures seemed so bright, before life had the chance to rob them of their rose-colored glasses.

"And Angel? She must be in high school."

"Thanks for reminding me," she said sardonically. "Let's take the stairs. I need the exercise. You make me feel old."

"You're not old." They started up the decaying stairway. "The Defense budget must not include building maintenance," Derek said, pointing to a big hole in the puke-green wall.

"If in doubt, buy a truck. That's their motto."

She led him down the corridor to the A ring, the innermost ring. It was akin to going from suburbia to ghetto. "Let's stop a minute. This is the last window." They looked out over the park setting to the white gazebo at the very center. The trees had donned their autumn colors. "The gazebo restaurant is only open in the summers."

"How come you're not down there?" Derek asked as he pointed out the noontime joggers.

"Should be. And you could watch with them," she teased, pointing to a crowd of cigarette smokers on a balcony overlooking the park. "You do still smoke, don't you?"

He patted his suit pocket. "Afraid so."

Natalie opened the door marked "684," snaked through a maze of cubbyholes, and stepped around a pile of discarded computer parts. "This is my palace." The room — about the size of a jail cell — was narrow and window-less with a desk at the far end and a table running along one of the side walls. The walls were covered with soundproof ceiling tiles. The ceiling boasted big areas of peeling green paint. Derek suspected the makeshift office had once been a computer room. The army takes care of their own; after Tom's death, a job was found for her. She pulled out a chair for Derek and then sat behind her desk.

"Judging from the computer equipment in the hall, you haven't been in here long."

"Six months. This is the government, Derek. You remember the government?"

They talked of old times, Tom's death, and her kids. A quick glance at his watch launched Derek from the chair. "I've got to go."

"I'll be here when you're ready to sign out."

"Thanks, but I can get out alone. No fuss." He gave her a kiss on the cheek and started for the door. "When I get back to New York, I'll drive up to the Point."

"Don't tell him I'm worried."

He winked. "We thought we knew everything back then. It never would have occurred to me that my parents might have worried."

Derek climbed to the fifth floor and then hurried through the corridors to the E ring. Unlike the offices where Natalie worked, these were glass sealed and in top maintenance.

"Derek Turner." He held his wallet to the glass.

The Marine guard looked hard at Derek's I.D., then his list. He picked up the phone. Derek amused himself by counting texture bumps on the wall while he waited. He'd gotten to well over two hundred before the glass doors opened and a man in a gray suit walked toward him, his hand extended. "Thank you for coming. I'm Adam Pershfeld."

"Derek Turner," he said, shaking the hand.

Adam signed him in and clipped a badge with a red-striped bottom to the lapel of Derek's navy suit. "Follow me."

The office was large and well appointed. Oak

24

bookcases rimmed the side walls. The books looked like the kind bought by the pound. Green plastic plants were strategically placed around the room. The large picture window behind the oak desk overlooked the Potomac.

"I was afraid you wouldn't come," he said as he motioned to a chair. He took the chair behind the desk as if for the first time.

"Well, I am curious as to why you sent for me."

Adam tapped a gold Cross pen against the side of the desk. "It's really a very simple matter. A woman under the Witness Protection Act has been murdered."

"Witness Protection Act? Why am I at the Pentagon? I thought the U.S. Marshal's office was downtown in the Justice Building."

"I'm with the Defense Intelligence Agency. We're involved due to the nature of her testimony." Adam watched Derek's face for signs of interest; Derek made sure there were none. Adam flipped the pen to the desk. "We need to know if her death was related to a treason case."

"So?"

Adam laced his hands. "It happened in a small town in Wyoming, and we haven't been able to get anywhere with the local yahoos. We sent a man out, but he came back empty-handed."

"Why?"

"The coroner. Wanted a court order."

"Surely you can get one."

Adam nodded. "We want to keep a *very* low profile."

Derek laughed. "So why call me, the town crier?"

Adam leaned over the desk. "You know the coroner."

"I don't know anyone in Wyoming. Let alone a coroner."

"Your stepmother."

Derek's back went ramrod straight. "My father's second wife, not my stepmother." He fumbled for cigarettes. "I thought she lived in San Francisco. What's she doing in Wyoming?" It took six tries to ignite his lighter. Longer for the tip of the cigarette to catch.

Adam leaned over and retrieved his pen. "She owns a buffalo ranch. Thought you might do a feature story on her."

Derek drew deeply on his cigarette, tasting the warm nicotine. He blew rings of smoke toward his host. "I'll pass."

Adam stabbed at the blotter centered on the desk. "You can voluntarily accept, or I'll see that you're ordered to."

"You going to call the feature editor and have her order a foreign correspondent to do a story on a Wyoming rancher? I'd buy a ticket to see that."

"Langley. We know you're CIA. We'll call Langley if we have to."

Derek took a last drag, then crushed the cigarette into oblivion. "You do that."

Derek had fortified himself with Scotch on the

plane, but he would have had to be in a drunken stupor to enjoy the hundred-and-forty-mile drive from the Billings, Montana, airport to the Turner ranch in northern Wyoming with Jake Immatoby, the silent, old Indian who drove the dusty pickup in a slow, weaving fashion. Although Sheridan had its own airport, Derek wasn't able to book a seat on a commuter flight, nor could he for another month. Hunting season.

They got off I-90 at Sheridan. Derek had to admit that it was one of the most picturesque places he had ever seen. And he'd seen plenty. The Big Horn Mountains towered over the green valley to the west and curved around to the south before leveling out on the eastern plains. They continued on a two-lane road about ten miles to a spot-in-the-road called Big Horn. A corner Texaco station, a general store/post office, and the Last Chance Bar made up its commercial enterprises. After another five miles they turned onto a blacktopped service road. Derek's sixth sense told him they were almost there when Jake turned onto the dirt road; a sick sense questioned that as they continued on and on. Finally, they slowed as they approached a cloud of dust, then stopped. Suddenly a figure on horseback appeared next to Jake's window.

The woman slid from her horse. Slight, medium height, twenty-five or so. That part of her pale blond hair that the wind hadn't blown wild was drawn into a tight knot. And neither the absence of makeup, the dust-powdered skin and clothing, nor her somber expression could diminish her beauty. Her marital status was hidden under gloves.

"I swear, Jake, I'm going to give you leave to shoot them the next time they jump the fence."

Jake got out of the pickup in the same manner he had driven, without a word.

She slid behind the wheel, drove the right set of wheels down into the ditch, and accelerated through the cloud of dust caused by the herd of buffalo. Derek's heart climbed to the right side of his throat. Her lead foot was the only thing keeping the pickup from flipping over.

"Did you have a nice flight?" she asked, swinging the pickup back onto the road ahead of the buffalo.

He nodded absently, and looked back at the buffalo that were now eating dust. Then he glanced at her, deciding the trip might not be a total waste after all. "I'm Derek Turner."

She whipped her head around, a strange expression flickering across her face. Her eyes didn't quite meet his. She turned them back to the road.

"Is something wrong?"

"No."

"You seemed surprised."

"It was the familiar . . . you have John's voice."

Her words dashed his enthusiasm. He should have known who she was. Looking out the window at the too quickly passing scenery,

Derek realized he was losing his touch. She wasn't in her twenties. She was thirty-four, four years younger than he — something his older sisters had never let their father forget.

Derek had been even more surprised that she agreed to the interview. Almost as surprised that he had been ordered to take the case. He suspected she still harbored some ill feelings over his sisters' threat to take her to court. After their father's death she had split the estate four ways, but his sisters didn't think she deserved even that. Their mother's lawyers were quick to point out that even if they could break his will leaving everything to the new wife, Samantha was still entitled to half. No more was ever said, which suited him just fine.

The woman made a quick left and zoomed up the red shale driveway bordering a rushing creek. She pulled to a stop in front of a large cedar house. "I'll show you to your room," she said over the sound of the water as she hurried to the front door.

Derek lifted his suitcase and his small laptop from the back of the pickup. Both were covered with a layer of red dust. A yellow dog, waist high, sniffed appraisingly before sprinting toward his mistress.

The house couldn't have been ten years old, and failed miserably in its attempt to be both rustic and luxurious. He followed boot and paw clicks along the Mexican tile in the hallway. He caught up with them at the threshold of the library. The pine walls were covered with built-in bookcases haphazardly filled with books and journals. He recognized the wicker furniture; it had graced the porch of his family's summer cottage in New England for more years than he cared to remember. The Star of India rug had been his grandmother's. They hadn't been allowed to walk on it. Now he could see where hot sparks from the fireplace had left char marks.

Samantha opened the next door. The coldness of the closed room slapped him in the face. "Your room. I'll build a fire in the stove," she pointed at the Franklin stove in the corner of the room, "when I get back from the hospital."

Before he had a chance to tell her he could build his own fire, she skirted around him and opened the door across the hall. "Here's your bathroom."

He looked into the bathroom and wondered what she expected him to use for towels. She was halfway up the stairs before he had a chance to ask. He heard her hurried footsteps overhead, the creak of the bed, first one then the other boot skip across the floor. He couldn't understand what his father saw in her; she was so . . . unsophisticated.

Derek set his laptop on the floor by the door and carried his suitcase to the bed. His clothes had come straight from the cleaners and were on hangers. It was a good thing: the closet was bare. The exposed pipe in the closet gurgled from the running water of a shower overhead. He placed his hand on the pipe, feeling only the cold steel.

He looked around the spartanly furnished room. A bed and a stove competed for his attention. A dresser would have been a nice touch, or even curtains on the floor-to-ceiling windows. Perhaps she thought the evergreens shrouding the house offered enough privacy. Whatever, he didn't like the room, and he didn't like being in her house.

Dop kit in hand, Derek placed his suitcase on the closet floor and then started across the hall to the bathroom. He caught a glimpse of a pair of trim ankles between the hem of a denim skirt and black flats. Four paws followed down the stairs.

She shook her long, damp hair. Still no makeup, and somehow he sensed it was because she couldn't be bothered. Her curly eyelashes and arched eyebrows were several shades darker than her hair, though still blond. No wonder she had been able to bewitch his father. Her high cheekbones gave her an aloof regalness. Her eyes were blue or green; Derek wasn't certain, since she couldn't seem to raise them to his. She wore a wedding ring, not that he cared now.

"I have to go back to work. I'll fix a couple steaks for dinner when I get back." She hurried down the hall, then stopped. The light glaring off the twenty-foot window bank turned her into a shadow. "Your father's car is in the garage if you want to go anywhere. The keys are in the glove compartment."

31

He managed a smile. "Thanks. I'll just hang around the ranch."

After she left, he wandered into the garage. He was not disappointed to find a silver Mercedes 450 SL convertible. What better car for a man trying to recapture his youth?

3

Sam drove the thirteen miles back to the hospital by rote, glancing at Boomer on the seat beside her. "It's uncanny, isn't it? You could see it, too."

Wiping a vagrant tear from her eye, she pressed harder on the accelerator. "Do you think he has any idea how much it hurts me to look at his face?" The facial lines weren't as deep, and his hair hadn't started graying, and he appeared to be even taller than John's six feet, but otherwise Derek was the spitting image of her late husband.

Somehow she expected him to be a boy, not a man in his own right. More tears slipped down her face as she remembered the warmth of John's protective arms and the crackling fire as they sat in their beach house listening to the roar of the ocean. He adored his children. And she loved listening to him talk about them. She laughed when he told how exasperated he and Derek's mother had been when at the age of two Derek became a renowned climber. After months of finding him on top of cabinets, on the washer, straddling doorknobs, he finally met his Waterloo as the chandelier in the dining room plummeted through the table with the child still clinging to it — even as it shattered over the marble floor. John had made a point of adding that it had been the same table that later bore Derek's initials.

The stories flashed one after the other through her mind. Picking him up at the police station after he and some other Boy Scouts had broken a street lamp, graduation from West Point, watching the young officer receive a bronze star for gallantry in Vietnam. It had broken her heart to listen to his stories and know that their estrangement was her fault.

Sam slowed, seeing the police car waiting at the school crossing. The clock on the dash read 4:30, the time when the twenty-mile-an-hour school zone reverted back to thirty, but she didn't want to take the chance of getting another speeding ticket. The police department derived special enjoyment from issuing her tickets. So much so that the state had sent her a little missive saying she would have to appear before a board of inquiry the next time she was ticketed.

She crept along. They wouldn't — couldn't — take a medical doctor's driver's license, but she hated to think of the humiliation of having the whole town read about a board of inquiry calling her in and slapping her hands. And the local newspaper loved printing such news.

When the marked police car disappeared from her rearview mirror, Sam floored the accelerator. A few blocks later she made a sharp right into the parking lot and pulled to a stop in the doctors' parking area. The attending physicians would still be in their offices. Only she and the radiologist were hospital-based, and his car was noticeably missing. She supposed that meant no doctor was in the hospital. She rolled down Boomer's window and jumped out.

The sign in front of her Jeep read: "SICK GRASS — absolutely no visitors"; Sam vaulted it, momentarily catching the hem of her skirt on a corner. She ran across the autumn-blanched grass and dashed through the emergency-room door.

"They pay you two for —" Sam left the thought dangling in air as she worked her way over to the nurses' station for a closer look. "You two need to ask for a raise if you can't afford two books."

Carol, the heavyset, older nurse, waved the second half of the paperback. "Sherry couldn't find another copy of *Gone With the Wind* at the bookstore. I'm giving her her daily ration."

Sherry, by comparison, was a frail, wet-behind-the-ears nurse. Her lips curled into a smile as she held up her meager pages. "Carol could read a little faster."

Sam slapped the top of the counter. "Makes sense to me. Well, this isn't getting my work done."

Sherry sprang from the chair and followed Sam to the door. "I've got to get back to the floor anyway." She waved the pages at Carol. "Get busy and read, you hear?"

"I'll bar the door and let no one in," Carol called as the pair passed through the swinging doors.

Leaving Sherry at the elevator, Sam said, "Let me know if the South wins this time."

"If Carol ever gets that far," Sherry said. She tapped the up button as though she was sending Morse code.

"Just remember, tomorrow's another day." Sam hurried to the front desk to turn on her house light, signifying her presence in the hospital. Hers was the only light lit, which meant positively that there hadn't been even one doctor in the building. It was a sore subject; the hospital needed a full-time E.R. doc, and she would continue to press for one. "Hello, ladies," she said to the five women behind the business counter. "Where's Ken?"

A small woman with a fetching British accent answered, "Said he was going home for a few minutes. About an hour ago."

"Must be slow over in Radiology. Wish I could say the same for the lab," she said, hurrying off.

Although her office in San Francisco had been discreetly hidden in the bowels of the prestigious hospital, Sheridan's lab sat smack-dab between the busy E.R. and the even busier Radiology department, with the administrative offices directly behind it. It was another sore subject.

She paused a moment at Larry's door. The illustrious administrator was slumped over his desk, reading or napping. His polished scalp reflected the light overhead. "Larry?"

He snapped awake.

"You must have been sweating bullets. But rest

assured. Now that I'm here, you have a doctor in house."

Larry pretended interest in the computer printout in front of him. "There's a whole row of doctors across the street."

"All anxiously awaiting your beck and call. Forget that they have patients wallpapering their waiting rooms." He pretended not to hear. "One lawsuit, Larry. Just one lawsuit will cost more than an E.R. doc's salary for ten years." He didn't respond. She slapped the wall and hurried down the hall.

Sam snatched the messages being held out by the lab's secretary. "Thanks, Kate."

Kate threw the plastic cover over her typewriter. She was nothing if not punctual. Come five she would be out the door. "Did you get your big babies back?"

"Think so. Jake's with them," Sam called over her shoulder as she grabbed her lab coat from a hook behind her cubbyhole door.

"What's he like? The guy from New York." Kate placed a sheer scarf over her billowy-styled, frosted hair, reminiscent of the sixties. It was so plastered with hair spray, it didn't move.

"What's he like?" *Like my husband.* "Tall, dark, and handsome." Sam went into the lab.

Kate, killing the fifteen minutes until she left as best she could, stood over Sam as she peered into the microscope. "What was he wearing?"

Sam held up a finger and put the Pearlcorder to her lips. "Bronchopneumonia. Two foci of pneumonic consolidation. A bronchus is filled with exudate. The intervening alveoli contain edema fluid and intermittent white cells. Overall intense vascular congestion." She turned it off. "What was who wearing?" she asked with enough irritation in her voice to silence anyone but thick-skinned Kate.

"The guy from New York." Kate buttoned up her coat.

Sam looked at the next slide. "I didn't . . . A navy-blue suit."

"Really? He wore a suit? My husband doesn't even own a suit." As if in a trance, Kate started for the door. "I want to go to New York someday."

Go to New York? Sam had half a notion to stop Kate and tell her that disappointments come when one lets reality get in the way of one's fantasies. But she knew the advice would fall on deaf ears and only cause Kate to be a good second late leaving work. After a few more slides, Sam felt a tap on her back. "I'm leaving now, Dr. Turner."

"Good night, Jerry." Sam slipped the slide into the box and took out another.

"Call the boiler room when you're ready to leave. Someone will walk you to your car." The chief tech knew her well enough to know she wouldn't bother. The odds against being attacked in Sheridan were even more astronomical than being killed by a Scud missile. "You'll call?"

"Certainly."

38

The code over the P.A. interrupted their conversation. "I don't believe this," Sam said as she brushed past Jerry. Running toward the E.R., she checked her watch. Sure enough, just after five. It would be a coronary. Some poor sucker trying to finish up his work had keeled over. One day it would be her, but not today; she didn't have time.

Carol had just put on the EKG leads when Sam arrived, pushing through a knot of hospital workers, each having come with the noble intention of giving a helping hand, but none high enough on the pecking order to take the reins of command. After a split-second evaluation in which she noted a weak, thready pulse that suddenly arrested, Sam started calling the shots. "Start the clock." To the paramedic she knew from the YMCA's weight room, Sam said, "Start compressions, I'll bag him. Carol, get the lifepak and set up a drip."

Time both stood still and flew during the five critical minutes. In slow motion the clock's second hand swept as Sam's mind raced. She watched the ashen-faced man's chest rapidly rise and fall.

"Thought you were going to bar the door."

Carol shrugged. "He slipped in when my back was turned."

"And I was going to nominate you for employee of the month." She watched the ventricular fibrillation rhythm on the cardiac monitor. "Get the paddles." Sam grabbed them as Carol took over the bagging, then smeared them with jelly. "It's two hundred on three." The room was stuffy with onlookers. The Ice Capades couldn't gather a larger crowd. "Stand back, one, two-everyone-clear, three." She put the paddles to the man's chest.

Holding the paddles up, Sam continued to look from the patient to the monitor. She was losing him. "Three hundred-watt seconds. Again on three." She looked around. "Stand back, one, two-everyone-clear, three." The paddles again jolted an electric shock through the man's body.

"I'll take over, Dr. Turner." Sam craned her neck around to see the out-of-breath internist. Apparently George was the doc on call and had dutifully dropped whatever he had been doing in his office to hurry over, just as Larry expected. Handing over the paddles, Sam melted into the crowd and then silently and swiftly left the E.R.

It had been one hell of a day. She had started the morning down at Buffalo's hospital looking at frozen sections of a breast biopsy. The afternoon brought an autopsy at the V.A. hospital and, of course, the phone call from her neighbor telling her the buffalo were grazing in his pasture. Now she had to hurry home to feed John's son.

What a shock the letter from him had been. She believed . . . no, she knew John's family thought she had leprosy. Not one of the children bothered to see John after the marriage; nor did any of them attend his funeral. Derek had written to say he had been out of the country, but the other two offered no excuse — though they were plenty quick to have their attorney write about John's money.

Night had long since blanketed the town when Sam finished spot-checking the pap smears. She turned out her light at the front desk as Dr. Miller turned his on. Sam smiled up at the tall, husky man, then frowned. "What's medicine coming to when the radiologist has to work after five?"

"That's a pretty low blow, coming from a pathologist." He ran his fingers through his silver-tipped blond hair. "I could expect that from the OB's or the internists, but I thought we were soulmates."

Sam really liked this jolly family man. "Say, speaking of soulmates, where were you during our usual five-o'clock E.R. break?"

"Shit . . . again?" His smile dissolved. "Fuck."

Sam winked at the switchboard operator stationed beside the doctor's lights. "Dr. Kenneth Miller, for an educated man, you certainly have a very small vocabulary." She laughed as she turned on her heels.

He caught her arm and whirled her around. "Did you save the patient?"

She shook her head. "George came over . . . but the man was gone."

"Well, at least he had a chance with George."

41

Sam shot him a warning look. She knew his remark wasn't a slam against her abilities, and she knew who he meant. She also knew that not all doctors were created equal, and she knew he knew, but there was no reason to say so out loud. "Well, I've got to go."

"Say, do something different for a change and drive home slowly. The streets are full of some very strange-looking little goblins."

"I just got it," she said slowly. "That's why you're here so late . . . X-raying the Halloween candy."

Ken snapped to attention and placed his hand over his heart. "My civic duty."

Sam crossed her eyes. "You just want to read your name in the paper tomorrow giving statistics on how many sacks of candy you examined."

"Better there than in the court calendar for a speeding fine."

One of the girls behind the counter stifled a giggle. Sam licked her finger and placed an imaginary mark in the air. "That's one for you, you S.O.B."

In his best John Wayne imitation, Ken said, "Smile when you call me that."

Sam put another mark in the air. "I've got to go." She started backing through the automatic doors. "I have to go home and feed company."

Ken beamed. "Female? Or as in male companionship?"

"A hermaphrodite, you asshole."

"Transverse pseudohermaphroditism, I hope."

"The gonads being female, you mean?" She took a couple of steps forward to close the door. The chilling wind was sweeping in behind her. "Enough about his anomaly —"

He pretended to snatch something out of thin air, then looked conspicuously into his cupped hands and opened them as if he were freeing a trapped butterfly. "His. You said his. A male visitor."

"Doctor Watson should be so astute." She backed out against a gust of wind. "Anyway, have to get going if I'm to be back before the trick-or-treaters get all of Bob and Betty's popcorn balls." The old doc and his wife put on the best Halloween extravaganza this side of the Mississippi, maybe both sides.

"Don't you have any taste? Get the carameled —" The word "apples" was lost as the glass door closed between them.

4

Derek walked the grounds around the house. It wasn't until he told his mother he was doing a feature on Samantha Turner that he learned all this had been his father's fantasy. Retire and move to the wilds of Wyoming and live the slow-paced life of a rancher. Derek's mother had laughed at the idea, and his father had never retired nor left the Bay Area, but obviously his father's young widow had realized his dream.

He strolled down the path to the stable. The small cedar shack beside it was Jake's Place. So said the sign over the door. Jake was nowhere to be found. Not that Derek expected to engage him in stimulating conversation even if he did stumble across him.

Leaning on the corral fence, facing southwest toward the Big Horn Mountains and the setting sun, Derek felt a euphoric sense overtake him. He took pictures of the herd of buffalo, peppered with a few elk, as they ate hay from three large steel-framed racks. The magazine would love the pictures. No sense in not doing the feature; he had to be here anyway. He told himself to forget personal feelings; this was nothing more than an assignment. A cushy assignment at that. Lisa Henderson's death had set off a frenzy of security questions. They had reams of papers on everyone associated with the case, but they had no answers. He would get whatever he could and slip quietly out of Sheridan.

The herd of buffalo was framed by red-rimmed clouds against a blue mountain backdrop. He only wished the pictures could describe the deafening quiet. Everyone in Manhattan should have a chance to listen to it.

Derek went in when the crisp autumn wind chilled him to his bones. He lit the fireplace at one end of the living room and a Franklin stove at the other. He started a fire in his bedroom, then wandered into the kitchen. The house had electric heating, but the thermostat was turned way down. He toyed with the idea of turning it up, but her words earlier indicated she would build a fire. When in Rome . . .

Left to his own devices, he found enough vegetables to make a tossed salad. Obviously, she never threw anything away until it had grown a culture, and so he passed on carrots, celery, and a head of lettuce with brown liquid oozing out of the plastic sack. The pint box of cherry tomatoes was iffy. A loaf of French bread on the counter had soaked up the blood from the thawing steaks beside it. He fixed the dry part.

He was hungry, and as much as he wanted nothing to do with her, he wished she would come home. He was tempted to broil one of the steaks over the countertop grill and eat alone. It was something that had become second nature during his childhood. Doctors, even pathologists, weren't reliable. His father had missed many birthday parties, baseball games, and pinewood derby races.

A car screeched to a halt outside. He threw on the steaks.

She talked to the dog and cat, promising to feed them, all the way down the hall, then he felt her presence in the kitchen. After an uncomfortable few moments of silence, he turned; she stood frozen in the doorway and looked as if she'd seen a ghost.

"Something wrong?"

She pinched her lips together, and then shook her head slowly. "It was just . . . from the back. Your father did all the cooking and . . ." She turned away to get the dog and cat food out of the pantry.

Derek turned back to the steaks.

"No, Boomer. You're such a glutton. That's the cat's. This is yours." The cat's stomach dragged on the floor. Derek suspected it didn't miss too many meals.

Sam leaned against the counter. "Did you find everything you needed?"

Her eyes were green. "Think so. How would you like your steak?"

She started setting the small kitchen table. There was a massive dining-room table dividing the huge living room in two. Apparently she preferred the more casual kitchen table tonight. "Rare."

He took one off the grill.

"Listen, as soon as we're finished, I have to go back to town. You're welcome to come along."

"I'd like that," he said with about as much passion as a schoolboy reciting a love poem.

"Wouldn't go out at all, but I fined one of the docs two popcorn balls for calling me back from lunch last week." She laughed, amusing herself mightily. She placed the sharp edge of the steak knife toward the plate. Knitting her brows, she turned it over. "I told him I'd be over soon to pick them up." She flipped the knife over again.

"I didn't quite follow that."

"It's Halloween," she said, as if that explained it all.

How well he knew. The first holiday after he had been told to follow up on the Lisa Henderson murder. There had been no murder on Labor Day, but if there was anything to the holiday-murder motif, this was the time for him to be here.

The dog sat with its chin on the edge of the table throughout dinner, while Sam seemed not to notice or at least, not to care. When she had finished, she placed her plate on the tile floor, and the dog snatched the bone from the plate and carried it into the living room, where he settled down on the carpet under the large table. The fat Siamese cat jumped down from its perch on top of the china cabinet with a loud thud and joined the dog. After a few growls and snaps, the cat ran off with a small scrap.

Derek pushed back from the table. "What was

that you called your dog?"

"Finished?" She picked up his plate and placed it on top of hers. "Boomer. Short for Boom A. Wrangler."

"Boomerang lure."

"Boom capital A Wrangler. He's a Western retriever. Everything that goes out, he fetches back.

"Watch the house, Boomer." She put on her coat and headed for the door. Derek had never known a woman not to first consult the bathroom mirror before going anywhere. He rushed to his bedroom and got his coat. She had started the car and was revving up the engine when he stepped out the front door.

"Do you want it locked?" he yelled.

"If it takes your fancy," she called back. "No, wait." She got out of the car and brushed by him. "I forgot my radio." She returned carrying a large beeper. She drove down the tree-lined path as if in the Indy 500.

"A pathologist who takes calls." Derek hoped that would stimulate meaningful conversation while he had the dubious honor of being in the copilot's seat as she broke the sound barrier.

"I'm the coroner . . . and this is a holiday." Sam kept her eyes on the road. Little consolation.

"There are more deaths on the highways during a holiday?"

"What?"

"You have the radio because you expect a fatality on, say, a county road because of the holiday."

48

"Oh . . . yes. No. Halloween isn't statistically noted for heavy highway travel. Those are the long-weekend ones. Like Labor Day and Memorial Day weekends." She sighed. "We've been plagued with a series of murder-rapes. The first was on Valentine's Day, then Easter, then the Fourth of July."

"Labor Day?"

Sam shook her head. "Let's cross our fingers he forgets Halloween. Maybe he's moved on and there won't be any more."

"This stirs my journalistic juices. Tell me about them."

"Nothing to tell."

He glanced over. She was nothing more than a shadow in the darkness, but something told him their interview had drawn to an abrupt close.

She didn't speak again until they arrived at a house transformed into a haunted mansion. "Trick or treat," Sam said through the screen door.

A short round witch opened the door. "My goodness, Sam, you've just proven Big Bob's maxim . . . the later the hour, the taller the goblins."

Derek, following them into the foyer, looked around the darkened room lighted by flickering candles. A card table at the foot of the stairs bore a depleted supply of popcorn balls and an empty punch bowl. A skeleton with a pulsating red heart stood on the landing. The stairway was draped with cobwebs.

"Did you have many trick-or-treaters?" Samantha asked the witch.

"This is all that's left. We made three hundred and forty carameled apples and six hundred fifty-seven popcorn balls."

Samantha, with exaggerated quickness, picked up two popcorn balls. "I'm taking mine before they're gone." She caught Derek's arm and pulled him closer. "Betty, I'd like you to meet Derek Turner. Derek, this is Betty Wallace."

"Turner. You related?"

Derek withdrew his hand. "No."

"We . . . we . . . met for the first time this afternoon. Derek's here from New York to write an article about us." Though misleading, every word was true. The sign of a master at deception.

"I'm impressed. . . . New York." Betty turned to the back aperture and pointed one of her blood red, glued-on fingernails. "Why don't you take your visitor on in to meet Big Bob?"

A little man with a generous paunch and a scant fringe of white hair rose when he saw them enter the family room. "Sam, I wondered if you'd come."

"Would I miss this for the world?" She pulled Derek close again, so close he could feel her still shivering from being out in the cold. "Big Bob, this is Derek from New York. Derek, Big Bob." She winked at Big Bob. "Betty's got the lowdown on him."

"Then I'll ask her," he whispered as he winked back.

Derek loosened the hand that clutched his arm, and Samantha jerked away, her face reddening. She must have confused him with his father again.

"Would you like something to drink?" Big Bob asked.

She made a face. "You aren't pushing that homemade cherry brandy again this year, are you?"

Big Bob threw back his head and roared, his stomach jiggling like jelly. "Peach."

"Peach! That's the pits!" she exclaimed, giving her host a bear hug.

The witch appeared in the doorway, hands on hips, eyes hooded. "Sam, what are you doing to my Big Bob?"

Samantha backed away and soberly turned to Betty. "Not my fault, Betty. He's trying to pawn off peach —" She doubled over in laughter.

"Oh, you guys. What's Derek going to think of us?" Betty took Derek's arm and led him to the bar. She smelled of strong musk perfume. "Here, let me fix you a drink. What's your pleasure?"

Derek turned around to see Big Bob and Samantha with their heads together, snickering. They were certainly enjoying themselves. "Peach brandy, by all means." He hoped his tone was not too sardonic.

"It's really good. Don't pay them any mind," Betty went on happily. "Sam liked the brandy last year so much, we had to put her to bed upstairs." That produced another round of laughter.

"Friends don't let friends drive drunk," Big Bob said in a feeble attempt at imitating a TV announcer.

To Derek's way of thinking, a true friend wouldn't let that woman drive in any condition. He lifted the glass to his nose; it smelled like brandy. He tasted it. "It's good."

Samantha stepped forward. "It's also about four hundred proof."

"Trick or treat," a tall, husky man said as he ducked under the door frame to allow the little princess teetering on his shoulders to clear. It surprised Derek. Apparently the local custom was to walk right in without knocking.

"Watch her —" Derek warned.

"Daddy, my hat," the little girl cried as her gothic cone-shaped headdress tumbled to the floor.

"Good show, Daddy," Samantha teased as she went around them to pick it up. "Here, it's as good as new." She started to hand it up. "Put Lindsey down, Ken, I can't reach."

Lindsey scrambled down, retrieved her hat, and gave Sam a hug.

"Where's Mary?" Betty asked.

"Giving away popcorn balls to some poor waifs we found on your doorstep. I told her not to give out the apples."

Betty refilled Derek's glass. "Not much chance of that. They've been gone for hours. Kind of late for tricker-or-treaters, anyway. Ken, have you met Derek?"

"No." The big man walked over to the bar and shook Derek's hand. "Ken Miller."

"Derek Turner."

"Turner?"

Betty jumped in. "No relation. A reporter from New York. He's doing a story here."

"On Dr. Turner's buffalo," Derek clarified.

"Mary," Betty called as a pregnant woman came into the room, "come over and meet Derek."

After introductions, Ken turned to Witch Betty. "You could have saved an apple for me."

Mary sat on a bar stool and leaned over the counter, tucking her swollen midsection under it. "Really, Betty. The poor man's just gotten home from the hospital. Been there since early morn. Didn't even have a chance to eat dinner."

"That's not —" Samantha bit her lip. "That's not enough to get sympathy in this crowd. It's worthy of one popcorn ball. Right, Big Bob?" Derek didn't buy that. He didn't know what she started to say, but the last bit was a clumsy cover.

"Betty, go get the apple I put aside on the counter," Big Bob said.

"Got two broken legs, Big Bob?" Samantha asked.

"Wait a minute." Ken put his hands in the air, stopping everyone. "I don't want a carameled apple. What I'd really like is a drink. Got any of that cherry brandy Sam's so fond of?"

"Peach," the three of them said in unison.

"Well, give me some before Sam finishes it off."

"Mary?" Betty asked.

"Nothing. I'm fine."

"Sam?"

Samantha sat down on the last stool and lifted Lindsey to her lap. "A Diet Coke."

"Don't think I have one."

"Give the skinny broad a real Coke," Big Bob ordered.

"That's fine. I'll share it with Lindsey. How does that sound? Us skinny broads have to stick together."

"What's a skinny broad?"

"Well, it's something akin . . . like . . . being called a beautiful princess. That's what you meant, wasn't it?" She looked up at Big Bob, her voice harsh.

"I don't know him," Lindsey said as she pointed to Derek and hid her eyes in Samantha's blouse.

"I'm sorry. Lindsey, Derek. Derek, Lindsey." Lindsey kept her eyes hidden. Derek smiled politely.

"Lindsey, Amy was here earlier." Lindsey looked up at Betty with a big grin. "She said to tell you hello if you came over." Betty turned to Derek. "Amy's our granddaughter."

"How come she left?" asked the princess.

"Bob Junior had to go back to the hospital and catch a baby," Betty explained.

"My mommy's going to have a baby."

Betty propped her black sleeves against the bar as she looked at the princess. "I know. Is it going to be a boy or a girl?"

"Yes," the three doctors answered gaily. Derek took it to be an inside joke.

Betty raced from the room at the sound of the doorbell, her black train sweeping behind her, and made another couple round trips while the rest merrily went on.

Derek had long since stopped following their conversation when Big Bob said: "Sam, do you think we'll make it through the night?"

"Yes." Samantha's voice had a metallic ring. "We got through Labor Day."

"Maybe the man moved on," Mary said hopefully.

"Sure . . . most likely he moved on." Big Bob's voice echoed Samantha's. No one believed the killing spree was over.

"What man?" Lindsey demanded.

The room became unnaturally quiet.

"What man, Sam?"

"A yellow-bellied sapsucker."

Lindsey covered her mouth with her veil and giggled. "He sounds funny."

"Yeah, he's funny, all right." Samantha handed the child to Ken as she slipped from the stool. "We've got to be going. Derek's still on New York time, and he looks like he's acquiring a taste for Big Bob's brandy."

"We have made a noticeable dent," Ken said, looking at the light through the bottle. He picked up Samantha's empty glass and sniffed.

"Real subtle, Ken." Samantha punched him in

the arm, making an ice cube jump from the glass. "If you'll notice, I'm walking out this year . . . and on only two appendages."

"And I so enjoy watching you crawl." Ken ducked behind his daughter.

Samantha turned to the rest of the group and cocked her thumb in Ken's direction. "He'd be a natural for a hospital administrator."

"What's Larry done now, Sam?" Big Bob groaned.

"Don't ask." Sam grabbed her coat. "Good night, everyone."

Derek shook hands with Big Bob and Ken, and then the little princess at her insistence. Big Bob walked them to the front door. "Now you come back," he hollered as they hurried through the mist.

"Thank you for the hospitality," Derek called as he turned to wave. "And the brandy." He had enjoyed the brandy.

5

Finding the house hadn't been difficult, with two marked cars lit up in front of it. People had gathered like flies to manure. The neighborhood under different circumstances would have seemed quaint. The little houses up one side and down the other were all shaded by large evergreen trees. The whole neighborhood seemed well cared for, belying the stereotypical belief that murders occurred in seedy places.

Bill Louis popped an antacid tablet into his mouth. Not being able to find the killer was the worst thing that had ever happened to him. He'd dragged in every criminal in the county, and still he couldn't make it work.

Even the newspaper guy had gotten out of bed. That's all he needed to get the town riled up. Weren't they paranoid enough? Every single woman — hell, every woman under eighty — wanted police protection.

"Chief, is this another victim of the Holiday Murderer?"

Bill looked at the wiry newspaper man and smiled. "It's Halloween, isn't it?"

"Any leads?"

Bill shook his head. "Giving it top priority."

"Who found the victim?"

Bad enough having to get out of bed, talking to

the press was too much. "Just got here, Sherman. Maybe you could call me in the morning at the station. I'll have a nice little statement for you. Even tie it up in a big bow."

"How 'bout taking me inside?"

"Don't want no pictures. Might panic folks."

Sherman nodded. "How 'bout off the record? If I don't take pictures?"

Bill put his arm around the kid's scrawny shoulders. "Why not?"

The putrid smell filled the tiny frame house. Bill covered his nose with his handkerchief and followed the voices down the hall into a small bedroom.

"What a shame." He wished he'd met the dark-haired beauty, stretched across the double bed, under different circumstances. Unlike the other two he saw, her shapely body was clad in a little black frilly see-through number. Crotchless, he noticed. "Where's the broad?"

"Haven't called her yet," Skip answered.

Just as well. She was as worthless as all get-out. If they'd had a real coroner like Thaddeus instead of a woman, the case would have been long solved. And the last thing he wanted was to stand around waiting for her to give him orders in that holier-than-thou voice of hers.

Bill rubbed his chin. "Well, just leave a message at her office. This one's clear enough. I'm going back to bed."

Jeffrey Talbot's radio woke him from a restless

sleep. His life had gotten out of control. His already burdened schedule mushroomed with a record number of hunting violations added daily to the docket.

The tired face in the mirror showed his sentiments. He ran a hand over the razor-sharp stubble that appeared each morning; the hair on his head should be so thick. And each morning he conscientiously lathered up and scraped a Bic across the foam. But his daily ablutions ended abruptly when he heard the seven-o'clock local news.

He put on his gray suit. He needed a cup of coffee, a pot. He made a mental note to call Sam. "The Halloween murder," he repeated as he swirled his red-striped tie around his hand.

The Rapid City camera crew was waiting by his reserved spot at the courthouse parking lot. Gripping his briefcase like a vise, Jeffrey stepped out of his car and greeted them.

"Mr. Talbot, what is your reaction to the statement made by the director of the Women's Center that, quote, the county attorney's lax approach to law enforcement has put every woman in this county at risk, unquote?"

It was the first he'd heard of it. "It's not worthy of a comment." He fixed his eyes on the camera. "However, I would like to say that I will prosecute — to the fullest extent of the law — the guilty party when he is apprehended by the authorities."

He cut his eyes to the interviewer. "If you'll excuse me now, the docket is extremely heavy today." As he walked briskly away, Jeffrey wondered if his life would ever return to normal.

"Am I disturbing you?"

Sam jumped. Clutching her chest, she wheeled around to see Derek standing in the doorway of her office. "Derek!"

"Sorry, I didn't mean to startle you."

"No, my fault . . . no, you're not disturbing me." She tossed her tortoiseshell reading glasses on top a pile of papers. "Here," she said, scooting her chair across the linoleum to remove a stack of journals from the only other chair in the cramped room. Out of the corner of her eye she saw Kate eyeing them over her typewriter.

"Thanks," Derek said as he sat.

She shifted nervously in her chair, waiting for him to speak. He didn't. "What's up?"

"Oh, I've just been giving your town the once-over. Thought maybe you wouldn't mind the journalist following you around a bit." He lifted a leg. "Like my new boots?"

Sam smiled, seeing for herself the little boy she'd heard so much about. "Great boots, Derek." She wondered how much wear he'd get out of them on the streets of New York.

"So this is where you work."

"Rather bleak, isn't it?"

"Well, it does seem disproportionate to your responsibility," he said, pointing to the spiderweb crack in the skinny window just under

60

the ceiling. It had been like that for months. Calling maintenance about it had become part of her daily routine.

"I'm beginning to wonder if I have any responsibilities. The nincompoops at the police station forgot to call me to last night's murder." She struggled to contain her anger.

"I heard about it over the radio."

Sam glared at him. "Yeah, so did I!"

After fumbling in the pockets of his khaki jacket, Derek pulled out a crinkled pack of Camels.

Sam grabbed a folder and waved it at Derek. Unable to find words to communicate her frustration, she threw it back on her desk and stared at the spiderweb crack.

He tapped the cigarette against his palm. "What if I hadn't had the radio on?"

A tired cigarette drooped in the corner of his mouth as he struck a match and touched the sputtering flame to the end. Smoke curled from his nostrils. "Do you have an ashtray?"

Sam jerked alive. "You can't do that."

"What?"

"Smoke."

He looked around for something to put it in.

"Here." Sam took a Styrofoam cup from her desk. "It's cold anyway."

He took another drag before dropping the cigarette into the coffee. "Sorry."

"Guess I could write a prescription."

"Come again?"

"If you want to smoke, I'll write you a prescription."

Derek smiled. "I still don't understand."

"To smoke in the hospital, you need a prescription. All the hard-core cases have prescriptions." She laughed. "It was the only time the administrator treated me like a real doctor . . . when he wanted a prescription."

"You wrote him a prescription to smoke?"

"No, but I wrote his secretary one."

Derek stared at her. His eyes were the same coffee color as John's, except John had a pie-shaped black flaw in his right iris. "Is that what you didn't want to talk about last night?"

"You mean at Big Bob's? About him liking to see me crawl?" She loved that flaw so very much. "No."

"That's it? Just no?"

"Yes."

"Write a prescription. You're making me nervous."

Nervous? How did he think she felt? Sam couldn't let herself think of John like this. Not with John's son here to see the tears. She sprang from her chair. "I have a better idea. Let's go to lunch." She took a five from her wallet and stuck it in her lab coat pocket and hurried from her office. "Kate —" Sam turned and motioned to Derek. "Come on, Derek." Whirling around, she said, "Kate, we're going to lunch."

Kate leaned both elbows on the desk to prop up her lacquered head of hair. Giving Derek the once-over, she asked, "Is this your reporter from New York?"

"Sorry . . . Kate, Derek. Derek, Kate."

"How do you do?" Kate extended her hand, palm down. Derek looked at the hand, looked at Sam, looked at Kate, then bent over and kissed it. A shriek of excitement passed through Kate's cherry lips. "Ah, he's just exactly how I pictured New Yorkers."

Sam swallowed a smile. "We'll be downstairs." She grabbed Derek by the arm and whisked him away. "And I bet she's exactly how you pictured a western gal."

He looked back over his shoulder. Sam was confident Kate was still staring at him. She was certain when he waved. "Well, not exactly." He pushed back a wisp of hair that had escaped the twisted knot at the nape of her neck. It was an uncomfortable moment for her. "As a matter of fact, you're more like my stereotypical westerner."

"That's how wrong stereotypes can be. Born and reared city gal."

"But you always wanted to be a country girl?"

"Never." They started down the stairs. "I'm expecting a couple of calls. Otherwise we could have gone out. The food's not half bad, though."

"You changed the subject. You were telling me why you moved to the country."

She stopped and looked up at him. "I was not."

"Well, I'm asking now."

Sam turned around and continued down the stairs. "Why would you be interested?"

"So what did the administrator do yesterday?"

"Don't you forget anything?"

"Not when you so skillfully avoid the question."

"It's not a big deal. Some neighbors wanted to give the hospital five million dollars to add a geriatric wing. Larry told them he'd be happy to have the money but he'd decide what was to be done with it."

"What does he want to do with it?"

"Doesn't matter what he wanted. The hospital in Buffalo was tickled pink to build them a wing."

She noticed him looking around the cafeteria. "Probably seems small by New York standards."

"No, some of my favorite eating spots are this small."

"Doubt if you'll add this one to the list." They started down the ten-foot buffet line, which boasted three entrée choices.

"What are the numbers between the food and the price?" Derek pointed to the blackboard as they stood in line.

"Calories. Not that it matters. A good rule of thumb, if you like it, it's high in calories. If you hate it, it has no calories and it's probably good for you."

"Look at the brownie. I'm never going to eat one again. You know, a blackboard like that might be just what the doctor needs."

"Why's that?"

"To set up in your office." He leaned over and whispered. "Track your killer."

"For everyone and his uncle to see?"

He shrugged.

Sylvia, the cook, stuck a pot holder under her meaty arm, covering most of the ring of perspiration. "What can I do you out of?"

Sam twisted a loose strand of hair as she decided. "The tomato soup and a small salad."

The soup sloshed over the sides of the bowl as Sylvia placed it on the glass covering the steam tray. She flipped a package of crackers onto the wet plate. Another pack landed in the salad. "Anything else?"

"More crackers, please." Sam looked down at the floor while she answered.

"They're a nickel apiece."

Three signs said as much, not to mention she reminded her daily.

"I'll have three," Sam said as she wiped the wet package on her napkin. "And a brownie for him."

Derek ordered the poached fish and a tossed salad.

Bertha, the cashier, rang up their order with lightning-quick fingers. "One seventy-five."

"It's not Sardi's, but where else can a dollar seventy-five buy two lunches?" she asked as she dug in her pocket for the five.

"Is that right?"

Sam nodded, then motioned to his fish. "And in this crowd you'd be considered an expensive date."

"I'm willing to pay my way. I'll even spring for the crackers."

"And they said chivalry was dead."

Bertha counted out the change and turned to the next in line.

"Come on, let's go down to the doctors' lounge. I want to be near a phone." Leaving the room was like swimming against the tide. "We got there just in time. Look at the line."

Sam had taken her first bite when she heard the page. She hurried to the phone and asked the house operator to transfer the call.

"Dr. Turner here."

"Sam, Bill. You called?"

"Yes, Bill, indeed I called. I'd like to remind you that I'm the coroner." Her temper got the better of her as she spoke to the police chief. "I'd like to know where you get off deciding when to move a coroner's case. I'll decide, thank you. We're trying to find a murderer, or have you forgotten?" Her voice was raw from yelling.

"Now, Sam, it was just like the others. I didn't see a need to bother you so early in the morning."

"Bother? Bother? You want to talk about bother? Bother is when you hear the news over the radio on the way to work." She fanned herself with the front of her lab coat as she felt the perspiration roll. She'd be looking like Sylvia any time now. "Dammit, Bill."

"Now, sugar, don't get your feathers ruffled."

"You ever do that again and I'll have your

66

balls. And don't call me sugar!" She slammed down the phone. "Sorry," she said, slipping back into her chair.

He slid his package of crackers toward her.

"Thanks." The crackers turned to powder as she crushed them. "I think my blood pressure's elevated." She ripped open the package with her teeth and dumped the crumbs into her soup.

"You said a couple of calls. I can hardly wait for the next."

She burst out laughing. "I'm afraid you'll be disappointed. It'll be the county attorney and he'll be the one screaming. County coroner! If you only knew what I had to go through for the honor of being county coroner, a ten-thou-a-year job."

"What did you have to do?"

"Beat out the undertaker. And it wasn't what you might call a landslide."

"Surely you have a lucrative practice as a pathologist. Why did you want to be coroner?"

"Ever work for an undertaker?"

He shook his head.

"I spent more time begging him to call an inquiry on a suspicious death than it would have taken to conduct the damn thing." How well she remembered. It was not more than a month after she'd moved to Sheridan. A six-year-old girl. By law an autopsy was performed. Many healed broken bones, absence of a hymen. Accidental drowning, you bet.

After lunch they walked outside to Butt

Heaven, the accepted gathering place for smokers. The red brick wall was lined with employees. Sam introduced Derek around, saving Larry for last. "Still smoking, Larry. It's a bad habit, you know."

He mumbled something she didn't hear, his vacant eyes looking beyond her.

"Larry, I'd like you to meet Derek from New York. Derek, Larry, our illustrious hospital administrator."

They shook hands.

A cloud of choking dust from the vacant field behind the hospital whirled around them. Cigarette ashes flew. "Well, I'm going back inside. Derek, I'll be in the lab when you're finished." She swiped at the ashes on her lab coat, only to make black smudges.

Derek pitched his half-smoked cigarette into the red shale chips already littered with hundreds of butts. "I'm finished."

Sam checked her watch as they strolled down the hall. "Going to have to give up on Jeffrey's call."

In the lab, Sam rummaged through the cabinet under the sink and pulled out a black toolbox with a radiation sticker on the side. "You parked in the front or back?"

He pointed toward the front. "What's in the box?"

"Autopsy kit. The sticker's to keep everyone out."

"A great deterrent, all right."

She stuck her head around the corner into the reception area. "Kate, I'll be at the funeral home." Sam led the way through the lab into a dark corridor. She waved at Larry as they passed his huge, well-appointed office. It was another sore subject with her. The work areas were short of space and he didn't need such a large office. He said it was needed for conferences with the town's dignitaries. Good excuse. After turning off her light, she slipped out the front door, Derek at her heels. "You do want to come, don't you?"

"I'll even drive."

6

The funeral director escorted them into the preparation room. The coldness between the man and Samantha could be cut with a knife. Derek supposed this was the undertaker she replaced as coroner.

Samantha gave the victim a perfunctory glance and seethed. "I'm going to kill him. With my bare hands I'm going to kill him. I'm going to kill you, Bill. With my bare hands I'm going to kill you." She turned to the funeral director. "Let me use your phone."

After she left the room, Derek walked over to the stainless-steel table and eyed the corpse. He'd seen many dead people, and she was definitely one. She also looked pretty good, for a dead person. Whatever had riled Samantha wasn't obvious to him.

Derek was tiring quickly of their scattergun approach. A team of experts probably couldn't help these bumbling locals now. He returned to the corner and hunkered down against the wall. He took out the crumpled pack of Camels and pulled out the lone cigarette. He looked over at the corpse. "You don't mind if I smoke?" He nodded. "I didn't think you would."

When she returned, Samantha ran a hand along the corpse's skin. She opened the toolbox and worked diligently and agilely with the detachment of a seasoned medical examiner.

Derek thought his purposes better served by silently waiting. His wait was short.

A man Derek surmised was the chief of police rushed in. He was followed by two uniformed officers. "Okay, Sam, what's so urgent?"

She banged the stopper into a test tube with the flat of her palm. "Bill, does this really look like the others to you?"

He gave her a questioning look.

"Bill, come a little closer." Her voice was as smooth as glass.

The chief inched forward.

"Come on," she coaxed.

He moved, not so bravely, to her side.

She took his hand and stroked it against the woman's skin. "Feel how moist the skin is?" Her words were slow and drawn out. "See how red it is? And the eyes . . . they're not bulging." She trilled to a scream. "They're shriveled!"

"So?"

"Bill." She paused. Her voice was nothing more than a whisper now. Rage must have taken her beyond screaming. "Bill, this body's been frozen."

The chief quickly wiped the hand that had touched the corpse on his pant leg.

She glared at him. "But overlooking that minor detail, this still isn't like the other three. It looks like an accidental death occurring during a deviant sexual practice." She ran a hand along

71

the dead woman's black, silky, and very sexy garment. "Look how she's dressed. I wouldn't be caught dead . . . Forget I said that."

The three men from the police department didn't forget. Instead they howled, repeating her blunder over and over and asking her what she wore to bed.

"A 49ers T-shirt, you assholes!"

That produced another gale of laughter.

"You won't have to worry about being the Thanksgiving turkey if that's —"

"You know, Skip, that's not half bad," she said to the youngest officer. With an Adam's apple more like a chin in his long neck, he looked a little like a turkey himself. "That's almost clever. I'm absolutely amazed that you could come up with a retort of such caliber. And all this time I thought you were just another moron. My apologies, Skip."

Derek tapped ashes into the empty cigarette pack as he watched the put-down float over the young man's head, over all their heads. He wondered if they would ever stop squabbling and get back to the point. "She's got you by the short hairs now." His ears heard what his mind thought.

Everyone in the room turned toward him. "Who's this?" Bill asked as if noticing him for the first time. "How'd he get in here?"

"He's with me," Sam stated, staring white-hot daggers at Derek.

Bill snarled. "You bringing company with you now?"

"He's a reporter from New York . . . doing a

72

story on my ranch," she mumbled.

The three police officers looked at each other, then over at Derek. Derek sensed this was great sport for them and wished he'd kept his big mouth shut.

"Well, well, a reporter from New York, eh? What do you think?" Bill sauntered over until they stood toe to toe. "Is this like all your Big Apple sexual-deviant cases?"

"Funny thing, the New York Police Department has never invited me to one of their murders. I'll have to speak with the mayor about it when I get back."

The acid of sarcasm burned through the chief's skin. His eyes scorched Derek's as if to say, "This is my town, not yours."

"But I think Dr. Turner has a point." Derek had already overstepped, a little more couldn't hurt, and he needed some answers now. Could all this be an elaborate hoax to make Lisa Henderson's murder seem unrelated to the treason case? "The woman was obviously expecting a close friend."

"Yes." Samantha took another stab. "Sadomasochism ranging on a scale from one to four — one being acts such as biting and scratching, while four is being able to accomplish orgasm only while strangling his sex partner — isn't totally unheard of."

"Say what?"

Samantha frowned. "Haven't you ever been scratched, Bill?"

"What does that —"

"Like in snuff films," Derek offered.

Snuff films he understood. "Oh, I see." He scratched his cheek as if it helped him think. "But it's Halloween."

Her face reddened with anger. "Bill, I don't give a flying fuck if it's your birthday. She wasn't murdered by our man and she wasn't murdered on Halloween."

"You want us to believe it's just a coincidence that she was found on Halloween?" Bill snickered and winked at the boys.

She made a fist with both hands. "Read my lips, Bill. She was frozen! She was thawed for Halloween."

Her words inspired another round of laughter.

Bill shook his head. "I've got to get back. Skip, you wait for the evidence. Gary and I are heading back to the station." They started for the door. "Thawed for Halloween. That's a good one."

Exasperation and disgust was written on Samantha's face as she silently returned to her work taking samples for the state crime lab. Derek wandered over to Main Street to buy a pack of cigarettes.

He was in the car when she hurried out of the white building. She hollered something to Skip as he was climbing into his squad car. He flipped her off when she turned away to cross the street.

"Sorry," she said as she slammed the door. She placed the toolbox on the floor by her feet and waited. Her face was red from the biting wind.

"Seat belt?"

"Sorry." She put it on and shifted in its confines.

He picked a dried leaf from her hair. "What was it you said to Skip just now?"

Her face flushed all the more. "To make certain the samples were Fed Exed before three. Why?"

"Journalistic curiosity." He started the car and pulled away.

"I'm sorry about all this. It's not helping you get your story."

"There seems to be an even better one in the murders."

She nodded. "I guess you never really know a person . . . though, now that I think about it, I can see Pamela wearing an outfit like that."

Derek let it soak in a minute. "You knew the victim?"

"Pamela used to work for me in my billing office. I let her go a year or so ago. She was telling everyone in town my business . . . even how much money I make. Wish someone had told me when I was so hot to get into med school that I'd have to run a business. How to pay all those hidden taxes, fight with Medicare, fund a pension plan per the government's say-so, and stroke disgruntled employees. Ad infinitum. All of the things John did so well."

People here had a real penchant for going off on tangents. "Did they know you knew her?"

75

She shrugged. "If it had somehow slipped your grasp, they don't care what I think. They're the good ol' boys, and I'm a woman."

"The part about your being a woman, now *that* I did notice."

His teasing tone hit a nerve. Sam pursed her lips and glared at him. He quickly turned his eyes back to the road.

Derek steered her back in the direction that he thought would do both of them the most good. In a tone appropriate to the seriousness of the situation, he asked, "Samantha, what are you going to do about this?"

"I'll tell the county attorney. Jeffrey can deal with the good ol' boys. I wonder who she was seeing."

"You're positive this one's not related to the others?"

"Positive. Different as night and day."

"Are you sure the other three murders were all related?"

"There's no question about it. Skin tissue under the fingernails match, same blood type, the pubic hair found on the women match, spermatozoa found only in the vagina, saliva match up. Absence of the same things . . . fibers, head hair. The evidence is overwhelming. We just can't find the creep."

"Have the local authorities considered bringing in outside help?"

"What! Admit failure?"

"Anything unusual about the other three?"

76

"My, your journalistic tendency serves you well."

"Sorry. That's how we are, curious to a fault." He couldn't help noticing the stares the Mercedes drew. Most vehicles were pickups, Suburbans, or Jeep products, like Samantha's other one. "Were there?"

"Were there what?"

"Differences in the other three?"

"No. The last victim was curious, though. She was a natural blonde who had dyed her hair brown. Her body was claimed by her parents back East, but when I called the contact number left at the funeral home, it wasn't a working number. Though it wouldn't surprise me if Thaddeus got the number wrong. But still . . . she had no photo albums, no address book, no personal letters, and no long-distance calls on the telephone bill I found."

"Why were you calling her parents?"

She shrugged. "Guess journalists don't have an exclusive on curiosity."

"You went to a great deal of trouble."

"Not so much. Some hotshot from Washington was asking a lot of questions about her. It made me curious, that's all."

Derek decided not to ask any more questions; no sense piquing her curiosity again. They rode the rest of the way back to the hospital in silence. When he pulled into the lot, he asked: "May I tag along, or are you too busy for company?"

"Come on in. I'll buy you a friendly cup of

coffee before I have to get busy."

All the tables in the cafeteria were empty save one. "Come join us, Dr. Turner," they heard from this table, at which four hospital employees were seated.

Samantha obliged. She introduced Derek to a clerk from Records — who considerately wore a name tag with Susan written on it — then to two X-ray techs, Barbara and Penny, and to a man from the boiler room she explained was married to one of the techs, though Derek couldn't remember which one.

"This has to be a great culture shock to you, Derek," said one of the techs.

"Actually, it's been a breath of fresh air," he admitted, flashing his best smile, the one he reserved for not-so-pretty ladies.

"I'm going to take him over to Heritage Towers and let him ride the elevator when he gets homesick." Winking, Samantha turned to Derek. "It has five floors . . . I think."

The conversation died of its own inertia.

"Did you see the movie on television last night?" Barbara asked the other tech.

"Which one?"

Barbara took her lip off the coffee cup. "I don't know . . . something about getting back to the future."

"*Back to the Future*. It had some great lines," Samantha said enthusiastically. "Like calling him Calvin Klein because it was written on his shorts."

Barbara frowned. "I don't remember that part."

"How about when he asked the soda jerk for a Tab and the guy said, 'You have to order something first.' " Samantha laughed.

Barbara scratched her nose and looked at Samantha. "I must've been handing out candy then. My favorite was when he walked into the bar without a tie."

Samantha bit her lip. It was a habit he noticed when she was trying to think something through. "When was that?"

"When he was looking for the key to his motorcycle."

"What motorcycle?"

Derek interrupted. "You two ladies aren't talking about the same movie."

"What channel were you watching, Dr. Turner?"

A hoarse groan caught in her throat, Derek heard it as self-effacing laughter. "Actually, I wasn't. I saw it in the theater several years ago . . . *Back to the Future*. I had to take Derek trick-or-treating last night."

The conversation moved on to trick-or-treating pranks, and, at a lull, Susan from Records said to Samantha, "That must have been awful for you . . . seeing Pamela like that. I sure wouldn't want to be coroner."

Samantha twirled the Styrofoam cup between her hands. "It didn't exactly make my day."

"Yeah . . . Keri's so upset she couldn't even

come to work today." Susan reverently shook her head. "Thinks it's all her fault."

Samantha looked up from her cup, but Barbara spoke. "Now, how could it be *her* fault?"

"Don't know. Said something about trying to call her. Apparently she hadn't been to work all week — hadn't even called. Thinks she should have called the police, especially when she went over and smelled something rotten."

"She must've been lying there rotting all week!" Barbara shivered at the thought.

Samantha was biting her lip again. "What smell?"

"She must have looked awful," Barbara continued.

"What? No . . . no, Barbara. She was as beautiful as always. The smell must have been something else."

"I'm glad to hear that. Bad enough she's dead."

"Derek, I just remembered some work I need to do."

"I'll go with you." As they got up, he added, "It was nice meeting all of you."

The women stumbled over each others' words trying to say something memorable. The man from the boiler room gave him a quick salute.

Outside in the hall, Samantha handed him her coffee and sprinted to the doctors' lounge. She was just hanging up the phone when Derek backed through the door with two cups in hand.

"The police are going to meet us at Pamela's."

Sam paced back and forth in front of the house. Yellow leaves crumbled underfoot. The sky had clouded to a steel gray, and the angry wind had numbed her ears. The taste of moisture filled the air. Derek leaned against the car, a cigarette in hand. He had picked an inauspicious time for his visit, but she didn't know what she could do about it now. She should have thought to tell him to come a week later. But Halloween wasn't a holiday she celebrated with any regularity, other than visiting Bob and Betty. On the other hand, it wasn't a holiday of choice for her killer either.

At last Skip arrived with the keys. Sam waited impatiently as he unlocked the door, then she burst in. The smell in the air vindicated her. Another reason she should have been called to the crime scene. It may not have meant anything to Bill, but it certainly did to her. She headed straight for the kitchen, whirled around, and went into the attached garage. The tiny space boasted only a dark Honda Accord and a white windsurfing board flattened against the wall by suspended hooks. The smell wasn't as heavy here.

"Samantha, it's in the basement." Derek held the door to the garage open for her. She smiled her thanks. Not only for the courtesy at the door, but for being smart enough to realize what the smell meant. But why wouldn't he be? He was too much like John for it to be any other way.

Derek led her to the basement door and opened it for her. The putrid stench made her gag. Sam felt her way along the wobbling stairs until Derek found the light switch, then she raced to the bottom. He followed, a step ahead of Skip.

It was there, just as she knew it had to be. They lined up in front of the deep-freezer and Derek lifted the lid. The frozen foods were twisted and warped. Sam picked up a mangled, gummy Lean Cuisine box. She slapped it into Skip's hand. "Show that to your chief."

Sam turned on her heels, leaving Skip open-mouthed, then stopped at the foot of the stairs and looked around Derek to see Skip. "Tell him to eat it with my compliments."

She waited until they were out in the fresh air to say: "Wish I could be a fly on the wall when Bill sees that."

"Well, looks as if you were right. She was frozen and thawed for Halloween."

Sam groaned. "Don't even smile when you say that."

"Seriously, would the murderer have gotten away with it if he'd just cooled the body — say, by putting her in the refrigerator, instead?" He took her arm as they started to the car.

"Maybe. He would stand a better chance, anyway. The pathologist might not think to check the potassium levels in the vitreous humor, which would have contradicted the other findings."

"Humor?"

He opened the car door for her. He had his father's manners, and it felt like putting on a comfortable pair of shoes.

"Eye." Sliding into the car, she added, "The potassium levels are temperature independent."

"That's sneaky." He closed the door and walked around the car. His stride was somewhat different from John's. More official; his military training, she supposed. She missed John so.

"About as sneaky as putting a body in the freezer." She sighed. "Truthfully, the trip was unnecessary."

Derek leaned over and patted her knee. "But it felt good."

"Made my whole day." She hadn't noticed his smile until now. It wasn't John's. "And juries like that sort of thing more than boring calculations related by expert witnesses. Then, too, there's always the chance of another screwup in the state lab."

"You mentioned Federal Express before. I take it you don't do your own lab work?"

"Do you really think a hospital that doesn't even have a morgue would have the proper equipment for a test done once, maybe twice a year? Personally, I'd rather see them hire an E.R. doc."

"I don't know. If the murders keep up it won't be such a low-priority item."

It was late afternoon when Jeffrey walked into the lab. A young child squirmed and fussed in his mother's lap as a tech attempted to draw blood.

An old man stood behind them, waiting his turn to sit in the chair. Sam was leaning over a microscope in the corner. She gave the attorney a warm smile when she saw him.

"I've been trying to reach you all day, Jeffrey."

"I know. Court's been a bear." He looked around the busy lab. "Could we go into your office?"

Sam put the slide back into the tray. "Sure."

They walked silently toward her tiny office. Jeffrey closed and then leaned against the door as Sam straddled the edge of the desk. "Well, now, I had a nice long telephone conversation with Bill. Would you like to say anything?" Before she could answer, he added, "I'd really like to hear that part about his birthday, again."

Color rose in her cheeks. "Darn it, Jeffrey. He blew it." She jumped up and paced the entire width of the room in two steps. "First he moved the body. For some reason, I thought I had been elected coroner. He couldn't even tell the body'd been frozen."

"Frozen?"

"Well, previously frozen. The body had been thawing at room temperature for a day or so." She threw up her hands. "Sound's like we're talking about a turkey. And that's another thing . . . Never mind. Anyway, Pamela was dressed for intimate company. She knew her killer."

"The victim knew her killer?"

"Is there an echo in here? Didn't I just say she knew him?"

Jeffrey held up his hand. "Just let me play devil's advocate for a moment." He looked away. "Perhaps the rapist liked the newspaper calling him the Holiday Murderer. Maybe he just wanted us to find her on Halloween."

"No, no, no! The physical evidence is entirely different. It's a different man. An accident, I'm sure. Wait and see what all we get back from the lab."

"What kind of evidence?"

Sam shook her head. "That's what I like about you. You're always interested in the legal evidence. You make me feel appreciated." She brushed back a lock of hair. "We were lucky this time. Got quite a lot. The good ol' boys found fibers at the scene. And I found a couple of hairs stuck to her skin."

"Good. You sent them to the lab according to procedure this time?"

Sam pursed her lips.

"I'll take that as a yes." She still wasn't talking. "All right, one more point. If this is a copycat, where's the other body?"

"What other body?"

"From the Holiday Murderer. Halloween's a natural."

Sam sneered. "You're as bad as the newspaper guy who coined that name! Maybe he had to work last night. Maybe he's moved away." She slammed her fist against the desk. "What's wrong with you, Jeffrey? You never used to be stupid."

"I'm sorry." He kissed her cheek. "Let me know when the results come back." He opened the door, then closed it again. "And meanwhile, stop verbally assaulting the boys in blue. They're no match for you."

"Was that a compliment," she called after him, "or should I be insulted?"

Jeffrey smiled and waved as he left the lab.

7

The sky spit snow throughout the night. Now a brisk November wind hurled a skiff of snow through the air in a spinning pattern just as Sam, Derek, and Boomer emerged from the house early Saturday morning.

Sam shivered and shoved both hands deep into the pockets of her down parka. "Nice way to start off the day," she said, looking around at Derek. "Got jelly for brains?" She grabbed his arm, turned him around, and dragged him back inside.

"What have I done?"

"You mean, what haven't you done?"

His new boots clicked across the kitchen and into the hallway. She pushed her way through the coats in the hall closet until she found a navy-blue parka at the back.

"My jacket's warm enough," he said dryly.

Sam had heard that tone often enough. Men were such boys. She put John's jacket to her nose and took a deep breath. There was the faintest scent of him still.

"You must have . . ." he cleared his throat, "loved Dad deeply."

"Until the day I die. He's the first thing I think about when I get up, and the last when I go to bed." She tossed him the coat. He transferred his camera to John's coat, then meticulously hung up his light jacket. "Come on, we don't have all day." She hurried outside ahead of him. She didn't like sharing her memories of John, not even with someone else who loved him.

They didn't speak again as they fought the elements, finally getting to the barn, where it was only slightly warmer. Sam had intended to saddle both horses but Derek insisted on saddling his own. He knew what he was doing, she soon discovered. Every little gesture, every movement he made, reminded her of John. She didn't know how much longer she could stand his company; fortunately, he'd be leaving tomorrow. She could make it that far.

She would do anything to have John back, and blamed herself for his death. She should have called 911 first, then started CPR. Instead, she had pounded on his chest until she was too tired to continue.

Their dear partner Chris had told her later that it wouldn't have made any difference, the coronary had been too massive, words that had brought her little consolation over the last three years. She was supposed to be able to save lives, so why hadn't she been able to save the one life that had meant the world to her?

"Derek, I wouldn't take off the halter until the bit's in place, if I were you."

She slapped the reins against her palm hard enough to raise welts. She hadn't been this nervous when she took her orals. Tomorrow he'd be gone. Tomorrow everything would be back to normal. "Ready?"

"Just about. Go ahead, if you'd like. I'll catch up."

Why couldn't he have his own voice?

Sam challenged the wind with exhilarated abandon, racing her horse through the pasture, around the buffalo, and up the foothills. Tears streamed down her cheeks. She galloped across the vast landscape, oblivious to everything around her. It didn't help.

She remembered how John had taken her breath away the very first moment she laid eyes on him. The chemistry between them couldn't be denied. She had been a young intern rotating through his pathology department. That was the day she had made up her mind to be a pathologist. She had planned to be a pediatrician, but all that changed with the sound of his deep voice.

A jolt returned her to the present. Her horse lost its footing on the corner of a prairie-dog hole, and Sam flew through the air, landing flat on her back, the fall knocking the wind out of her. She gasped, fighting to fill her lungs with the stinging cold air. Crisp snow, like tiny icicles, pricked her face. The leaden sky reeled. Finally, she became aware of a warm tongue licking her face. Boomer's.

"You all right?"

It was John's voice, and for a split second she believed. Then she remembered. She pushed Boomer away.

"I see you ride like you drive," Derek scolded. He dropped to one knee and leaned over her. "You're ghostly white. I don't think you're seriously hurt, though."

Such incessant chatter and all she wanted was to breathe. She raised herself on her elbows, shutting her eyes as she waited for a spasm to pass. "I think I was thrown."

"A marvelous observation." He ran a hand over her body.

She slapped away his hand, and fell backward for her effort.

He kept poking at her.

"Hey, I'm the doctor."

"A doctor who treats herself has a fool for a patient." He felt some more. "Nothing seems broken." He offered a warm hand. "Try to stand."

Her ankle buckled. Derek swooped her up, and before she knew quite what had happened, she was sitting astride his waiting horse.

"Does your horse have a name?" Derek asked, handing her the reins.

"Roseola. Just call her Rosie." She watched as he crept up on the skittish horse. Just as he grabbed for the reins, Rosie backed away. Sam leaned back in the saddle and roared. "Looks like my Roseola can't be caught by an adult, either."

He caught the reins and made sure Rosie's leg wasn't lame, then stepped into the saddle like he was born to it. "Now, what was that about not being able to catch your horse?"

"Nothing really. I have a penchant for puns. Her namesake is a childhood disease. A high fever that lasts just long enough to get the parents good and scared. Then just as the fever subsides — and hopefully before some young intern orders a spinal tap — a rose-colored rash appears."

"You named this poor creature after a disease?"

"She should be honored. Most diseases are named after people."

He shook his head. "I'm almost afraid to ask what you call the other horse."

"Alanine. It's an amino acid."

"Valine, Alanine, and Leucine."

"Your cousins." John's brother, a chemist, named his three children after amino acids. "I'd forgotten."

"Forgotten?"

"That you were John's son. For a moment there, I was thinking of you as a New York reporter."

"That's good." He rode with an easy slouch as they headed toward the grazing herd. "Why don't you tell me about the buffalo? For the article."

"Probably the first thing you should know is that they're not buffalo. They're bison."

"Bison?"

She nodded. "Not that it matters. The name 'buffalo' is so ingrained that it will never

91

change." Sam motioned to the herd. "There they are. Ask what you want."

He clicked off some pictures. "Do you ever put any down?"

"That's a funny question to start with. And so politely put." She laughed. "You don't want to know what they like to eat? If they lie down to sleep? Of course, you already know they like to run off . . . for which my neighbor . . . he just loves having them come calling." She grew serious. "No, this is where they come instead of being killed. But in all fairness I must say that I would put one down, as you say, if he were a threat to the rest."

"Like what?"

"Diseased. Did you know that the bison were disease free until cattle gave them brucellosis? Something akin to the white man giving the Indians smallpox." One of the larger animals broke into a run, stampeding the others. She stared hard. "That's Curly, I think."

"Curly. The disease of hair. Which one is Brucellosis?"

She laughed. "You aren't teasing me, are you?"

"Wouldn't think of it."

"Anyway, his story might be of interest to you. Curly made national news a few years ago. His owner was going to kill him until the community got wind of it and raised a fuss." She bent over to straighten her boot in the stirrup. Her ankle hurt more than she cared to admit. "See how his right horn spirals out to the side? He pokes the others

92

with it. Probably by accident. They're all nearly blind, you know."

"And so you took Curly in."

"Actually, I had to pay the scoundrel two thousand dollars." She held up an accusing finger. "But that's off the record."

Derek whistled. "Two thousand. That's hard to believe."

"That's what he would have gotten from a sport hunter for the honor of the kill."

"You don't approve of sport hunting?"

She leaned over and patted Alanine's neck. "It doesn't matter whether I approve or not. I have no control over anyone else."

They fell into silence as they circled the herd to be upwind of the thin prairie dust the herd was kicking up, to take more pictures, and to chase them back the other way if they made a break for Guy Walker's pasture.

"What's Jake's story?"

"Jake came with the first five buffalo. An Ogalala Sioux claiming to be a great-great-nephew of Crazy Horse." Sam saw recognition in his eyes.

"He doesn't talk much."

"Most Indians don't. Their culture is different from ours. Indians prefer to be unseen and unheard. They have a quiet way of moving, whether the pace is swift or slow. Indians traditionally obliterate every trace of their presence, while we feel the need to assert ourselves by scarring the land with permanent structures."

She couldn't read his expression, but she didn't think she was holding his interest. "Of course you know how important the buffalo were to the survival of the Plains Indian, but did you know the buffalo also hold religious significance for them? Seven is a very important number — seven sacred rights. As is four — four seasons. Seven times four gives you twenty-eight, which is of super significance. A moon's cycle, for example. Buffalo have twenty-eight ribs."

They rode up the mountain trail to the crest where her property ended. Her ankle buckled as she dismounted. She must have groaned, if she could go by the way Derek came to her aid.

"I'm fine. Just ground-rein them," she said.

Here was a commanding view of the frosted valley below, her reason for bringing him up. Beyond was a brown cloud hanging over the town. Pollution reigned even here. She loved the view here as much as she had the ocean view from their beach house. The wind had died down and the mildew-colored clouds had moved east, leaving the empty sky a soft blue. The frost and snow would melt quickly now.

"What do you think?" She motioned to the valley.

"Breathtaking. The world could come to an end and we'd never know." He clicked off some shots. "A buffalo haven extraordinaire."

"You know, my little herd seems so puny compared to the thousand-head one in Gillette. Why didn't you go there? Or to California?"

"I'm not related to any of the others."

He was quick to disavow relationship at Bob and Betty's, but she let it pass.

"Do you have any other buffalo stories I might be able to use?"

Under an old oak tree Sam rifled through a pile of soggy leaves until enough dry ones surfaced to sit on. "There's the one about the white buffalo that turned into a sacred woman who gave the Sioux a pipe with which they would multiply and be a good nation."

"Let's hear it."

"That was it. But when the White Buffalo Woman returns, Grandmother Turtle will crack up." She pushed her windblown hair away from her face. "That makes a lot of sense to me. Have you ever looked at the back of a turtle? It looks like a plate tectonics map. When the plates crack up, the world will see earthquakes of gigantic proportion."

"My readers will like a little doom and gloom," Derek said sarcastically. He reached into his shirt pocket for a cigarette.

"According to Sioux calculations, the White Buffalo Woman has been born. She'll reach womanhood at about thirteen, plus or minus a year or two, which more or less parallels Nostradamus' predictions of the great destructive earthquakes."

"That's pretty heavy stuff for a feature story." Derek struck a match. He drew smoke deeply into his lungs the way a hard-core smoker would.

It reminded her of one of her earliest patients. He was on oxygen but wanted to smoke. She was just a lowly intern, but knew enough not to mix oxygen and fire. After heavy mediation it was decided that someone would wheel him into the courtyard where he could blow himself to smithereens with no structural damage to the hospital or other patients.

"I'd be less concerned about earthquakes and the end of the world and more concerned about those cigarettes if I were you," she said as she pulled up a blade of grass and ran it through her teeth, tasting the autumn wetness.

He flicked ashes for his reply. Hard-core. He squatted down beside her. "Is all this worth putting up with the Good Ol' Boys?"

"I don't have to deal with them often. It's just this murder business. I just wish . . . this makes it all worthwhile."

"Think you'll catch the murderer?"

She shrugged.

"Want some friendly advice?"

"Why not?"

"Call in the feds."

"How can we? It's a local matter. No drugs. The victims weren't carried off, the creep obviously lives here and the copycat one is the same."

"You said some hotshot from Washington was asking questions about one of the victims. Why don't you call him?"

"I don't know who he was." She looked at her watch.

"Look at the time; we've got to hurry back. Got to get to town."

Her ankle buckled as she jumped up. Derek picked her up before she was aware he was beside her.

"Rosie?"

"Fine."

"You work on Saturdays?" He lifted her easily to the saddle and tucked her game foot into the stirrup. "Can you get the other one?"

"Done." She pulled the stirrup away, not that he could see. "No . . . going to the movies."

"I like movies." Derek mounted.

She clicked Rosie down the mountain trail.

"What's playing?" he asked when the narrow trail leveled out and he was beside her.

"I have no idea. There's four you can choose from. We don't care."

"We?"

"My father's going with us."

"You have relatives here?"

"I do now." She whipped her horse into a canter.

Her ankle was still bothering her when she got out of the Jeep at the nursing home. "Sit tight, be right back," she said, slamming the Jeep's door. She hurdled an evergreen bush, but came down favoring her left foot. She hurried to the door, trying hard to keep from limping. She didn't want to remind Derek of the accident. It was obvious he disapproved of her and everything she did.

She greeted everyone she passed. The walls were newly redecorated in a great-looking green-and-peach paper, but decoration couldn't mask the odor of years of urine. Sam found her father settled in his favorite green recliner in the television room. "Ready to go, Daddy?" Hard to believe her father was only two years older than John would have been. Alzheimer's was an awful disease.

"Am I going somewhere?" He absently fiddled with the zipper on his red jacket.

"Yes, Daddy. We're going to the movies."

He smiled like an excited boy, planting his tennis shoes firmly on the rug as she pulled him from the chair.

Sam took his arm. His gait was far worse than it had been three days ago. She would have to talk with Big Bob about the dosage of L-Dopa he was prescribing. "Take big steps, Daddy, I won't let you fall."

"Are we going outside to see the movie?" he asked at the door.

"Yes, Daddy. We have to go in the car. Take big steps."

Derek got out of the car and started to get in the back.

"No, Derek. He can't get into the front. On better days he likes doing the driving from the back."

"I bet 'slow down' is one of his favorite expressions."

"John Turner!" Her father was suddenly spry

as a colt. He offered Derek his hand. "Dr. John Turner." He turned to her and added in a low voice, "He's a doctor."

"Daddy, this is John's son, Derek. Derek, this is my father, William Davis."

"It's a pleasure to meet you." He shook her father's hand vigorously. She should have warned Derek, but he was taking her father in stride. And in a million years, she'd not have guessed her father capable of remembering John, let alone seeing the resemblance. Or maybe it was the voice.

They had gone only a few blocks when, in a frail voice, her father said: "Sharon takes me to the movies every Saturday."

"Well, I'm taking you today." To Derek, she added: "Sharon's my sister."

"Sharon lives here too?"

Sam gave a quick shake of her head, hoping to discourage further questions now.

William Davis was more talkative than usual. "Sharon's married to a lawyer. He's very successful. Sharon and I go to the movies every Saturday. She knows the meaning of filial duty."

"I'm Samantha."

"They have different birthdays," her father said with a note of finality.

Derek bought the tickets as Sam and her dad walked toward the concession stand. "Take big steps, Daddy."

"I own this theater," her father told Derek when he caught up.

"He owned a chain of theaters in Denver."

"Bakersfield."

"Denver, Daddy."

"Bakersfield."

"Whatever you say, Daddy."

The girl behind the concession stand didn't need to be told. A sack of popcorn, a small drink, and a Snickers sat on the counter. Sam flipped a quarter on top of two dollar bills.

"You must be a creature of habit," Derek said.

"Guess so. Here, Daddy." She handed the older man the Snickers. "What would you like?"

"It'll take a minute to decide. You go on in."

Sam was waiting at the rest room when Derek turned up with a giant sack of popcorn. She should have fed him lunch.

"Daddy can't pass a rest room."

"Where's Sharon?" Derek asked.

"New Orleans."

"Does she visit often?"

"A couple of times, but why should she? He thinks he sees her every Saturday."

"I'll check on your dad."

It was a quiet afternoon for Saturday, and he was locking up when they passed him as the movie let out. He had always been curious about the pretty woman and the bent old man.

At 1:45 every Saturday afternoon she would walk by with the shuffling old man. But today there were three of them.

He didn't like change and he didn't like

100

strangers. They both made him anxious. And this stranger reminded him of the ones his mother used to bring home from the Mint Bar, where she worked as a cocktail waitress.

They helped the old man into the car. She was always patient, always considerate. Just like his mother.

Far-off things brought close-in memory reflected in the shop window. He remembered hearing his mother at the door: "Shh, be quiet . . . don't wake my kid." He would throw the pillow over his head to drown out the muffled noises of passion that followed.

The other man touched the woman's elbow. *She let him touch her!* Rage bolted through him like lightning. He hated her like he hated his mother. No, he loved his mother. Yes, he loved his mother.

Even after one of the men married her — has it only been since the first of this year? — and moved away, she still remembered him. Hadn't she sent him a Valentine card and an Easter card, too? She called on the Fourth of July. That showed how much she really loved him. Yes. She loved him. She didn't want to move. She wanted to stay. But his job was there, not here.

He hated change.

8

Derek's plane didn't leave until late afternoon, but the good doctor had him on the road before dawn. She was going to show him something that was "worth writing about." A normal Sunday at home began around ten with a walk to the corner for *The New York Times*, the first few pages of which he read over a cup of coffee at the bakery. The rest of the day was devoted to the newspaper. He liked it that way. He liked it a whole lot more than the Mach II ride down the two-lane highway in the Mercedes. She pointed out the tree-stump-shaped structure miles off the road around ten eastern standard time. Too quickly after, they were standing at the base of Devil's Tower, where she was reading the Kiowa legend to him.

" 'Eight Kiowa children, seven sisters and their brother, were picking berries. Suddenly, the boy became a bear. The sisters were terrified, so they ran to a stump of a great tree. The tree told them to climb upon it, and as they did it began to rise into the air. The bear came to kill them, but they were just beyond its reach. It reared against the tree and scored the bark all around with its claws. Then the seven sisters were borne into the sky, and they became the stars of the Big Dipper.' "

Derek had no quarrel with the story. The rock formation looked like a giant tree stump with straight bear claw marks all around. He took some pictures to pacify her. This was all well and good, but what he really wanted to see was her records on the other three victims. He wasn't sure what recommendation he would make. What seemed like a simple random killing at face value might very well be an elaborate scheme to cover Lisa Henderson's murder. She moved to Sheridan in December; the killings began in February. Maybe too coincidental. "I thought there was a hole on one side for the spaceship to land."

"What?"

"You know, in *Close Encounters of the Third Kind*. A good moviegoer like yourself —"

"I knew that. I just forgot. Must have restored it after the spaceship took off again." She zipped up her down jacket and shoved her hands into her jean pockets. "That's the problem with having a father like mine. Every time I forget something, I think I've inherited Alzheimer's." She laughed heartily. Too much so. "Wasn't that the one where he had to go into the bar to get the keys to his motorcycle?"

"A steel-trap mind." He pulled her in tight against the gusting wind, wishing he'd worn his father's down parka. "I don't think I'm familiar with the Kiowas."

"They're a small tribe. According to legend, they came one by one into the world through a hollow log. A woman, heavy with child, got stuck in the log. After that, no one could get through."

"You women are so troublesome." He held tight as she tried to wiggle loose. She pinched up her face, ruining her looks. "No you don't. We're sharing body heat. Stay right here and tell me all about the Kiowas — in epic detail."

"They have handsome features — even the *men* — high cheekbones. In the Hollywood Westerns, the Kiowas have the right side of their hair cut to the ear and braided on the other side."

"I know their kind. They gave a 'How,' then tried to lift John Wayne's scalp."

"No, sir. Never John Wayne's scalp. Maybe all his friends' . . ."

"There you go." He kept searching for a way to talk about the murder cases. "Are the Kiowas on a reservation around here?"

"No, they were just migrating through the area in the late seventeenth century. They were mountain people from western Montana. They computed their stature by the distance they could see, and so, feeling confined, they left the area, with its deep lakes and dense timber, canyons and waterfalls. In Crow country, they picked up the culture and religion of the Plains Indians. And fifteen hundred miles later, they ended their journey in Oklahoma, around Rainy Mountain." She took a deep breath and choked on the cold, wet air.

Derek patted her back. "Be careful. Sheridan

can't afford to lose its only detective."

She choked some more.

"Bill would have chalked this murder up to the serial killer."

A throaty groan came between coughs.

"I was thinking maybe there's a true crime book in this. They're big these days. Maybe I could come back sometime. Look at your files. Maybe I'd stumble across something."

"Believe me, there's nothing in my medical files that would help until he's found. And I'd bet my last penny the good ol' boys have nothing either. It will be a miracle if he's ever caught." She glanced at her watch. "Derek, I'd love to stand here in the cold all day, but we need to get back if you're going to catch your plane. I can only drive so fast."

He didn't let the opportunity pass. "Maybe they'll catch him on a speeding violation."

"They'd give him a citation and let him go on his merry way."

There was more truth in that than Derek cared to admit. "That's how Ted Bundy was apprehended."

"A frightening man. He seemed so normal."

"Look for normal."

"A normal, bald man. I'll tell Bill," she added sardonically. As they headed for the car, she pointed east. "Somewhere over there — by Sundance on the eastern border of Wyoming — around the summer solstice, the Plains Indians would gather for the annual Sun Dance. Then, later, when the times got bad, they turned to ghost dancing."

"Ghost dancing?"

"To bring back the buffalo."

"You've brought back the buffalo."

"Hardly. A thimbleful compared to the sea of buffalo that used to roam the prairie."

They walked along in silence until Derek said, "Mankind just keeps screwing up."

She nodded. "The dinosaurs were better caretakers of the earth than we are. They ruled for millions of years. We'll be just a blink in time."

"I wonder to whom we'll pass the baton."

"Insects. Those living underground, protected from the radiation seeping through the ever-decreasing ozone. To survive, they'll have to cannibalize. And insects produce enough offspring to meet their needs."

"That's a bleak picture."

She nodded.

He waited until they were back on the road and gliding at ludicrous speed before he led her back to the murders. "Bald, you said."

"Bald? Oh . . . bald. Not a trace of evidence to the contrary."

"Maybe he wore a stocking over his head?"

She shook her head.

"No?"

"Too much saliva. He was kissing them."

"Maybe his hair —"

She leaned over and gave his hair a friendly yank. So sure of herself, she held her hand out in front of him without looking. "They all struggled. The first one's bald. Pamela's killer isn't."

"What else do you know about the first killer?"

She glanced at him. "You have quite a morbid streak. You didn't ask as many questions about my bison."

Time to segue. "Tell me more about the ghost dancing to bring the buffalo back."

Her pager went off about five miles across the Montana border. He'd already learned more than he ever cared to know about Sitting Bull and Wounded Knee. She was quite the little historian. It took her some time to pull over.

"Fifty-six, eighty over," she said into the radio.

The operator transferred the call. "Hello?" came the timid female voice.

"Dr. Turner here."

"Ah . . . I'm almost seven months pregnant, and about a half hour ago I had a gush —"

"Breaker, breaker," Samantha shouted into the radio. "I'm sorry. My radio went bad. Do you have a doctor in town?"

"No, we're just passing through. On our way to California where my boyfriend's got a job waiting."

"Where are you?"

"At the phone in front of Pamida."

"Go to the emergency room at the hospital. I'll call to let them know you're on your way. Do you know how to get to the hospital?"

"No," came the whispered reply.

She gave directions. "Good luck to you." When

the girl hung up, Samantha told the operator to patch her through to the hospital. She checked her watch while they waited. "Plenty of time."

Derek nodded reassuringly. Even a couple of cars she hadn't previously passed drove by. It would give her incentive, he feared.

At last the E.R. answered. "Connie, this is Dr. Turner. I've got one for you. Phone the OB on call. Tell him I suspect he'll need the plane." She hung up and placed the radio on the ledge behind the seats.

"Does that happen often?"

"First time. She probably picked my name out of the general section of the yellow pages, liking the *female* Christian name better than my *male* counterparts'." She started the car and merged onto the isolated highway.

"Well, after all, she *was* a woman. What would *she* know?" The car picked up speed. Derek shifted uncomfortably in his seat. "Seriously, though —"

"Oh, you weren't being serious before?"

"If you slow down just a little, I'll never say anything derogatory about the fairer sex."

The car passed a semi.

"I meant the smarter half of the population." The car didn't slow noticeably. She was one lucky woman having not crossed the path of a highway patrolman. "What's the fine for speeding?"

"Five dollars up to eighty-five. Let me know if you see a cop."

"Take some doing to get down to sixty-five."

"Eighty-five. Just change lanes. By the time they get another fix you're down to eighty-five." She pointed to a sign. "Now entering the Crow reservation. All of this for the next sixty miles or so was their reward for helping the white man subdue the Sioux and Cheyenne. Their bitter enemies, I might add. The Cheyenne have a tiny reservation on the east border. Another trick. Put the hostiles where the good Indians can police them."

No sense talking to her about speeding any longer. Apparently she was missing that part of her brain. "Just out of curiosity, and because I don't belong to the smarter half of the populace, why did you break in on the radio like that?"

"To protect her privacy. She thought I was on a phone instead of on the radio where every hunter in the area could be listening in."

"What's going to happen to her?"

"She'll go into labor within the next twenty-four hours. Hopefully, they'll have time to get the plane here and send her to Denver. The preemie might have a chance in Children's Neonatal Center. But sometimes I wonder if it's worth it."

Worth it to save premature babies or to have children? "Do you want children, Samantha?"

"John already had three children."

"I'm asking about Samantha."

She shrugged and pressed harder on the accelerator. "Academic questions are a waste of time."

About ten miles south of the Custer Battle-field, they came across a horse-car accident. Between the dead horse lying on the road and the gawkers, the sparse traffic had all but stopped. The shoulder was lined with cars and trucks with license plates from Colorado, Wyoming, Montana, Missouri. A semi had five rows of plates. An old Pontiac was turned on its side in the ditch.

"Anyone pinned in the car?" she asked the young Indian man who was directing traffic.

"The driver, but he's dead." His voice was frantic.

She pulled over, narrowly squeezing in between the semi and a Honda. She radioed for an ambulance before getting out of the car. "My bag's in the Jeep. Dammit."

A number of people, both Indian and white, were already giving chaotic aid to the injured Indian family. A middle-aged white couple, who looked to be vacationers, were holding and rocking two small children, a boy and a girl. Samantha ran to the nearest victim, a woman Derek guessed to be in her early thirties. She appeared to be catastrophically injured. The truck driver and two college-age girls were doing nothing more than standing over her. Samantha caught his eye and motioned to move on. Out of earshot of the victim, she said: "Chest injury. Nothing we can do for her."

Some men had gotten the driver out and carried him to the field. Samantha hurried over, dropped down beside him, and took his pulse. From ten feet away Derek could tell he was dead. She definitely couldn't help him.

A teenage boy was sprawled out on the thorny weeds, a piece of metal sticking out of his abdomen. He was bleeding so badly that no one was close to him. She dropped one knee in the pool of sticky blood and felt for a pulse. "Tacky, barely palpable."

"Shock?" Derek asked.

She nodded and took off her coat and pitched it. "Can you hear me?" She ripped off the shirt underneath. Pamela wouldn't have been caught dead in the simple bra Samantha wore. On the other hand, she filled it out nicely, something Pamela couldn't have done. "I'm a doctor. You're going to be all right." The boy didn't respond. "I need your shirt too." She padded the metal with the shirt to stabilize it.

Derek stripped out of his shirt.

She pulled her belt free and tore his shirt in two. He didn't complain. She was making a tourniquet with one of the pieces and her belt. "I need your belt." Sticky strings of blood pulled away as she moved to his other side. She was covered with blood. In these days of AIDS, her actions could be considered nothing short of heroic.

He kissed his belt good-bye.

She made another tourniquet. When she tightened it, she loosened the other; an impressive rotating tourniquet. "Derek, can you go check out

the kids and let me know if they need my imme-
diate attention. I need to make sure he stays in
the Trendelenburg position."

He left her manning the boy's tourniquets. He
might have gone his whole life without knowing
the Trendelenburg position had it not been for a
horse wandering out into the highway. On the
other hand, had the horse waited a little, he
might have been the one in the Trendelenburg
position, or worse. He wondered if this would
serve as a warning to her.

Derek squatted beside the woman holding the
little girl. There was an obvious break in her thin
arm. He felt above it. "Can you feel this?"

The little girl raised her big, black, watery
eyes. "I want my mommy."

His heart sank to the pit of his stomach. "Your
mommy's very busy resting from her injuries."

"Soon an ambulance is going to take you to
the hospital, where they're going to put a cast on
your arm for all your friends to sign," the woman
told her.

"I hurt. I want my mommy."

"Shhh," the woman said. Derek looked at the
boy. He had a little scrape on his left temple.

He reported his findings. Samantha had put
on her jacket, now also streaked with blood.

"We'll need a second ambulance. Could you
call?"

"The highway patrol's here. I'll let them
know."

The horse had been pushed into the median,

and after what seemed to be an eternity one ambulance arrived. Samantha ran to the attendant. "The boy over there needs to be shipped to Billings ASAP. The woman over there is a yellow prime . . . chest wound. The kids are all green and can wait for the other ambulance to take them to the Crow Agency hospital."

"What about the one over there?" the driver asked, pointing toward the father.

"He's black." Triage terminology for dead. Brought back Vietnam memories. None pleasant. Red — life threatening; yellow — serious; green — non-emergency injury. Derek hadn't heard the phrase yellow prime before.

After collecting the mother and teenager, the ambulance rushed off toward Billings. It took quite a while before the second ambulance arrived.

As the attendant closed the back door, Samantha and Derek hurried to her car. "Will they make it?" he asked.

"The boy has a good chance."

"But she isn't going to make it?"

"I doubt it. I'll go over and check on them after I've seen you safely off."

A car sped past, and Derek realized how vulnerable they were on the shoulder of the highway. "Why did you call the woman a yellow prime?"

"Chest wounds are classified yellow prime because . . . well, the boy was more salvageable. Some military triage systems even categorize a catastrophic injury like hers with the dead. We prefer to transport them ahead of patients with no urgent needs, though." She took a deep breath. "We aren't going to have time to stop at Custer Battlefield."

"It doesn't matter. This was more important."

The plane had started boarding when Derek arrived at the gate. Though she looked the worse for wear, she had insisted on coming into the terminal just in case he missed the plane. If he had missed it, though, he had no intention of driving back to Sheridan with her. He would have waited it out in a Billings motel. He placed his coat over the back of one of the empty chairs and embraced Samantha.

"Samantha, I'm so thankful that you and my father found each other. Thank you for making the rest of his life happy."

She pushed away. "Better hurry or you'll miss your plane."

"Drive home slowly, Samantha."

She nodded, but he knew she wouldn't. It worried him. He understood now why his father had fallen in love with her. Derek turned to wave when he reached the door, but she was racing down the concourse.

9

"Your ad said 'elk guaranteed.'" The whisker-stubbled dandy spun around on squeaky new boots and pointed an accusing finger at Frank.

Frank shifted the shoulder strap of his rifle and looked around the mountainous terrain. He'd been stupid to place that ad. But who'd thought there'd be a bumper crop of hunters in this sector?

"If Chuck and I don't get one today, we'll have to go back to California empty-handed," David spat. This one was part Mexican, Frank was almost sure.

"And you won't get the other half of your money, Frank," Chuck threatened, taking off his camouflage cap and running his sleeve across his sweat-slick forehead.

"We'll find one, don't worry," Frank said. The chances were getting mighty slim this late in the season. The few he'd seen had been down in the valley on that buffalo reserve. If there were only some way of scaring them back up the hill. He sure didn't want to lose his fee. Why'd he ever want to be a guide in the first place? A double Jim Beam would come in handy now. Well. "Let's head back to the pickup. I know where we'll find one."

Dusk was gathering when his pickup stopped

at the side of the dirt road. The two would-be hunters, armed with matching .375 Weatherbys, were one step ahead of him. He liked it that way. He was well out of their rifle sights when they crawled over the buck-and-rail fence. Frank followed when they were well situated on the other side. Their efforts were rewarded with the sight of a grazing bull at the other end of the draw.

The two men crept ahead. The elk's head sprang up just as Chuck shot. It ran. It jerked to the right and then stumbled as David's bullet pierced its left shoulder. David stood tall. Chuck gave him an angry smile.

"He's a big one," David said as he raced toward his kill.

Chuck followed with less enthusiasm. "Yeah, we may have to rent a packhorse from someone around here."

Frank would have to discourage that notion in a big way. He unsheathed his knife and squatted down beside the carcass. "One of you hold his front legs. We'll just take the head and cape, and the hind quarters."

"No, let's take it all."

They didn't seem to understand that they were poaching. He wasn't about to mention it, but he'd feel a whole lot better when they were out of there. "You wanna help over here, or what?"

Sam had a bad feeling about the out-of-county white battered pickup parked on the road above her house. The shots reinforced her fear. She gathered her denim skirt around her and jumped on one of the two four-wheelers and headed in the direction of the shooting.

The hunter gutting the elk stopped and watched her. His orange parka was grease-stained and his pants had a patch where one of the knees had sprung out. Compared to his buddies' matching camouflaged ensembles, his clothing was shabby. He had the look of an after-dark poacher, but the other two were more country-club types.

Sam got off the four-wheeler and stormed toward them. The large buck's entrails were exposed from crotch to neck and his throat slashed ear to ear, like the crossing of a capital T.

"Go ahead, finish the job," Sam said in a calm, steady voice. Her clenched fists were behind her back, lest they betray her true feelings.

"You and the hubby live near here, ma'am?" asked the deeply suntanned one, scratching three or four days' worth of brown whiskers.

"Right here," Sam answered, trying to keep both fear and anger out of her voice.

"Over in that house?" he asked, starting toward her.

Sam nodded and took a step back.

"Nice house. Chuck and I are contractors. You don't see cedar shake like that many places."

When the elk's esophagus was out, Sam placed hands on her hips and took a giant step forward. "Now you fuckers get off my land before I call the sheriff."

The shabby one climbed to his feet slowly, wiping the bloody knife on the elk's back.

Mr. Cedar Shake darted back to the elk. "Come on. Let's hurry and get him out of here." He spoke in whispers, but Sam could hear just fine. "She can't do anything. Get the cape at least."

"Just leave him where he is."

The shabby one stepped away from the carcass, sheathing his knife. The other two ignored her and kept on working.

A muscle twitched in her cheek. She added in a positively malignant tone, "You take him and I'll see you prosecuted."

"Oh, come on, lady! What's the big deal?" Mr. Cedar Shake asked.

"The big deal is that this is my land, and you're trespassers. That elk was a guest, unlike you. Now scram."

"Let's just go," the shabby one said, swooping up his pack. The other two deferred to his wishes.

A great sense of satisfaction swelled within her as they started off, but it vanished as she turned to see Jake's rifle leveled at the trespassers. She watched the hunters until they were out of sight. "Do whatever you want with the meat."

Depression at losing the elk turned to hatred as the hunters sat drinking at the beer-soaked table in Big Horn's Last Chance Bar. Frank had gotten that Jim Beam, and another. Now he was

118

helping polish off the pitcher of beer.

"Who does she think she is, anyway? That was my elk . . . I killed him," David said.

Drink riled his friend. "You should go back there and get it."

"No, it's gone by now," Frank assured them.

Chuck took the empty pitcher to the bar and returned with a full one. Foam sloshed everywhere. Unsteadily, David grabbed the pitcher with one hand and hooked a finger around his mug's handle with the other. He poured two parts foam and one part liquid gold. "I was really looking forward to mounting its head on the wall over the door." He slid the pitcher across the table.

Frank poured half foam, half liquid.

His partner agreed. "Yeah, that would've made a great conversation piece. We'd be the only construction offices in San Diego sporting an elk head." The foam had settled by the time he filled his mug.

They sucked on their beers.

"I'll tell you what would really be great on that wall," Chuck said. "A buffalo head."

"Yeah, like at Disneyland at that ah —"

"Bear Country place."

"Yeah . . . we could rig a speaker. He could say good-bye to all the folks."

"Yeah, just like the one at Disneyland."

Frank listened to the overzealous boys in disgust. The only thing he liked about them was their money. And their beer.

"What do you say, Frank?"

He looked over at him. "About what?"

"The buffalo."

Slowly it sunk in. "You want me to help you poach one of their buffalo?"

Chuck looked at him hard. The crinkle between his gray eyes deepened. "Well, you weren't opposed to poaching the elk on their land."

"No. Maybe they've already called the sheriff."

David pushed back his cap and leaned in closer. "We'll pay you double."

The bar turned stuffy all of a sudden. Frank coughed nervously. *Double. Would serve the bitch right.* "All right."

"Dr. Turner," Sam said as she picked up the phone in her office.

"Sam, it's Jeffrey."

"Hello, Jeffrey. What's up? Did they catch the killers?"

"Killer, please. No sense making everyone more nervous than they already are."

"Jeffrey, the Halloween murder was not — and I repeat, not — committed by our so-called Holiday Murderer."

"Sam, I don't need this right now. It's all I can do to tread water."

"Yeah, and how about Pamela?"

"Sam, I feel like the Dutch boy with his finger in the dike. I'm afraid if we say anything now a wall of water's going to drown us."

"Your allusion eludes me, Jeffrey."

"Listen, Sam, I didn't call about business. I called to ask you to serve on the Doctor-Lawyer dinner-dance committee."

Just what she needed. She hated that kind of stuff, but didn't quite know how to tell him no. "Sure, I'd love to."

The sky was as full of motion and change as was the seemingly still prairie beneath it. Jake, like his ancestors who had great love and respect for the land, watched with a happy heart as the prairie dogs played tag. Most ranchers would have poisoned the creatures to rid themselves of the holes the horses trip in, but not Dr. Turner. She loved all animals, and more animals than usual grazed her land, as if knowing it was a sanctuary from the hunter.

Racks of elk meat hung drying on the south side of Jake's shack. He had been saddened as he cut the thin strips, knowing what the killing of the elk had been to her.

A strange feeling tugged at him as he rode over the land. Hawks, circling to the south of the grazing buffalo, told him that something was wrong. Jake clicked his horse toward them with dread. All of the vulnerable buffalo calves were accounted for. He continued south.

The growling and snarling of the coyotes confirmed what he had already guessed. The sight of a headless, skinned buffalo brought tears to his eyes.

The white man would never learn.

Kate put her hand over the phone as Sam walked through the door. "Dr. Turner, Jake just called. Said to tell you that one of the buffalo died."

"What?"

"Just a minute, Mike." She covered the phone again. "Said to tell you that one of the buffalo died."

"Did he say anything else?"

"Just that he'd call the sheriff."

"What?"

"Just that he'd call the sheriff." Irritation crept into Kate's tone as her patience dwindled. "Listen, Mike, can I call you —"

"Never mind, Kate. I'll be at home."

Sam raced through the halls and out the front door without stopping to turn off her house light. Bent against the wind, she ran to the Jeep.

She'd gotten just beyond the school when she saw the flashing red light in her mirror.

Sizzling blood skated through her veins as she waited impatiently for Skip to get out of his patrol car. He didn't. She jumped out and raced back to his car.

"Would you wait in the outfit, ma'am?"

"Listen, Skip, I'm in a hurry. You want to just tell me what this is about?"

He cut her off by turning to the dash as if he could see the person whose voice came over the radio. "Wyoming three . . . two nine one four. Listed to Samantha Turner, M. D. R. R. One, Big Horn. No warrants, over."

Skip started to press down on the button to answer, but instead looked around at her. "Ma'am, please return to your outfit."

Sam glared at him, and he turned away, waiting for her to obey his order.

She stormed back to her Jeep. *Fine time to get his revenge.* Seething, she sat waiting for him. Having pushed the moment to its limits, he strolled up to her window.

"May I see your driver's license, ma'am?"

She slapped it against his palm hard enough to send a corner up under his jacket sleeve.

He studied it long and hard. He held it against her cheek to make certain the picture matched every pore in her face.

Sam could stand no more. "Do you want to tell me what this is about?"

Skip pulled the license back. "Ma'am, I clocked you doing forty-three in a school zone."

"Really? Are you sure, *officer?*"

"Yes, ma'am." He walked away, eyes glued to the license.

Sam drummed her fingers on the steering wheel while she waited for him to return. Between worrying about what had happened at the ranch, and the ribbing she knew she'd be taking from her friends when they found out about this new ticket, Sam was sure her anxiety level had reached an all-time high. A beta-block to slow her

123

heart rate might be just what the doctor would order.

At last, he returned. "Please read this carefully, then sign at the bottom . . . next to the X." He handed her the metal clip board slowly.

She scribbled her signature on the bottom and thrust it back, giving his wrist a whack for good measure.

Meticulously, he tore off the yellow copy and handed it to her. Sluggishly, he returned her driver's license. "Have a nice day, ma'am."

She raised the window. "It's turning out to be one hell of a nice day."

The sheriff's brown Bronco was parked in the driveway. She opened the pasture gate and drove along the creek's narrow bank until she saw the circle of brown uniformed men. Ignoring the buzzing from the Jeep, Sam rushed forward and pushed her way through the deputies.

Crouching, she looked down at the decapitated carcass of a male bison, feeling as if she'd been stabbed with a red-hot cattle prod. Insects jumped as she slid her hand up his hoof and then through the woolly hair on his leg. The trunk had been skinned.

Hank hunkered down next to her, but the stink quickly drove him back. "Can't imagine who'd do this, Sam."

"A couple of contractors would be my guess."

"You *know* who did this?" the sheriff asked, pulling his handkerchief from his back pocket.

"I should have given them the elk," she said

to no one in particular.

The sheriff covered his nose and mouth as he leaned in to hear her. "What?"

"Nothing." Sam climbed to her feet and walked away.

10

Sam left before dawn the following Sunday morning, making the mountainous four-hour drive to Worland — she'd remembered the county number on the license plate — in a little over three. She drove up and down every street in town looking for the battered white pickup. She'd called every contractor in Worland, but to no avail.

After covering every block of the small town, Sam started on plan B. She drove to a ranch-style house across the street from the elementary school. A child's laughter came from inside. She walked up the cement steps.

A little redheaded boy answered the door.

"Hello. Is your daddy home?" Sam asked.

The boy scampered off. A youthful-looking, sandy-haired man soon appeared at the door. "Dr. Turner." He opened the door wide. "Please come in."

"Thanks, Stewart." Sam wiped her boots on the doormat before stepping onto the green carpet. She looked around the clean, though toy-scattered, small living room, and took a seat while apologizing for troubling him. Then she told the supervisor of the Bureau of Land Management about the buffalo.

His faced reddened as he listened. She had

come to him because he knew what the buffalo meant to her, and he thought he owed her one for taking a couple of old ones off his hands a few months back.

Sam listened as he talked on the kitchen phone. "Howdy, Linda. Sheriff handy? Thanks." His tone changed. "Honey, can you and Andy go to church alone?"

Guilt overcame Sam as she looked down at the little boy crawling across the carpet. "You married, Andy?"

Andy ran the truck over her toes. "Yuck! I hate girls."

She twisted her feet under the chair. "Single. Good enough reason as any."

Andy's mother, armed with a comb, came looking for him. The big-boned woman grabbed the squirming boy's arm and sat on the edge of the rocker. She nodded her welcome to Sam. "Can't hardly get a comb through this," she said as she tugged.

Little Andy hollered as he inched away. Like a vise, his mother's legs locked around him. Except for the cowlick that stood straight up, the hair was pretty well slicked down. His freckle-blotched forehead somehow looked naked without the mop of red hair hanging over it.

"The sheriff's going to meet us there." Stewart kissed his wife, then swooped up Andy and pecked his cheek. "You be good in church, young man. I don't want to hear you were being noisy."

Andy turned his head away. Sam got the idea

he might not be the most patient little fellow. And church could seem mighty long even for the most patient.

They arrived at the taxidermy — a converted barn next to an old house just off the two-lane — ahead of the sheriff. The owner was sitting at a workbench laboring over an elk head. An odor of mothballs won out over the multitude of others in the dark room.

"May I help you folks?"

"We're just looking," Sam told him as she examined the animals adorning the walls. "Are these all for sale?"

"Most of them. Do you see anything you want?"

Sam tried hard to keep the sarcasm out of her voice. "Absolutely nothing." She failed miserably, if she could judge from the taxidermist's glare.

Stewart walked over to a closed door. "Have anything else in the back?"

Before he could answer, the bell over the door chimed and the sheriff walked in. The taxidermist paled noticeably.

The sheriff ambled over to Stewart. "See it?"

Stewart shook his head. "Maybe in here?"

"Mind if we look in the back room?"

The man stood up and threaded through the clutter. "What's this all about, Sheriff?"

"Looking for a buffalo head."

The man scratched his thin nose over and over again as he thought. With only a slight hesitation, he bobbed his head. "Someone brought one in a couple days back. Through there."

Stewart stepped into the dark room one step ahead of Sam.

"You need to pull the string," the man offered, suddenly trying to be very friendly. "Here, let me get it." He brushed past the sheriff, and felt the air for the string. "There."

Stewart looked around the crowded room. "Where is it?"

The man pointed to the far corner.

Sam skirted them and hurried to the corner. Blood-hardened newspaper snapped and pulverized as she stepped on it. She bent over and pulled off the sheet of newspaper that only slightly hid the buffalo head. The paper ripped as it caught on the spiraling deformed horn.

Jeffrey watched the busy hostess seat another party of luncheon customers. He glanced at his watch. Sam was late, and if she didn't arrive soon, he'd have to leave. He wondered what they'd charge for the basket of crackers he ate.

"I'm sorry I'm late," Sam said as she slumped into her chair. "Where's Harry?"

"His secretary left a message with mine saying he had to go to Casper unexpectedly."

"Great. We should have postponed the meeting until tomorrow or next March, whichever comes first." Sam flicked out her napkin and spread it on her lap.

"What we really ought to do is send our secre-

taries to lunch and let them work out the details."

"I second that motion."

"It has been moved and seconded. All those in favor?" Two hands flew up. "Opposed?"

Sam looked at the empty chair and shook her head. "Just like Harry."

"Two to one. Carried," Jeffrey said, tapping his knife on the tablecloth.

"I do so love the majority system."

"Busy morning, Sam?"

"Incredibly. And yours?"

He tried to motion to the waitress, but she went the other way. "I don't believe we've ever prosecuted more hunters. Had one this morning who dumped a six-pointer by the side of the road."

"He left the points?"

"Got a bigger one."

Sam leaned over the table and, in not much more than a whisper, asked, "And speaking of getting bigger ones, what's happening with the murderers? Any leads?"

"I wish you'd stop talking in plurals —"

"And why should I?" Sam's voice grew louder. "We both know —"

"We don't know anything . . . not legally."

"Fuck legal," Sam cried as she banged her fist on the table, flipping her spoon off the table.

Jeffrey bent over and retrieved the spoon, stalling until the occupants of the surrounding tables turned backed to their own conversations.

"We've already had this discussion. The lab claims they never received the evidence from the Halloween murder. And without that evidence . . ." His voice trailed off as he saw her face contort in anger. "If you could just understand —"

"All I understand is that there are two killers walking our streets." She took a deep breath and moved her lips as she counted to ten. "All right, let's not fight. You're the only ally I have. And I really do believe the Halloween killing *was* an accident. The guy is probably so upset over what he did that he hasn't so much as gotten a parking ticket. But the other killer is a time bomb. You and I have to do something about him. How many more women are going to have to die before our illustrious police force catches him?"

"Don't you think I want him caught just as much as you?"

Sam pushed the salt and pepper shakers to the edge of the table. "I know you do."

"Just tell me what you want me to do."

"I don't know. Call in the FBI, CIA, IRS, NBC. I don't know."

"If Bill could have his rathers, it'd be NBC."

"Dan?" Pleased with the pun, she ordered a chef salad. He got a French dip.

Once the waitress was out of earshot, Jeffrey started to squirm. "Sam, I don't think we'll be able to extradite the two poachers from California."

Sam's back became ramrod straight. She glared at him. "And why not? They killed Curly."

"It's too costly. Even if we did, they'd only

serve thirty days or so in the county jail." Seeing that she was about to explode again, he added, "I'll hang the guide out to dry, though."

"Gee, that's real white of you, Jeffrey."

Jeffrey picked up the bud vase. "My God, Sam, you've wilted the carnation!"

Her pursed lips and hooded eyes told him she wasn't amused. He quietly set it down. "I am sorry, you know."

"Yeah."

Her icy tone knifed through him. After a few minutes of listening to her silent irritation, Jeffrey chanced speaking. "Sam, what do you want from me?"

"I don't know." She ran her finger along the edge of the tablecloth. "Why do I feel as if I have to push twice as hard to get half as much accomplished?"

"Do you think you're the only one? You want to talk frustration? How'd you like knowing that almost half of the briefs you're spilling your guts over have already been decided under the table?"

"So I hear. Wish they'd move Stanley to traffic court."

She was not without a sense of humor. He reached over and took her hand. "Why don't you just slow down? You know you make their day."

"Words are easy."

He withdrew his hand as the waitress approached. When the waitress left, he said, "Maybe if you didn't drive a red car."

"What do you mean?"

"Red cars attract attention. You need a boring color . . . like brown."

"You think that would help?"

"That and slowing down. Get an old clunker that won't go fast. A 'forty-eight Rambler. I'd even let you give me a ride."

"How about a VW? Would you ride in a VW?"

He shrugged. "I'd certainly ride in a stretch limo with a chauffeur."

"How about a stretch Grand Wagoneer? Like out at the dude ranch. And a cowboy chauffeur?"

"Now you're cooking."

"Or an Indian. I could get Jake to drive me around town."

He held up his hand. "Stop right there. I'm not riding with Jake. Now there's a person who really should lose his license. He's as slow as you are fast."

"White man speak with forked tongue."

Jeffrey held up his fork. "White man eats with tonged fork."

Sam grimaced. "That was terrible, Jeffrey." She looked around. "I hope no one heard you."

"Me?" He pointed an accusing finger. "You started it."

"Well, the penalty for bad punning is life imprisonment." Her face turned sour. "Better to kill a buffalo. Or women."

He nudged the last of his French dip into his mouth as he looked over at her. After an uncomfortable moment, Jeffrey looked down at his watch. He shot up. "Stanley's probably dismissed the first four cases already."

"I've got to go, too." Sam grabbed for the check, but Jeffrey snatched it away.

"You can get the next one . . . a nice expensive one." He dropped a couple of dollars on the table as he rose.

"That's what I love about you, Jeffrey."

"My extravagance?" He pulled the chair out for her.

"Now *that* was funny."

He took the envelope from his mailbox before climbing the rickety stairs to his apartment over the Main Street coin store. He laid it squarely on the wobbly-legged kitchen table, hung up his coat, took out a saucepan, a can opener, and a can of Campbell's tomato soup.

After he put the soup into the pan, he sloshed water around the empty can, trapping the remaining residue. He took a loaf of brown bread from the multicoated white cabinet and untwisted the wire tie as he haunted the simmering soup. He placed two pieces of bread on the counter beside a bowl, then carefully sealed the cellophane package and put it away.

He stared at the envelope as he sipped his soup. His mother's writing was so sloppy, almost as if she had written his address in a hurry. An empty bowl and a few bread crumbs later, he ran his finger under the flap. He didn't read the printed Thanksgiving verse, just the short scribbled note:

"The store starts its Christmas activities Friday after Thanksgiving, so shall be busy. So sorry you can't get away for turkey day, but will look forward to seeing you at Christmas. Take care of yourself. Love, Mom."

He read it over several times, then the verse. He stuck the card back into the envelope and then into the kitchen drawer containing her Valentine and Easter cards. He washed the dishes.

11

Friday, the day after Thanksgiving, was quieter than most at the hospital, with most would-be patients enjoying a four-day weekend. It was quieter, that is, until the phone call came after lunch. The victim was seventy-six years old.

Sam grabbed a rape kit out of the E.R. supply closet and headed out. Tucking the kit under her arm, she thrust her hands deep into her coat pockets. The sun was shining, but it gave little warmth against the chilling wind. She couldn't remember when she was this cold. Nor could she remember where she'd left her gloves.

The trailer court Mrs. Taylor had lived in was like any other: crowded. Sam found number forty-one the easy way, by looking for the yellow tape strung across the property. She was mightily surprised to see neighbors standing in small clusters around the mobile home. They must have been freezing.

Mrs. Taylor's walkway hadn't been shoveled, and the trampled snow had turned icy in spots. Skip stared at her with unfocused resignation. She nodded and brushed by him. The storm door creaked open as far as a drift of snow would allow. She squeezed through the aperture.

A sixtyish woman sat crying on a gold plaid couch in the narrow living room and another woman of about the same age rocked briskly in a matching chair, a wet tissue at her nose. The place was tastefully done in Early American maple furniture. Both women looked up at her and then turned back to the television where they were watching, or at least staring at, Dr. So-and-So tell Monica that her husband's Mittelschmerz condition was terminal. He was the first man Sam had ever heard of to be dying of ovulation discomfort. But then, the Hollywood doctor was probably a specialist in such matters. He held Monica's hand very convincingly.

Sam crossed between the women she assumed were crying over Mrs. Taylor's fate, not Monica's husband's, and headed down the hallway.

Bill was ringmaster of the circus, which included a couple extra clowns. The man from Washington, who had wanted her records back in August or September, was beside Thaddeus. Up until she walked through the door, Thaddeus had been bending the man's ear about how he would handle this case if he were still coroner. Mobile homes were not known for their impenetrable walls. The Washington man's face was thick with baby fat, and he wore his khaki trench coat over a gray suit like a boy in men's clothing. The trench coat wasn't warm enough — he was a bit blue around his goiter. Sherman was taking pictures of Bill next to the lump under the flowered sheet for his newspaper. A Bible was strategically placed to be in the shot. A police officer, Gary, stood waiting with his Polaroid to take official pictures.

Sam slipped behind Bill and the overturned lamp and lifted a corner of the sheet. Loose skin all but obliterated any signs of the stocking around the neck. But the top end of the stocking covered her blue hair like a scarf. Her eyeballs bulged under heavily crinkled lids. She would wait until Sherman was gone before looking at the rest of the body. "Who are the women in the living room?"

"Friends of the deceased."

"They found the body?"

"One of them did." Bill spoke behind unmoving lips as he smiled for Sherman. "She was supposed to go to a church circle with them. They honked and honked. One came in and found her."

Sherman reached out and pulled on Sam's arm. "Now one with you and the doctor."

Bill put his arm around her. She broke away while he was busy posing. "Sam, get back here. He wants a picture."

Sam stopped in front of the G-man and offered her hand. "I wish you had left a card, I would have called."

He shook her hand and opened his mouth to say something.

Bill spoke. "He's been here all week waiting for this one."

"Why's that?"

"It's a holiday, Sam," Bill explained as if to a kindergartner.

"So were Halloween and Labor Day. This is

the first from our man since July."

Sherman's ears perked up. Bill rushed him out of the room. "Now, Sherman, if any of those turn out, you be sure to send me one. My wife keeps a scrapbook, you know."

The G-man didn't look surprised. Sam took it to mean Bill had explained that Pamela's murder was unrelated. It was a huge concession on Bill's part.

"Who was Lisa Henderson?"

The outsider stared blankly at her, his right eye twitching.

"She didn't have any memorabilia. What's your interest in her?"

"It really doesn't concern you."

Sam noticed Thaddeus smile. It was something he rarely did. Well, one doesn't really smile when dispensing sympathy to the grieving widow, even when the lavish funeral will put braces on Junior's teeth. "I'll be the judge of that."

His pale-blue eyes disappeared behind slits, the twitch hardly noticeable. "I don't believe so."

"Do you know who the killer is?"

He shook his head.

"Little hard to see the picture when you're hiding a piece of the puzzle, don't you think?"

"I'll ask the questions."

The arrogance of the man was beyond belief. "Ask all the questions you want. Just don't expect answers. At least not until you've answered mine."

The unseasonable cold snap continued into December, reaching into the minus-fifty-degree range with the wind-chill factor. The landscape offered a monotonous sameness, a blanket of white snow shrouded by a damp, icy cold, steel-gray sky. Furious blasts of blowing wind whirled ice pellets high into the frozen air.

Depression stemming from the bleakness of both the murders and the cold made the days, which were actually growing shorter, seem longer. And the townsfolk weren't caught up in the festivities of the Christmas season, but were preoccupied with gloom. The Thanksgiving victim's being an old woman didn't help.

The sheriff tracked Sam down at the V.A. hospital; another coroner's case. Sam followed his directions and found the small ranch on the border of the county line.

She parked between the deputy's LTD and the sheriff's brown Bronco. She walked briskly through the blowing snow to the house, her bag listing in the wind. She hadn't been given specifics and had no idea what to expect but would welcome anything a warm house had to offer. She stomped snow from her boots and looked into the incredibly messy living room. The weathered hardwood floor creaked as she stepped inside. The sheriff left a sobbing man sitting at the kitchen table and hurried over to her.

"Hank." Sam nodded, unbuttoning her coat.

"It's a real mess," he whispered, his jaw thrust at a serious angle. He looked back over his shoulder toward the kitchen. "Poor man got home this morning from Lander to find his whole family . . . dead."

"How many?" she asked, slinging her coat over the back of the couch.

"Five."

She seethed. She wished she had some magical words of condolence to soften the blow, but she knew there were none. Only time could partially heal such pain. "Where are they?"

Hank cocked his thumb. "Both bedrooms."

"God, I hate this!"

Toys and rubble choked the passageway to the bedrooms. Sam took a deep breath before entering the nearest bedroom. A young woman's body was sprawled across the blood-soaked bed. Shot in the eye and upper left quadrant. She must have been in a sitting position if Sam could go by the splattering of blood and brain tissue on the headboard, wall, and seascape.

Albeit repulsive, it was nothing compared to how she felt seeing the yellow crib with the aqua and pink bunny mobile swaying in the cold draft from the window, which was raised an inch. The stench of death lingered anyway.

She worked her way around a basket of laundry, two boxes of Pampers, and a pile of newspapers and woman's magazines. The crib held a tiny new infant. She instinctively closed her eyes, but the image of the corpse didn't fade.

It took a moment to separate the clinician from the woman. She opened her eyes slowly, trying to absorb the horror a little at a time.

"Did you find the baby somewhere else?"

He shook his head. "Why?"

She crooked her finger, summoning Hank. "It's a head wound. But I don't see much blood. You sure the baby wasn't in bed with the mother?"

"Not when we got here . . . and Mr. Woods said he hadn't touched anything. Maybe the nephew did."

"You're right. See the black powder burns on the sheet?"

He looked over her shoulder. "Why'd the kid have to kill the baby, anyway? It couldn't talk."

"You guys know who did this? What's the story?"

"The woman's nephew. Went crazy and killed everybody in the house, then turned the gun on himself."

"Where is he?" Sam asked as she started out of the room.

"In the children's room." He followed her out.

A flutter of horror bolted through her as she looked down at a skinny kid lying on his side, legs bent awkwardly at a right angle. She could almost make out the printing on his T-shirt. *Life's A Beach*. "And then it's over," she mumbled under her breath. He was at the foot of one of the twin beds with a gun in his hand. "What is that?"

"A .38 revolver."

She squatted next to the head to get a better look at the gun. "Give me your pen." She lifted the boy's index finger. "Hank, look at this. The rigor mortis is broken."

Hank hunkered down beside her and pushed back his Stetson for a better look. "Isn't that funny?"

"Real funny."

She climbed to her feet and worked a kink out of her back.

She stepped over the scattered toys and dirty clothing and walked to the farthest twin bed. There she found a boy of about ten, with a bullet hole in his back. His Superman pajama top was stiff and dark with blood. Flecks of crusty brown blood fell away as she put a finger to the bluish puckered hole. Another bullet had penetrated the colon. The stench of feces persisted. He had tried to hide under the bed.

"Ownership of the gun?" she asked.

"Mr. Woods. Said he kept it on the top shelf of the hall closet, out of the boys' reach."

"Too bad they weren't able to reach it. Might have been able to defend themselves."

In the other bed was another little towhead boy. A round entering the occipital bone posteriorly had shattered the left mandible and embedded in the little fellow's scapula. Sam allowed her mind to view him only clinically. She did not wish to think of him as a little boy who'd gone to bed two nights ago with the now blood-speckled Winnie-the-Pooh under his arm.

"A .38 revolver shoots six bullets?"

He nodded.

"He had to reload to shoot himself, then. I count seven." Sam skirted around the sheriff. "Let's get out of here so I can breathe."

She leaned up against the hall wall, wishing she were anywhere but there. "How long was the father out of town?"

"He left early the day before yesterday. Got back early this morning."

"Where was the nephew sleeping?" Sam asked, walking into the unscrubbed bathroom between the two bedrooms. She went straight for the medicine cabinet.

"In the little shack across the road."

Sam pulled out a vial and held it out. "My arm's getting too short for this. Going to have to start wearing my glasses on a chain around my neck."

"What is it?"

"A prescription from Dr. Wallace."

"Old Doc Wallace?"

She shook her head, only half hearing. "Little Bob."

"The wife swears by the old doc. Brought all three kids into the world. Took out my appendix back in '64. He really got Sarah when the first one came along. In a Donald Duck-like voice he kinda said 'Mama.' Sarah said she just about fell off the table in surprise."

She smiled. "He's a character, all right." Sam put the vial back into the cabinet. "I want to visit with Mr. Woods."

Hank led the way. "Mr. Woods?"

The tear-swollen faced turned up to reveal red-rimmed gray eyes under horn-rimmed glasses. His face was leathery, as are many ranchers; Sam suspected this was what made him look centuries older than his thirty-some years.

"Mr. Woods, this is Dr. Turner. She'd like to speak to you a minute."

He nodded.

Sam sat across the table. "I can only guess how difficult this is for you, Mr. Woods, and I'm so terribly sorry I have to bother you like this."

"It's all right," he assured her in an old man's voice.

"Was someone helping your wife with the children while you were out of town, Mr. Woods?"

He took off his glasses and wiped tears from his face with the back of his hand. "Just her nephew."

"You didn't move any of the bodies, did you?"

"No —" His head thumped against Formica as he broke down and cried.

Under a mountain of fatigue, Sam rose. She put on her coat and buttoned up before leaving the house. She made her way through the blowing snow toward the shack where the nephew had lived. The sheriff followed on her heels.

"Why do you want to see it? We already checked it for a note." He raised the collar of his jacket against the wind. "Clean as a whistle."

Sam shrugged. "Just humor me."

The one-room shack was surprisingly clean. She stood over the narrow bed, staring down at it for a very long time. Lifting a corner of the floral bedspread, she peeked under. "Ever in the service, Hank?"

"Marine Corps. Korea."

"Come look at the corner on this sheet."

He squatted down next to her. "Military, all right."

"They teach that in Boy Scouts?"

"Boy —"

"Never mind. Rhetorical."

Sam sat on the edge of the bed, leaning back against the wall. "Wrong angle." She sniffed, and then turned to look at the scrubbed wall. "Pine-Sol." She ran her fingertips over the wall, feeling the bumps of texture. "You sleep with a pillow, Hank?"

"Doesn't everybody?"

"One would think he didn't." She motioned to the head of the bed, then got up and sat down in dilapidated gold swivel chair in front of the television. A loose spring jumped up and bit her. She vaulted out of the chair, rubbing her thigh.

"Whatcha doin'?" His face wore worry. "Hurt yourself?"

"Spring pinched me. That's all." She looked hard at the chair before sliding back into it. She held the spring down and listed to the right for extra measure. She let her legs go limp and noted the angle.

"All right," Sam said, easing herself out of the chair. "I'm satisfied. Let's go." She buttoned up her coat and pulled on her new gloves before going outside. Hank didn't have gloves, just a Sheriff's Department-issue fleece-lined jacket.

"Just can't imagine who could do a thing like this."

She could imagine. But she'd rather tell him over the phone when she was back in her warm office. It was damned cold.

"Poor Mr. Woods."

"Don't poor-Mister-Woods me."

"Huh?"

She stopped in the middle of the road and tugged on his sleeve. "Want to hear my version?"

"Yeah," he replied, his voice laced with surprise. His hands were deep in his pockets, lending his stooped shoulders an even greater hump.

As if doodling, she drew the toe of her boot across the red shale the county truck dumped to add traction to the snow-packed county road. "Mr. Woods, probably by accident, suffocated the baby. He must have been the prime caretaker for the last two weeks . . . since his wife's confinement to bed. To cover up, he killed the rest of the family in their sleep."

"What! You crazy? He was out of town."

"Should be able to trace his comings and goings. Had to buy gas somewhere. Yesterday morning, hours after he killed the wife and kids, he decided to blame it on the nephew. He went across the road and shot him in bed."

"This is the most absurd —"

"He moved the body to that damn chair in front of the television in order to tidy up the mess. Must have carried the body over after dark last night."

"But there weren't any traces —"

"Did a neat job . . . too neat. Too bad he couldn't have helped his wife as much."

He shook his head. "No, it's unbelievable."

"Unbelievable? Perhaps. But that's what the evidence looks like to me. The infant was dead before it was shot. There's almost no blood in the crib . . . because the blood wasn't circulating through the body. It had already congealed."

He nodded in agreement. "That's why you asked about the baby being in bed with the mother."

"Remember the rigidity of the nephew's bent legs. Rigor mortis didn't set in while he was on the floor. He would have been molded to the surface if it had. It set in while he was sitting in that chair. Bet I'll find a bruise on his butt, too." She shivered. "Mr. Woods must have had a hell of a time getting the fingers around the gun. Remember the broken rigor?"

"But —"

"I'll post them in the morning. Hate doing autopsies on kids." She started toward her Jeep.

"Hey, Sam," the sheriff called over the wind. "Why was the woman confined to bed?"

"Now *that* I don't know, but two weeks ago she had a prescription filled for a muscle relaxant . . .

and by the looks of the house, she hasn't been out of bed since."

Sparks flew as Bob Wallace, Jr., ripped his blood-soiled gown away from the sweat-slick green surgical garb. He threw the gown in the red Dumpster, then pushed through the swinging doors of the obstetrics wing, intending to head for the doctors' lounge. A hot shower and street clothes would be the ticket. It had been a restless night and a busy day. But nothing lifted his spirits more than handing a healthy newborn to loving parents. It made the long hours worthwhile.

He noticed Sam turning on her house light. He'd wait for her. She looked upset. "There you are. I was looking for you earlier. I want you to tell Boomer he's quite the stud . . . did a fine job."

Sam stuffed her gloves in her coat pocket. "Have the puppies come?"

"Ten of them early this morning, before sunup." He twirled a side of his handlebar mustache. They were always splitting or drooping, and needed more wax than Karen's hair needed mousse. "I can't even get my own family to deliver during the day."

"I hope you won't be offended if I don't feel sorry for you." Sam took off her coat. She was standing in a widening reddish puddle, her worn boots covered with red shale and melting snow. It looked as if she'd been wrestling with her buffalo.

"I'd gladly change places with you . . . you eight-to-fiver."

"You'd have loved it today." Her tone said otherwise.

"Another woman?"

She shook her head. "By the way, why did you give Mrs. Woods the Parafon Forte?"

Sheer terror struck. All of Sam's patients were dead. "It killed her?"

"Indirectly." She laughed and took his hand. "Just kidding, but you should see the color of your face. Casper's sheet should be so white." She sighed. He waited with bated breath. "She was shot . . . and so were her kids. Plus a nephew."

The panic of a malpractice suit subsided a little, though his knees were still shaking. Shot? He was born and reared in Sheridan. It had always been a mecca of peace. What was happening? What kind of environment was his little Amy growing up in? "The Holiday Murderer?"

She shook her head.

Who would kill like that? And such a nice family. He had a hollow feeling in the pit of his stomach. Those two little rambunctious towheads were dead. And he'd just brought the baby into the world a month or so ago. They'd been so happy when he told them it was a girl.

"Well?" Sam asked. "What was the prescription for?"

"She fell down a flight of stairs leaving church. Sprained her back and broke her pelvis."

"That's enough to make atheists of the best of us."

Life had played a cruel trick on the family. "How's Mr. Woods taking it?"

"Not great."

"Did they catch the killer?"

Sam shrugged. "I'll come by in a couple of days . . . ah, sometime soon to look at the puppies."

He took her arm. "Come on. I'll walk you as far as the showers."

They started down the corridor. "I'll be sure to tell Boomer about the puppies . . . though I doubt if he'll care. His motives were entirely different from ours."

"You're so catty."

"Punny, Bob. Real punny."

"Sam!" It was Larry's voice.

They stopped and looked at each other.

"I bet my horoscope said to stay in bed today." She backed up and looked into the administrator's office. "You called?"

"Come in and sit down a minute."

Bob started to leave, but Sam pulled him back. "Come in with me. Let's hit him up again for an E.R. doc."

"You are an eternal optimist." He followed her in.

"Glad you have a moment to visit, Larry. Bob and I were just this minute talking about this great E.R. doc down in Denver. He wants to move to Sheridan."

This great doctor was a figment of her imagination, but Bob would play along. "We think he should be invited to join the staff." Larry didn't bat an eye. "Maybe on a trial basis."

"Just one lawsuit," Sam raised a finger for a little visual aid, "would pay for his services a good ten years."

"So you keep telling me." Larry rubbed his already polished scalp. He cleared his throat; it was his way of controlling the conversation. "A supplier's coming up the day after tomorrow. Says he can undercut the current supplier ten percent. I want you, representing the hospital, to take him to dinner."

"For the lab?"

"X ray." He shortened his eyes to a letter on his desk.

"X ray! Talk to Ken."

"Ken can't. He's busy Friday night."

"Then you take him."

"I'm busy."

"I'm busy, too."

Bob was busy three. They were all being busy together. It was his birthday, and Karen was throwing him a surprise party. He should offer to take the supplier to dinner just to throw in a monkey wrench. "Karen and I'll take him to dinner."

Sam looked at Larry, her eyes slits, her lips pursed as though she was waiting for him to kiss her. Or maybe waiting to build enough saliva to spit in his face.

Larry cleared his throat. "If you do this for me, I'll free up some time to talk to you about this Denver doctor."

"You mean it?"

"Well, we can discuss it. No promises."

Larry was such a diplomat. Bob couldn't understand why Sam bothered. She could pour a can of gasoline over her head and set fire to herself and the administrator would still be unmoved.

"All right," she said, nodding. "I'll take him to dinner, if you take me to lunch. Friday."

The phone rang as she was reading the want ads in the back of the *New England Journal of Medicine*. A quick look at the clock and even quicker addition told her that it was after midnight in New Orleans. That was so typical of Sharon.

"You got out of singing again this year, I see. Well, go get your earplugs."

Silence.

"Sharon?"

"Samantha, it's Derek. . . . I could call back later if you're waiting for a call."

Sam felt the heat of embarrassment rise through her. "No, I wasn't, wasn't a . . ." Her tongue was tied. "I wasn't expecting a call. I thought it was Sharon." She groaned and then took a deep breath. "It's after midnight in New York. What are you doing up?"

"Oh, I'll turn in soon. Listen, the pictures

didn't take. Must have sent them through the X-ray machine at the airport or something. Anyway, do you think I could come to Sheridan for Christmas?"

"Sure."

"I'm not keeping you from a vacation or anything?"

"No. Dad, Jake, and I will be having Christmas dinner here. We'll set another plate."

"How about the Friday before Christmas?"

"That's fine . . . and there's a dance Saturday. Do you have a tux?"

"Every self-respecting New Yorker has one. Actually, I own three."

She silently mouthed the word *three*. She had only one evening dress, a fifteen-year-old black number made from flimsy summer material. "Well, bring one along."

"Will do. I'll call you about the fine-tuning. Thanks."

"Good night."

"Good night."

Sam returned to the journal. She read the same column twice before giving up and turning off the light.

"The puppies." Sam leaned over the side of the bed. "Boomer, thanks for the great birthday present."

He sighed.

12

Sam kept one eye on the clock over the bar as she listened to the X-ray supplier. Dinner had been easy enough — though she was still steamed that Larry had slithered out of lunch — but getting away after dinner had proven futile.

"This really is a nice little town. I'm happy I came myself instead of sending one of my salesmen."

Bob's surprise party was well under way by now. Sam picked up her wine goblet and drank as if she were looking for the bottom.

"Ever get to Denver?"

"Not much." Sam didn't want to tell him that she had been born and reared there, knew it like the back of her hand. She just wanted to finish her drink and leave.

"Sheridan reminds me of it, somehow."

"Probably the mountains." Sam took another swallow.

He nodded. "Yes, the mountains. Probably so." He looked around. "Nice bar. Nice quiet music."

"Yes, the music's nice. Soothing." Though nothing could soothe Sam's anxiety over being late for Bob's birthday party.

"Yes, soothing." He twirled his drink. "Nothing I like more than sitting in a quiet bar, listening to good music, drinking a nice cold dry martini with a beautiful hot wet lady."

Sam choked.

He leaned across the table. "Are you all right?"

She nodded as she coughed. "Sweet."

"What?"

"Sweet. The opposite . . . of dry is . . . sweet." Still coughing, Sam picked up her purse and fumbled through it. Throwing a ten-dollar bill on the table, she rose. "Good night."

He grabbed her hand. "Wait a minute. Larry said —"

Sam whirled around, pulling her hand free. "Larry said?"

He looked around wildly, at anything but her.

"I'm interested in knowing what Larry said."

He remained silent.

"Actually, I don't need to know what he said." She started out, then returned. "And thanks."

The picture of the bewildered X-ray supplier stayed with her as she drove the snow-packed road to Bob and Karen's. *I'm going to get you for this, Larry.* "I'm going to get you for this." The lights and gaiety of the party spilled out into the darkness.

Sam went around to the garage door instead of the front door, wanting to see the puppies. Scratching Beauty behind the ears, she counted. "You sitting on one?" No, there were only nine. One must have died. "You're a good mother, Beauty. Boomer sends his love. Said good job." Beauty seemed nervous. "Yeah, what *do* men know about such things!" The dog started to get out of the box. She was young, and it was her first litter. "No, no, just stay where you are."

She found Karen in the kitchen. "Need help?"

"Hi, Sam. Not really. Just going to light the candles and carry in the cake. Why don't you go on in and say hello to the birthday boy."

Sam found Bob leaning against the piano chatting with Mary and Ken. "Ah, Sam. Wondered if you'd make it." He swept her into his arms, a trace of liquor on his breath.

"Fortified, I see." She pushed him back. "Here." She handed him a present wrapped in Snoopy birthday paper.

"A bomb?" he asked, shaking it.

"Yeah, Bob . . . a bomb. I was going to get a thick black dog collar with big spikes, but I settled for a bomb."

Ken broke in. "He probably could have found more use for the collar."

"Or ten. Did you get to see the puppies yet?" Mary asked.

"Now, is this an innocent woman or what?" Ken winked at Bob as he put his arm around his wife's shoulders. "The collar's for Bob, dear."

"But the leash is for Karen," Sam added.

"Well, anyway, I hope it doesn't explode in my face." Bob slid the package across the piano. "I'll open it last . . . in the privacy of my bedroom."

"Bathroom. It's really a plastic duck." She laughed.

"Another decoy." Ken poked him in the ribs.

"Hunting season will be great next year."

"Thanks, Sam. Karen said if I bought any more decoys she was filing for divorce. She didn't say you couldn't. Could you give me five pintails?"

Sam motioned to the package. "If you don't mind the small inflatable kind." She turned pensive. "One of the puppies died, I see."

"Really?" Bob started toward the laundry room, but Karen came through the archway with the lighted cake, stopping him. He would have known if there had been a carcass to take out of the box. She redefined Beauty's nervousness. In the midst of singing, Sam slipped from the room.

She took the stairs two at a time, turned on the hall light, and ventured into Amy's bedroom. The light spilling in from the hall illuminated the angelic face of the three-year-old. Sam tiptoed over and lifted the covers. *Mystery of the missing puppy solved.*

Sam felt the thudding heart of the tiny creature looking more like a rat than a puppy as she carried it downstairs. She intended to take it back to the litter, but she saw her opportunity to catch Big Bob, who stood like a lone thorn in a bed of roses.

Sam pulled him aside. "Big Bob, I need a —"

He looked down at the puppy. "Sam, their eyes aren't even opened yet. I don't think you should be —"

"I rescued it from Amy's bed." Catching Bob's eye from across the crowded room, she held up the puppy and mouthed Amy's name. "Anyway, I need a favor."

"Name it."

"Can you get Tommy and Larry together without looking suspicious?"

He looked around the room. "I'll try."

"Thanks, you're a sweetie. Be right back . . . think Beauty's looking for this one."

Sam placed the puppy next to its mother. "Well, Beauty, found the baby for you." Beauty quickly licked it. "No wonder you were so nervous. Kidnapped right under your nose." She turned, hearing the swish of the door. "Hi, birthday boy."

"Is he all right?" Bob asked, dropping to a knee.

"Its little heart was pounding to beat the band."

"Well, Beauty isn't shunning it, anyway. I'll have a talk with Amy in the morning." He helped Sam to her feet. "Come on, let's get back to the party. You haven't had a drink yet."

"That's what you think. Had an after-dinner drink with that X-ray supplier. And it's revenge time. Find Ken and wander over to Larry. Tell Ken to agree with everything I say."

"We always do, love." He kissed her cheek.

Sam worked her way through the crowd. Larry was deep in conversation with Big Bob and Tommy Redding, one of Bob's ranching neighbors, and more important, a member of the hospital board.

"Larry," Sam said, tapping him on the shoulder. "Sorry, we had to cancel lunch. Thought you'd like to know, though, about my dinner."

"Sam, do you know Tommy Redding?" Larry asked, trying to hint that she not talk shop in front of him.

She offered her hand. "Yes. It's nice to see you again, Mr. Redding."

"Tommy," he corrected as he squeezed her hand.

"Tommy." She turned back to Larry. "Anyway . . . I'm really excited about the new contract." She had to cover her mouth and pretend to cough as she saw the panic in his eyes. "Excuse me. Got something caught in my throat. Anyway. I told him he'd have to stop by to get your signature on the contract, but that it was just a formality."

Larry shot Tommy a look.

"Oh, Ken," Sam pulled him closer, "you'll be interested in this. I was just telling Larry about the exclusive contract with the new film supplier. Larry asked me to represent the hospital —"

"Well, actually . . ." Larry interrupted.

Sam turned to Tommy. "I can't tell you how exciting this is. Larry found this supplier who can save the hospital a good ten percent . . . maybe even fifteen." Looking at Larry, she added, "You'll have to sign a ten-year contract —"

"Ten years —"

Sam stepped on Larry's words. "Well, you can work that out. Anyway, the reason he's so cheap is that the film doesn't use silver. Can you believe the modern technology? No silver. Just think of the savings."

"Isn't that something!" Bob said as he nudged Ken. "No wonder silver's at an all-time low."

"The Japanese discovered the process. It'll revolutionize the film industry," Ken said, looking confused.

Sam rubbed her chin. "Maybe I should have agreed to the twenty-year contract, after all."

"Well, Sam," Larry cleared his throat, "the board will actually have to —"

Sam glared at him. "That's not what you told me. You asked me . . . no, you *begged* me to have dinner with him. Even dangled the possibility of —"

"You must have misunder—"

"An E.R. doctor." She turned to Tommy. "Heaven knows, the salary of an E.R. doc would be cheaper than the first lawsuit settlement for a wrongful —"

"Sam, I don't think —"

"A wrongful death because there was no doctor in the house."

"I think you're right, Sam." Ken turned to Tommy. "Sam and I usually have to cover the E.R. until they can round up a doctor who knows what he's doing."

Bob shook his head. "A pathologist and a radiologist. The lawyers could have a field day with that."

"Really?" Tommy asked.

Big Bob laughed. "One tells his patients to hold their breaths and the other one knows they will."

Bob patted his father on the back. "They're really a pair to jump-start hearts. Sam never sees anyone till they're stiff and Ken just looks at their pictures."

Larry's face was white; they might have overdone it a tad. She turned to Ken. "You don't keep the X-rays very long, do you?"

Ken shrugged. "Seven years."

Sam clutched her chest. "You're kidding." She looked at Larry. "Why didn't you tell me that, Larry?" Her tone was accusing. "What have we done?"

"What's wrong?" Bob asked, trying to sound serious.

"But without the silver, the pictures dissolve."

Ken's face lit up as if he finally understood the game. "That's right! The pictures dissolve. What if there's a lawsuit? How will we prove our innocence?"

Bob jumped in. "Larry, for a measly ten percent, you'd put us —"

"Wait a minute. I have no intention —"

"What have we done? A ten-year contract!" Sam's shoulders slumped as she wandered away. "What have we done?" she mumbled to herself as she left the room.

Sam grabbed her coat from the top of the pile and took a quick peek at the puppies before she let herself out.

Bob caught up to her before she reached her car. "Sam, that was great. Did the crime fit the punishment?"

"I don't know. Is he sweet-talking his way out of it?"

"Said he'd straighten out everything to-morrow. But Ken asked him why he had you rep-resent the hospital instead of someone from Radiology."

"What did he say?"

"I don't know, I came out here . . . where it's damn cold." He batted his arms together. "Redding seemed interested in the E.R. doc, didn't he?"

"I'd hate to think I made a fool out of myself for nothing."

Bob pulled her into his arms and hugged her. "You were great. And so very warm."

She pushed him away. "Get back inside before you freeze. Got no smarts?" She turned around and continued up the road.

"See you Monday," he called. "And thanks for the duck."

"It's a flea collar."

13

Sam paced back and forth, waiting for Derek's plane. She had rushed all day, and then hurried to the Sheridan airport to meet his three-thirty flight. Now it was after four, and at four-thirty she'd have to be suited up and ready to bowl. Her team was in first place; she couldn't let them down.

The Convair 580 was on approach, they said. Whatever that meant. She wasn't the only one anxious. Some sat nervously, others paced, and one man looked out the window, searching the blue sky while a couple of small children played tag around the rows of multicolored chairs.

"There," the man said, pointing. A woman ran to his side just ahead of Sam. The woman's hands clasped and she shrieked as she saw it. Excited geese made less racket than the people waiting as the plane touched down and rolled the length of the snow-scattered runway. It taxied, then pulled to a stop in front of the building. The plane's door opened and the stairs were pushed out. The propeller made one final, tired revolution before coming to a stop. The second hand on her watch clicked away.

An older couple burdened with Christmas-wrapped packages came out first, followed by a young couple, each carrying a toddler. The stream of holiday visitors slipped and slid over the icy surface as they gingerly made their way toward the terminal. A blast of wind edged in as a uniformed attendant propped the door open. It rolled in after that. Sam shivered more than the others who were being bear-hugged.

She had just about given up on Derek when he appeared. Sam couldn't remember the last time a flight attendant hugged her when she left the plane. She fiddled with the keys in her pocket. She was going to be late.

Derek saw her, and threaded through the embracing families. "There you are." He gave Sam a hug, his laptop thumping her in the back.

"Love the smell of the perfume you're wearing," Sam said in her most smart-aleck tone.

"I like yours better." Derek held her at arm's length. "Now, let's have a look at you." What was there to see? She was dressed in a plaid shirt, faded jeans threatening to spring out at the knees, boots, and a Levi's down jacket. She always wore jeans on Friday. Can't bowl in a skirt. "I'm glad to see you're wearing a shirt."

Sam felt the blood rush to her face remembering how she had used her shirt to make a tourniquet the last time they were together. His, too. "That's right, if someone needs it, we'll give them the shirts off our backs."

He laughed. "We Turners are just like that."

That made her feel good somehow, as if he had accepted her as a family member.

She studied his features as they waited for his

luggage. He looked so much like John, and even though she missed John so incredibly much, she'd been having trouble remembering exactly what he looked like. In her dreams he'd become a fuzzy shadow. She glanced at her watch. If she got there by the third frame, they'd let her bowl. "I don't have time to take you home. Just drop me off at the bowling alley. I'll find a ride later."

"Bowling? I wouldn't miss that for the world." He tapped out a cigarette. "Can't quite picture you bowling." The baggage carousel started rolling with a tinny crash and a handler started shifting the luggage. Derek slipped the cigarette back into the package and picked up his bag.

"Yeah? Shows you how little you know about me."

Derek looked hard at the brown Jeep in the parking lot. "Is this a new car?"

"Just painted the old one."

"Why?"

"I was tired of the red." She lifted the back for him.

He dumped his bag and carefully laid down his laptop. "It looks awful with the red interior."

"Thanks."

Cold air seeped in through the vents and there wasn't anything to be done about it. She'd waited inside so long, the heater had cooled off.

"Sorry about all this. But a winter scene with Curly and the gang will be just as nice."

"Curly's dead."

"Dead? What happened?"

She told him as she drove to the bowling alley. She was too late to bowl the first game, and her team lost by five points. They had to use her average minus ten points; all the more reason to feel that she had lost the game for them. Susie couldn't have cared less; she only came bowling to visit with her V.A. hospital co-workers. Her husband, however, cared a great deal. Sam bought Tony and Hugh another round. She should have gotten Derek to pay for it; he made her late.

"It's only a game."
Derek filled her beer glass and wondered if that would have been the reply had they not won the last two games. "Another piece of pizza?"
"No, thanks." She pulled the pins out of her hair and shook it, sending sparks flying. This was the first time he'd seen her hair loose since Halloween. She was world-class beautiful. Even more so for not trying.
"I'm sorry about Curly."
"Me too."
"Any other deaths?"
She shook her head.
He'd have to be less subtle. "Your Holiday Murderer didn't strike again?"
"Oh, I thought you meant the buffalo. Yes, at Thanksgiving, naturally."
"Sorry. Thought getting through Labor Day and Halloween was a good sign."
"Me too."

"Was she as pretty as the copycat Halloween one?"

"No. She was old and in terrible shape. The skin under her arms sagged a good four inches."

"Same M.O.?"

"No foreign saliva in the mouth, but she'd been raped, despite total procidentia."

"Which means?"

"The entire uterus protrudes through the introitus."

"What causes that?"

"Having lots of kids. Proves rape is an act of violence and not sexual."

"How about the Halloween case? What did the lab have to say about it?"

Samantha pursed her lips. "They supposedly didn't get it. Tried to trace the Federal Express number, but came up empty."

"What could have happened to it?"

"I think the police department did it out of spite." Sam's face contorted.

"You sound a bit paranoid."

"Just because you're paranoid doesn't mean they're not out to get you."

He gave that some thought. "What about your friend Jeffrey? Did he talk to the police for you?"

"Yeah, he was a big help." Her tone said otherwise.

"Why?" he asked as innocently as he could manage.

"I tried to give him the other samples I have, but he refused to send them. Would be inadmissible evidence in court, he said."

"I'm sure he's right."

"So fucking big deal. Once we have a suspect we can run a DNA check and when we're certain, we can go after him some other way. Link him to Pamela, make him confess, something like that." She smirked. "Said we'd spend the rest of our lives in civil court on invasion of privacy, et cetera, et cetera, et cetera. He's so persnickety about technicalities."

Derek bet he was. The one blemish on his sterling record was a murder-for-hire, over ten years ago. Jeffrey was fresh out of law school, working in the D.A.'s office in Denver. He didn't follow procedures to the letter and lost the case on a technicality. He lost his job and ended up in Sheridan. "You know, for a picturesque little town, you sure have a disproportionate amount of violence."

"Kind of reminds me of New York."

Derek offered her the last slice of pizza. She shook her head. Having missed lunch, he felt justified in polishing it off. "Did you have some trouble in New York, Samantha?"

"I've never been there."

"You're maligning my home and you haven't even been there?"

"Well, you know, muggers and all."

"Oh, yes, muggers. I was mugged once . . . in Paris."

"It's a dangerous world out there."

"And Sheridan's not?"

Sam and Jake spent the early part of the morning feeding oats to the herd while Derek captured them on film. He wouldn't be able to use any of the great pictures he'd taken at Halloween, not unless he wanted her to know he'd lied about losing them.

"Had enough punishment yet?" Sam called to Derek.

"Yes, I think I can now write about the cold . . . using vivid adjectives," Derek said, pulling his borrowed cap down to his tingling nose.

"Cold, desolate, bleak, stinging icy needles, stabbing —"

"Crystal sharpness, clear, freshly fragrant," he added.

"My, don't we have a selective memory," she said with a laugh.

He liked her laugh, liked the way it made the tiny lines around her eyes crease. Matter of fact, he just plain liked her. "We prefer to call it creative writing."

"Well, if you wish to enjoy more of this clear, fresh fragrant, crystal sharp air, you'll have to do it alone. My body's frozen through and through."

"As a supreme sacrifice, and wanting to be the perfect guest, I'll escort you back."

"Shit, it's cold."

"Didn't I say that?"

"Karen," Sam called as she, her father, and Derek headed toward the theater, "how are

170

those puppies doing? Amy sleeping alone?"

"They're all over the place, and growing bigger every day." Karen pulled her stocking cap over her ears. "And Amy's backside acts as a reminder when she wants company."

"Karen, I'd like you to meet Derek Turner. Derek, this is Karen Wallace. We visited Karen's in-laws on Halloween."

"So this is Derek. I've heard a great deal about you from them. You made quite an impression on Big Bob."

"Probably because I liked his brandy."

"Or at least pretended to." Turning to Sam's father, Karen said, "Mr. Davis, it's nice to see you again."

His head listed to the left as if trying to remember. "Oh, yes, I lived with you in Bakersfield."

"No, Daddy, you met her at my place last Easter."

"Oh yes, you have the little blond girl who showed me her Easter basket full of spectacularly decorated eggs."

Sam shook her head. Sometimes he amazed her. He'd be just like his old self. Not a person alive he couldn't charm. "That's right." Of course, that wasn't what remained most memorable about Easter in Sam's mind. She'd gone to the funeral home to post the second victim.

Karen smiled. "Well, I'd better get going. It was nice meeting you, Derek, and I'll see you at the dance tonight. Sam, remind me to ask you something. Good-bye, Mr. Davis."

14

Sam slipped the cold diamond necklace around her neck. It hadn't been worn in a while; not since before John's death. She shivered remembering the tickling trail of kisses he'd left all the way around her neck when he'd surprised her with it. And the scent of his after-shave, the fingernail down her spine. They'd been late for the residents' graduation party.

She twisted under the light, throwing a prism of colors all over the room. None of her friends here had anything like it. She undid the clasp and threw it back into the musty-smelling, gold velvet box. Another reminder of San Francisco.

The dress was too long. She should have taken it downtown to the Stitch-in-Time place. She hiked the dress and descended the stairs.

Derek, thumbing through a medical journal in the library, did a double take at seeing her. He whistled and tossed the journal back on the shelf. She surely was blushing all the way down to her bare bodice. "Wow, that's spectacular," he said, twirling her around.

She was having a static-cling problem. She used to have an old spray can of something or other, but it was too late to dig around under the sink to find it. "Thanks, I've certainly got my money's worth. Marked down for the umpteenth time to ten dollars."

Derek grabbed her around the waist as she tripped on the tile in the hall. "It could be a little shorter," she mumbled as he turned her to him. It made her uncomfortable being so close.

"You know, you could have it altered."

"Yes, but then it wouldn't have cost ten dollars." She squirmed away.

In the hall closet, Sam pushed through the coats to find her burgundy down coat.

"Now, this I know wasn't ten dollars." He took out the red fox jacket.

"A present from your father." She continued her search.

His hand stopped her. "Here, let's see what it looks like on," he said, guiding her arm into the sleeve.

"But —" She wanted to tell him that she'd never liked wearing something that had belonged to an animal first. In fact, she and John had fought over it that Christmas morning. She wanted him to take it back and exchange it for a trench coat; he'd refused.

"The other arm, please." He swept up a loose lock of the hair and did something to make it stay with the rest of the hair she'd piled high on her head. Derek offered his arm. She'd been outfoxed.

Derek left Samantha standing at the door in Jeffrey's care — she was unwillingly playing hostess — and crossed the empty ballroom intending to prop himself up against the bar. He was happy. A Scotch in one hand, and a cigarette in the other, he watched the first partygoers arrive.

He'd never suspected Sheridan was capable of such elegance. Glittering crystal chandeliers, mirrored walls, large round tables covered with white linen and floral centerpieces, and soft music floating out of hidden speakers. He might as easily have been at a New York gala.

As Derek stood admiring Samantha's gown from afar, a gray-haired man with a bad case of the fats pried himself loose from the other end of the bar and walked over.

"I don't think I know you." He took a cigar from his mouth and spit brown phlegm into his cocktail napkin. "I'm Stanley Moots." He shifted the napkin to his left hand and extended his right. "You must be one of the doctors."

"Derek Turner." He was hesitant about taking the proffered hand, but took it anyway. "Visiting from New York. I'm with Samantha Turner."

"Sam I know. She's testified in my courtroom many times." He rolled the wet end of his cigar between his chubby fingers. "I didn't know she was married."

Derek told him that she wasn't, then explained that he was here doing a story on her buffalo.

The big man rocked back on his heels and came forward on his toes. "I understand she's seeking the death penalty for the vandals who killed one of her buffalo." He chuckled.

174

Derek made himself smile. "This town has had its share of crime lately."

"If it's not one thing, it's another," the judge said, sticking his cigar back in his mouth as if to punctuate his words and end the conversation. He drifted back the other way.

Samantha eventually came and whisked him away from the crowd at the bar to their table, where he was introduced to Bob Wallace, Junior. He knew the others at the table set for eight. Ken and Mary from Halloween, Karen from the street, and ol' Jeffrey.

"Ken, there's something wrong with this picture. See if you can tell us what it is." Sam pointed at Jeffrey, "Boy," and pointed to herself, "girl, boy, girl, boy, *boy*," the finger was accusing when it pointed to Ken, "girl."

Ken scratched his head. "Mary's out of place?"

"Isn't that just like a man!" Karen exclaimed.

"We'll have to be crass, because I'm not moving." Mary gave a sigh and patted her heavy stomach. "And if I did, it would be over one to sit by Jeffrey. I wouldn't want to sit between *those* two," she said, pointing to Bob and Ken.

"A woman with taste," Samantha said, leaning over the table and showing impressive cleavage.

Bob covered his eyes with his arm. "Ken, did you think to bring your sunglasses this year? She wore it again."

Ken jumped in mock surprise. "Sam? For a minute there I thought the glare was from the snow-covered Big Horns."

"That doesn't surprise me, Ken, since you only get to see *pictures* of boobs." Samantha bent over again. "Get a good look. There will be an exam later."

"I'm good at breast examinations," Ken said, wrapping his arm around Mary.

Samantha shook her head. "I don't know. Looks like you got carried away, if you ask me."

Ken licked a finger and chalked one up for her as the rest of the table laughed.

"If it's an oral exam, I'll take it for him," Bob offered, grooming his mustache.

Samantha laced her fingers under her chin, concealing most of what had interested them. "Where'd you get *your* M.D., Bob, the Floating University of the Seven Seas? You have to pass the written exams before they let you take the orals."

"Could you take your elbows off the table, Sam?" Bob asked as he reached for the bread basket. "Ken and I are still consulting. Your incision —"

Samantha shot up straight as an arrow, arms folded over her chest. Her pearlescent skin reddened in big blotches. "You could see it?"

Bob and Ken laughed.

Karen nudged her husband. "That was cruel, Bob."

Mary shook her head. "No, just some wishful thinking."

"Ken could. He's got X-ray vision."

176

Derek strained to look down her gown. The scar interested him, and he wondered why she'd turned skittish about it.

Jeffrey's eyes were unfocused.

Samantha hiked the front of her gown as she leaned over Derek to speak to Karen. "I like your new hairdo."

Karen combed her fingers through the straight hair, cut just below the earlobes. "I like it, now that I'm getting used to it. It was something I had to do . . ." Her voice trailed off.

"It's very becoming," Derek said.

Bob leaned over and kissed her cheek. "She looks like a high-fashion model."

Shushing him abruptly, Karen turned to Derek. "You'll have to ignore them. We can dress them up, but we can't take them out."

Mary, placing her hands high on her bulging middle, agreed. "Karen, next year let's leave them at home."

Karen nodded. "Save on baby-sitting. And maybe Sam will loan us Derek and Jeffrey."

"A dream come true," Mary said, giving her husband a little smile.

When the music started, Jeffrey and Samantha took to the dance floor. The doctors were busy planning an ice-fishing trip. Derek danced first with Karen, and then returned to guide the awkward eight-months-pregnant Mary onto the dance floor.

"Derek, I don't think —"

"Come on, just one dance. It's nice and slow,

and I have my reputation to protect."

"Oh?"

"I'd hate for it to get back to New York that I let a pretty one slip away without so much as a dance."

"Has anyone ever told you you're something of a tease?"

"No, but I'd have taken it from someone as pretty as you."

Mary turned to face him, holding her arms out. He snuggled her in close. After only a couple of steps, she stopped abruptly and looked up at him. He just held her closer and started up again.

"I've had some complaints about my dancing, but no one's ever kicked me before."

She giggled. "I'm really sorry. He's an active one."

Derek slid his hand around until it rested on her side, feeling the baby's constant movements. "Does it hurt?"

"Hmm. It's a nice hurt." Mary looked up. "And by the way, I don't believe you've received a complaint in your life."

Jeffrey wandered off toward the lawyer side of the room after Derek arm-wrestled Samantha away from him.

"He seemed a little quiet," Derek said of Jeffrey as he took Samantha into his arms.

She nodded.

Derek stroked her bare back, feeling its smoothness. "So . . . tell me about your incision."

Samantha wedged her hand between them and tugged at her bodice. "It's nothing."

"The way it makes you so self-conscious makes me think it's something," he said, placing her hand back on his shoulder.

"It's really nothing. In order to see it, all of me would have been hanging out."

"I like your friends," Derek said, trying to ease her obvious discomfort. He'd only seen the tough professional side before.

"And you're making quite a hit with them," Samantha replied, just before tripping on the hem of her gown.

Derek lifted her off her feet. "About two inches, I'd say."

"What?"

"Have them take two inches off the hem," he scolded.

"Maybe I'll just bag it, and buy another one with higher décolletage."

He stroked the silky smooth skin of her back. "Don't ever get rid of it. Bargains like this are hard to find."

15

A ringing sound seemed to be somewhere in the foggy distance. Sam threw the pillow over her head and continued dancing on the billowy cloud in John's arms. Something screeched, making Sam break away. It wasn't John. She had to find John. The clouds at her feet rose around her. She couldn't see. She ran and ran, but nothing around her changed. All fog. She couldn't see, but she had to find him. There was something she had to tell him. She saw him behind rows and rows of Arabian veils. She called to him, but he couldn't hear. He drifted away. She had to catch him, she had something to tell him. She would walk through one of the silky curtains only to have another appear ahead of her. John was nothing more than a dark shadow beyond them.

"Samantha." Derek leaned over the bed, shaking her. The dog growled. "Samantha, wake up."

"John, I have to tell you something." Slowly, the clouds rolled away. Even sleep-drugged, she knew something was wrong.

"Samantha, you need to get up."

Someone was standing over her. She screamed. The noise drove the cat out from under the covers and over the side of the bed.

"It's all right, Samantha. It's Derek."

Sam sat up, grabbing the covers and clutching them to her. "What is it?"

"There's been another murder. Get dressed . . . I'll warm up your car."

By the time she was awake enough to ask details, Derek had left. She threw on a pair of jeans and a sock. Hard telling what Boomer had done with the other one. Sam tugged one boot on, then struggled to put the other on over her bare foot. She tucked the tail of her nightshirt into her jeans as she ran down the stairs. Her foot slipped against the inside of her boot. It was uncomfortable and felt like being trapped in a cardboard box.

She put on her down jacket and pulled her stocking cap down to her eyebrows and ran out the door. The wind was stinging sharp. She had both gloves on before she reached the Jeep.

The dome light went on when she opened the door. Boomer was sitting in the back wagging his tail. "You didn't happen to bring my other sock, did you?" Boomer looked innocently back, as if he didn't have the slightest idea what she was talking about. She bunched up her toes, for all the good it did.

Even the slightest twist or bounce from the snow-packed road felt like an exploding bomb. "You sure you don't have my sock?" Boomer wagged his tail. Derek was quiet. "You didn't give me the details. You said murder?"

"I'm sorry, Samantha. It's Karen Wallace."

"Karen?" Her blood turned to ice. Her voice sounded hollow even to herself. "Are you sure?"

He took her gloved hand and squeezed it. "I'm sorry, so very sorry."

"But Bob —"

"Was at the hospital."

A shudder crept over her. She focused her unseeing eyes on whatever came into the headlights. "I need to stop at the hospital first."

She tried to crush down her personal feelings. She had a job to do.

Hazel Adams's watch read five-thirty when she heard the alarm sound. It had been a busy Saturday night in the E.R., with all of the Christmas parties and the slick roads. Why people thought they could drink and drive was beyond her. Soon the morning shift would arrive and the doors would be open again, but in the meantime she would superintend and marshal all admissions.

Rising on swollen ankles, Hazel left the nurses' station and walked to the locked door. Her gray mood turned to deep depression when she saw the pathologist. As she opened the door, Hazel felt the chill of night touch her face.

The nurse couldn't find her voice to answer the greeting as the doctor pushed past her. It had to be another murder. A pathologist didn't have pressing matters to take care of, unless the pathologist was also coroner.

It wasn't even Christmas yet. She had learned

over the years that holidays were a time of depression for the lonely, but now the fear of holidays clutched at the hearts of even the happiest people.

Hazel locked the door even though she knew the doctor would be leaving again in minutes, supporting herself against it, as if trying to bar the evil forces. She watched the doctor disappear into the supply room.

"Are we out of rape kits?"

Hazel crossed to the supply room. She was slow climbing the stool. Her ankles were trying to tell her it was time to take a desk job, and she probably would if she weren't so deep in hock. She found a kit on the top shelf and handed it to the doctor, opening her mouth to speak, but the flutter of thought didn't come in words that could be expressed.

"Thank you."

Sam had unlocked the door and disappeared before Hazel caught up and pulled it closed, locking out the foreboding darkness. She leaned against the door and took a cleansing breath.

The cold winter night came to a close as morning's crimson light glared against the windshield. The road Sam and Derek traveled led east out of town, toward the streak of pale light beyond the snow-covered rolling hills.

Pulling into the sharp turn next to the pasture, the car followed the narrow drive until it settled next to an ambulance. Sam looked at the sparkling Christmas lights around the house. "It will be a truly memorable Christmas for the Wallaces."

Derek caught up with her and slipped a supportive arm around her shoulders. He drew her closer. She nuzzled against John's down jacket, hoping for a little comfort in its warmth.

They went through the garage and in the back way. Beauty was nursing her puppies in the laundry room. They didn't stop to look closer, but the puppies were much bigger than they were the last time she had seen them. In the family room, they found Bob sitting in the rocker cuddling Amy in his lap. The decorated Christmas tree in the corner made it all seem sadder.

Sam dropped her bag on the floor behind the couch before going to them. She fell to her knees next to the rocker and slid a hand over Bob's sweaty green scrubs and placed another on Amy's fuzzy pink sleeper. "I'm so, so very sorry," she whispered.

"Mommy's gone to heaven." The innocence of the child's words slashed through her like a saber.

Sam kissed them both as she got to her feet. She picked up her things and followed the voices to the master bedroom. Tensely, and with as much detachment as she could manage, she walked slowly to the bed. She needed to see Karen in stages, get used to the sight. Something akin to the reverse of beholding a Rembrandt.

She squinted, as one would in bright light, and opened her eyes slowly until Karen's naked body came into full view. She gagged at the sight of the black nylon stocking around her neck. "It's black."

Hank pointed to the dresser. "There's her other one."

He'd strangled her with her own stocking. It made it all that much worse. The terror of Karen screaming and scratching and fighting him off was etched solidly on the walls of her mind. She must have been so frightened. What a horrible ending. She wouldn't wish it on an enemy, but a friend . . . Karen never did a mean thing in her life; she was loved by everyone.

Tears ran down her cheeks as she stood rigidly over the bed. Sam inched her eyes upward until Karen's bulging lifeless eyes stared back at her, crying out for help. "Have you taken pictures yet?" she asked Hank.

"Yeah."

Karen's eyelashes tickled her palm as she pulled the eyelids down.

She sat on the bed trying to get used to Karen this way. Her tears continued to fall, though she was hardly aware of them. Derek pressed a facial tissue into her hand. He wandered over to the windowsill and leaned against the frame. The white and purple print curtains, matching the bedspread twisted along the foot of the bed, pulled tight against his weight. Karen had been so proud of them.

"Sam, if you don't need anything, the boys and I are going to have a look around outside. Sun's up good now."

"That's fine, Hank," she said in a whisper. She noticed the sheriff glancing at Derek on his way out. She didn't bother with introductions.

"Let's go, boys."

Derek fished in his pockets. She expected him to bring out a pack of cigarettes, but he didn't.

"Go ahead and smoke if you want. I don't care."

"I left them on your kitchen table. Use the Kleenex, Samantha."

Sam wiped her nose and wadded the tissue.

He sat down on the edge of the bed next to her, careful not to move Karen's hand, and took the tissue and wiped her face. "Isn't there someone you can call to do this? Someone in another town, maybe?"

She shook her head. "The rest of them are all funeral directors. Most pathologists don't want to be bothered. Besides, I want to do it." She looked into his eyes. "This is his last victim. I'm going to find him." She got up off the bed and opened the rape kit. Derek moved back to the window. "I'm going to find him, Karen. I'm going to find him."

Sam steeled herself and cultured the mouth, where she expected to find his saliva, then took seminal fluid from her thighs and vagina. Nothing would be found in the rectum, but she followed the protocol. She clipped Karen's fin-

186

gernails and took samples of pubic hair, then lingered as she combed through the newly cut hair. The style Bob thought made her look like a model.

"Derek, would you mind getting the sheriff for me? I'm almost finished."

He left the room and returned with Hank in tow. Sam handed over the samples for the state crime lab, then tucked her personal samples under her arm.

"I want you to drive the samples to the crime lab, personally. We're going to nail the fucker this time."

"You know who he is?"

"Not this minute. But even if I have to knock on every door in this town looking for a bald-headed, blood-type-A Caucasian, I'll find him."

Hank raised an eyebrow. "Can't I just send them?"

"No. I want them hand-carried. And I want to see the receipt." Sam started for the door, then turned back to have one last look at her friend. "I'll find him for you, Karen. I'll find him, all right."

Bob was still sitting in the rocker when Sam returned, but Amy was shaking a present under the tree. "Would you like me to take Amy home with me?"

Bob looked up with sad eyes. "What?"

"I said I'm taking Amy home with me."

"No. I don't want her out of my sight."

"You have relatives to call and arrangements

187

to make. She doesn't need to hear all that." He was a broken man, and didn't protest. Sam knelt beside Amy at the tree. "Amy, why don't we go upstairs and get a few of your things together."

"I'll go with her." Derek was beside them. To Amy, he said, "You wouldn't mind, would you?"

She looked wishfully at a big green package with a red bow, then took his hand and led him into the hall. Derek blocked her view as they passed the master bedroom. It was something John would think to do. "Can we take the puppies?"

"We'll see," Derek said as they started up the stairs.

Sam turned back to Bob. "What happened?"

His voice was little more than a whisper. "I'd just gotten back from taking the baby-sitter home when I was called back to the hospital. An emergency C-section. Returned around four-thirty."

He buried his head in his hands. "I could feel a draft. The front door was ajar . . . snow was blowing in. I closed it, then crawled into bed. Karen was sprawled out. I nudged her to move over. She was so cold. I turned on the light. That's when —" He burst into tears.

"That's when you called the ambulance," Sam finished for him, even though she knew that wasn't what he had started to say. "Amy can stay with us as long as you like. Would you like me to call anyone?"

He shook his head.

"I'm going back to the hospital. I'll tell them to have Patrick cover for you."

Bob nodded absently.

Sam started upstairs, but met Derek and Amy coming down. Amy ran to the rocker to give her father a hug. Bob sobbed into the child's hair. Derek pried them apart, and Amy, who blessedly could not grasp his suffering, went running off to the box of puppies.

"Can we take the puppies, Sam?"

"No, sweetie, let's leave them with your daddy." She took the child's coat from its peg in the laundry room and bundled her up. Derek pulled her hat down over her ears while Sam struggled with the mittens that ran through the sleeves on a long piece of green yarn.

Derek scooped the child up under one arm, her suitcase under the other. Sam leaned over and picked up the tiny snow boots.

Amy's face lit up when she saw Boomer in the Jeep. Boomer licked her face.

"Back," Derek commanded as he fastened the seat belt around the child.

Sam looked up at the sky. It would be a clear, sunny day. Maybe not even too cold.

Not for Karen, though.

16

The funeral was held at ten A.M. on the twenty-third of December. The large Presbyterian church was filled to capacity.

A stream of melted snow from the boots of a rancher in front of Sam puddled around Derek's left foot. The trickling water reflected the image of Karen's body on the funeral home's preparation table. Sam had slit the death-paled skin at the nape of the neck, folding the scalp over the face and turning the new hairdo inside out.

She had taken a great deal of care in putting Karen back together, even used the same blind-stitching technique the general surgeon, Peter Nelson, had used on her incision. She wouldn't have known how to do it had it not been for Bob and Ken ganging up on her to have that silly fibrocystic mass removed. It was nothing and the only thing that came of it was learning the blind-stitch, which she'd probably never use again. But last night when she had viewed Karen in the coffin, she was happy she'd taken the extra time.

Derek pulled his handkerchief from his gray suit pocket and pressed it into her hand. Sam hadn't realized she was crying until then.

Amy, squirming from Big Bob's arms, climbed down and ran her little hand along the side of the copper coffin. She smelled the flowers and whined for a rose. Little Bob pulled one out for her and sat her on his lap. She was satisfied for a while, and then slid away and gathered a fistful of flowers.

All eyes were on the casket as it rolled down the aisle with six somber doctors trailing. An eerie silence filled the sanctuary as Karen's friends and family filed out. Sam felt Derek's hand at her elbow as she negotiated the salt-covered steps.

The silver Mercedes fell in line far behind the shiny black hearse. Moving at a snail's pace, the procession made its way north on Big Horn Avenue. Sam paid no attention as they passed her father's nursing home. She was only vaguely aware of Derek's presence next to her as she stood huddled against the wind — not quite under the tarp — watching the coffin descend into the cold, green carpet-covered hole.

Mourners scattered. Some visited. Others picked their way over the wet and muddy ground to cars. Sam stood in a trance. As Derek took her elbow, she pulled away. Something teetered on the tip of her tongue. A thought that wouldn't form in words.

"Are you all right, Samantha?" Derek asked in a voice laced with deep concern.

She shook her head. "For a minute there I thought I had it."

"What?"

"I don't know, but I think my subconscious

does." Sam turned into the wind and walked rapidly and resolutely to the car.

"Where are we going?"

"To the hospital."

She raced through the halls decorated merrily with Christmas themes, pushed through the lunch line, and went behind the counter. "Derek, help me with the blackboard."

"What are you doing?" Sylvia asked, one of her hands grasping the blackboard. "You can't take this."

"I need it to find Karen Wallace's killer."

Sylvia gave Derek a hand with it, until a couple of men in line took up the cause. Sam picked up the bigger pieces of chalk that had fallen to the floor and smashed, then hurried ahead to hold the elevator. Larry, who had returned from the funeral, looked up from his desk as the blackboard passed, but said nothing.

Sam rifled through files and pulled out folders while the blackboard was wheeled in. There was just enough room to turn around in after everyone but Derek left, but the door was trapped behind the blackboard. She struggled to close it; she didn't want Kate's supervision. Derek managed to get it shut, but the penned-in feeling was almost enough to make her open it again. Almost.

She grabbed her lab coat and used it as an eraser. "Look, they had tomato soup today. It's my favorite."

"No, the twenty-seven-calorie crackers are

your favorite. Why don't you start, and I'll go get you some soup?"

By the time he got back with the soup and crackers and a plate of meat loaf and potatoes, she had the names of the victims down the left-hand side and was trying to decide how much room and how many columns she needed. She started with physical characteristics, then went back and wrote the ages beside the names. She tagged the next column *Artifacts* to give a place for Mrs. Taylor's false teeth and Pamela's skimpy Fredrick's of Hollywood number. She thought about leaving Pamela off the board, but decided this would dispel any lingering doubts about Pamela's death, which was yet to be solved, as far as Sam was concerned. Who knows, she might even find Pamela's killer, though it was not top priority. The serial killer would kill again, and soon. Pamela's death was most likely an accident.

Derek put the tray on her desk and picked up the stack of pictures. "Let's see if we can find discreet ones to tape up."

"Covered by a sheet?"

"They're all pretty gruesome, I'll give you that. Sit down and eat your crackers while the soup's still hot." He studied the photos.

She sat at her desk. The other chair had been moved out when the blackboard was brought in. Sam patted the corner of the desk. "Have a seat."

He squared the photos and placed them beyond the food tray. "Wish I'd gotten the sandwich now," he said as he juggled his plate and fork.

"Just be thankful you don't need a knife."

"I know Karen was strangled with her own stocking. Same with the others?"

"No. He brought them. They were the same brand, but they're twenty, thirty years old. I figure he took them out of a stuffed pillow or something made out of red velvet."

He pointed to the top picture. "Your Thanksgiving victim is so much older than the others."

"I know. Now we have every blue-haired woman in the county . . . Shit." She grabbed the pictures and shuffled through them. "That's what was nagging at me. It was even written on her calendar." She got up and headed the next column *Hair*.

"What?"

"Mrs. Taylor's hair appointment. Under Wednesday she'd written *10:00 minibus, 10:30 hair*." She wrote *blue rinse* on Mrs. Taylor's line and stooped over to write *haircut* on Karen's. "Karen had a new haircut. Lisa Henderson was a natural blonde with dyed hair. I could still smell the chemicals." She started to write on Lisa's line, and then drew a big *X* across the board. "It's the hairdresser."

Sam pounded on the desk. "What's wrong with you, Jeffrey? The laboratory's findings show that the victims all used the same shampoo formula. Karen's will show the same when the re-

194

sults come back. Mark my words."

She went around behind his desk and picked up the five photos. "Look at the pictures," she said, shuffling them in front of him. "Look at their hair. A new perm. Braids. The natural blonde with the dye job. Blue rinse. And Karen's new haircut. You were at the table. Remember how proud Bob was?" She threw the photos on his desk.

"Sam, be reasonable. I'd be laughed out of court on such flimsy evidence. Besides, there were six victims. What of her hair?"

"No," she yelled, pounding the desk, "the one in October was a copy-cat murder."

"Now, Sam, you know there's no evidence to prove that. The lab lost the whole kit and caboodle, and any half-wit attorney would get the second duplicate specimens thrown out in the first five seconds of court."

"She wasn't killed on Halloween," Sam said through pursed lips.

"So what? The killer read about himself in the papers and wanted to continue the myth." Jeffrey squared the photos, put them in the folder, and pushed them across his desk.

"Karen wasn't killed on Christmas. How come he didn't freeze her?"

Jeffrey shrugged. "Because she didn't live alone?"

"Couldn't you at least have the police put a tail on him? He's bald, for chrissake."

"Sam, this is Sheridan, not New York City," he

195

said with a touch of sarcasm that told her he was still peeved about her taking Derek to the dance.

Exasperated and infuriated, Sam started for the door.

"I don't want you doing anything to jeopardize this case. When the results come back on Karen and *if* the shampoo formula's the same, we'll get that warrant."

Sam whirled around. "Now, is that before or after New Year's Eve?" She stormed out of his office, slamming the door behind her. Glaring at the secretary, she motioned to Derek.

In the hall, Sam said, "Not enough evidence." Rage broke from her throat. "He won't even put a tail on him . . . not until Karen's results come back."

Christmas was a cold, bleak day. But Derek was euphoric. There was a message on his answering machine that Frederick Wilson was clean. Clean wasn't the correct word for the serial murderer, but he and the treason case were unrelated. Derek's job was finished.

Insisting he'd cook the turkey, Derek had gotten up early and had stuck the fat bird into the oven. He had shoveled a path down to Samantha's ugly brown Cherokee and had brushed off the new snow. It had been so peacefully quiet. Even the roaring creek of October had settled into sleepy water that slipped silently around the pockets of ice. He had taken pictures all along the creek, then finished the roll with shots of Jake feeding the buffalo their Christmas oats. Samantha had driven to the nursing home after breakfast and had brought back her father.

Mr. Davis was sitting in front of the television in the living room, seeming to enjoy the college football game. Samantha was trying to persuade the Jell-O to come out of the mold. Derek tested the whipped cream.

"Don't," Samantha shouted as she slapped his hand with a spatula.

He still managed to lick the whipped cream off his index finger, as well as the back of his stinging hand. "You *are* a sadist." He jerked on her apron strings. The apron sagged and began sliding down her red and green taffeta skirt.

The Jell-O mold in one hand and a spatula in the other, she gyrated as if keeping up a hula-hoop, but the apron was around her knees before Derek pulled it free. "Me! Look what you've done to the Jell-O."

Derek pressed into her as he looked over her shoulder. "Don't blame me for that crater. I believe you'll find cranberries dangling from the side of that bowl you're holding."

"I'm talking cause, not instrument."

He wrapped the apron around her tiny waist, bowing deeply and fanning out all the folds. "Don't know how much this helps. Your skirt's a good ten inches longer."

She moved to the sink and ran water into the mold. "Let's see, two inches off the black one, ten inches off this one?"

"Hmm." He leaned back against the cabinet, admiring her trim ankles. "I'm not sure. I like the way it clings, and besides, for all I know, you might have knobby knees."

She lifted her skirt above her knees.

"Make it an even foot."

The skirt fell.

"Where's the tablecloth for the dining-room table? I'll set it for you." It was a gentle hint. She'd set out four blue woven place mats on the kitchen table.

"In the china cabinet . . . in one of the drawers."

The pink tablecloth in the drawer wasn't long enough, but his grandmother's lace one was. Derek studied the pattern on the Wedgwood china. His mother had never liked it, but Derek thought the intrinsic blue pattern urbane. He took out four plates. One had a chip from when his milk glass collided with it. The plate fared better than the glass, if memory served. The silver was the same pattern as his mother's — he would keep his father's secret. The crystal was an Early American Fostoria.

"Where'd you get thick crystal like this?" he asked as he carried them to the sink to rinse off the dust.

"I don't know. Mom had them. When she died, Daddy gave me the crystal and her diamond. Sharon got the china and the silver. I like it because it's not so fragile."

He squeezed a little soap into the running

water. "What was the incision for?"

Samantha put the lid back on the steaming peas and onions. "You're never satisfied. Had a mass against the chest wall. Ken couldn't get a good picture of it, and Bob couldn't aspirate it. They talked me into having it taken out, over my better judgment. The quacks. It was benign. Kind of pretty, had about twelve bluish cysts around the fibrous tissue. Looked enough like a sapphire broach that I sent it to Chris Newman to show him what I made."

"Uncle Chris." Derek shook his head. "I can remember him bouncing Renee and Donna on his knee."

"That sounds like the old goat. Last week?"

He laughed. "No, when they were little girls. Ol' Uncle Chris. Still in San Francisco, is he?" She didn't answer. Derek turned around to see her stealing from the room. "Fragile," he said, sticking the drying towel into one of the goblets.

At two they sat down at the dining-room table to a Christmas dinner of turkey with stuffing, mashed potatoes and gravy, peas and onions, cranberry Jell-O, and hot rolls. For dessert Samantha gave them a choice of white Christmas pie or pumpkin pie. They had a sliver of each, except her father, who wanted more than slivers.

"Now," Samantha said as she scooted her chair back, "before you all fall asleep from the natural sedative in the turkey, I want you to move over to the couch." Derek started gathering up the serving plates. "That means you, too, Derek."

"Be right there," he called over his shoulder as he carried plates into the kitchen, Jake following with the serving platters.

Samantha and her father were wrestling over a heaping spoon of butter when he returned from the kitchen. "Daddy, you don't want that. We'll save it for later. Let's open presents now."

Derek took the spoon as she helped her father to the couch. She played Santa first, giving a red package to Derek, a green one to Jake, a brown one to her father, and a red one, sporting a little bell, to the dog. She handed two more to her father. "These are from Sharon."

He took the presents. "Sharon's my mother. She's married to a lawyer."

Derek smiled and mumbled that that was nice.

Jake pulled three presents out from under his coat.

Derek hadn't been overly creative in his choice of gifts. Three two-pound boxes of Godiva chocolates sat on the coffee table. He leaned over and distributed them.

"Daddy, Derek, look at this." Samantha held up a coral and turquoise beaded belt. "Thank you, Jake." She fastened it around her waist and twirled around for everyone to see. The green and red taffeta didn't do much for the belt. "It's great, Jake. I love it."

"It's beautiful." Derek opened his present from Jake to find a container of homemade elk jerky. "You don't mind if I wait awhile to taste it.

Don't think I could eat another bite."

Jake smiled. Derek suspected he was experiencing the same discomfort.

Samantha inched between Derek and her father. "Here, Daddy, let me help." She unwrapped a pair of handmade moccasins with beaded tops. "They're lovely, Jake. Makes my Pendleton shirt seem shabby."

Derek leaned over and whispered in her ear. "How'd you like to have shown up with candy?"

Samantha pointed to the red package. "I only wish I had!"

He unwrapped it. "You'll have to tell me what it is," he said, holding the ashtray up close to get a better look at whatever the black thing under the glass was.

"It's a piece of a smoker's lung."

He patted her knee. "I'll cover the bottom with candy. No one will notice."

"More likely ashes."

Jake held up a Buck hunting knife. "Thank you. I broke the tip off my old one."

"I know. It's from the Ritz, if you want to exchange it."

He held it at the tip, feeling the balance. "No need."

Samantha's father devoured chocolates from both her box and his. "Thank you for the shirt, son."

"The wool shirt was from Samantha."

"Samantha?"

"Your daughter."

"He means me, Daddy."

Mr. Davis gave her a look of recognition. "Oh, yes, Samantha . . . Sharon's mother."

"We'll call Sharon now, so you can ask her what Santa brought, Daddy."

Derek watched Samantha help her father to the kitchen. He would miss her.

17

On the twenty-seventh of December, Sam put Derek on a plane.

When she saw the plane's wheels leave the ground, she turned on her heels and left without looking back.

Sam pulled into a parking space in front of a Woolworth's and backtracked to the Ritz. She stomped snow from her boots before venturing into the sporting-goods store, then paused while her eyes grew accustomed to the dim light inside, feeling the heat from a large vent on the wall. The pink streamers fluttered at ninety degrees. The lunch counter was filled with local boys at their ritual coffee — same seat, same time, day after day, year after year, until death created a vacancy. She wasn't sure how a vacancy was filled, but thought it something akin to an inheritance. Sam crossed the hardwood planks until she reached the gun case.

"He didn't like the knife, Doc?" the always-cheerful owner asked.

"I think he liked it. It's kind of hard to tell with Jake . . . I'm here looking for a gun," she said, looking past him to the picture of Queen Elizabeth. The Queen had bought a hunting jacket for her husband and a quilted vest for herself on her visit to Sheridan a few years back.

"Handgun or shotgun, Doc?"

"Handgun," she said, taking a fancy to a pearl-handled gun in the case.

"What kind?" He motioned at the vast number of western six-shooters.

"I don't know. One to protect me from a two-legged, yellow-bellied animal."

His expression became serious. He walked to the other end of the counter and returned with something. "This is the one you want. A .38 Special."

He laid it on the counter, along with a box of ammunition. "Have you ever fired one?"

She shook her head.

"Well, Doc, we've got to rectify that. Meet me at the shooting range tomorrow morning at seven."

"Six-thirty?"

"Six-thirty."

A bell tinkled above the ice-frosted door. A woman holding a handful of curlers offered Sam a chair. A young cosmetologist and her middle-aged client were chatting at the farthest station. The only other client in the shop was an older woman whose blue hair was being sprayed by a queerly shaped young man with narrow shoulders and wide hips. What little hair he had left was shaved, a dark shadow against his pale pallor. His mannerisms were fey.

When her turn came, Sam approached as if she were about to sit on an electric chair. With a smile on her face, she greeted Mr. Frederick.

A chill ran down her spine as Frederick Wilson wrapped a strip of soft, variegated paper around her neck. A kamikaze on his final dive couldn't have felt more vulnerable.

The shampoo burnt through her scalp like acid. "I'm happy we were able to work you in. New Year's Eve is usually booked up."

"I should thank the woman who canceled." She stared blankly at the light fixture on the ceiling. "I meant to come in earlier, but I had out-of-town company over Christmas," she said through a cotton-dry mouth. "I wanted to wait until my company left and I was alone again."

Warm water cascaded over her hair. "You're not having your hair fixed for a New Year's Eve party?"

Her voice left her for a moment, but when it returned, her words were strong. "Nope, I'm probably the only one in town who'll be at home all alone tonight."

Mr. Frederick gave no indication of hearing her as he put a small white towel around her head.

He ran the comb through her hair, working the snags out. "I see you walking to the theater on Saturdays."

Sam pulled her arms under the cape as she felt the goose-flesh rise. She glanced into the mirror, catching his hazel eyes. She quickly looked down, training her eyes on the Redken shampoo. The printing was small, but she had no need to read the label; she knew the ingredients by heart. "Yes, I take my father every week. He lives in a nursing home."

He nodded.

Her eyes darted to his reflection in the mirror, but he showed no reaction. She looked back at her own face, trying to relax the deep lines on her forehead. "It would be too difficult for him to live on my isolated ranch — thirteen miles is a long way to drive if he needed medical assistance."

Frederick gave no indication of hearing.

"And the road to Big Horn can be very treacherous in the winter."

"How much do you want taken off?" he asked, holding the scissors against his cheek.

"Just trim it . . . about half an inch."

She was listening to hidden meanings in everything he said. "You're not married?"

"I'm a widow," she answered, hoping he couldn't hear the pounding of her heart against her ribs.

His jugular stood out like piano wire. Her hands gripped the sides of the chair as an uncharacteristic deep bass voice rose from the depths of his chest. "My mother's been a widow since I was little, but she's married again now." After a pause, he added, "Tomorrow will be her first anniversary."

"That . . . that must be very nice for her. Does she live in town?"

He shook his head.

"Do you hear from her often?"

"Some. She likes to send Hallmark cards on special occasions."

Terror flashed through her like lightning. She could name those special occasions, she thought. Valentine's Day, Easter, Fourth of July, Thanksgiving, and the day he received the Christmas card. Motive. What kind of card do they have for Independence Day? She wouldn't ask.

A great wave of relief swept over her as he put down the scissors. Handing her the mirror, he twirled the chair around. "Is it all right?"

Sam's eyes didn't see. She forced a smile as she said, "Yes, it's very nice."

She held her breath as his hands slipped around her neck. She exhaled as he took the cape away.

He slid a finger down her throat and then unwrapped the crepe paper.

She closed her eyes for fear he would see her terror.

After she had paid and he turned his attention to his next client, Sam made herself walk slowly out. Once she rounded the corner, she leaned against a wall and took a deep breath of the cold wet air.

All four parts of the Westminster chimes played on the grandfather clock in the library announcing the top of the hour. Sam counted the gongs. Twelve.

"Happy New Year," she said with a half-maudlin laugh.

After dinner, Sam and Boomer had visited Jake. He offered her the only chair in his small shack as he sat on the edge of the buffalo robe that covered the bed, waiting for her to speak.

Sam looked around at his Indian handiwork, but its magnificence was lost on her this time. "Would you mind keeping Boomer tonight?"

He rubbed the dog's nose as he nodded. She knew he wouldn't consider questioning her.

She looked around blindly, gave an emphatic slap to her thigh, and then stood. At the door, she turned. "Please don't come up to the house tonight . . . for any reason." Their eyes locked. She slipped out the door.

Sam had watched television until ten. That is, her eyes were focused on the set, afraid to look out the windows. There was nothing to see but darkness and perhaps her own reflection, but she would have hated to frighten any Peeping Toms away. Thinking it was late enough to retire, if anyone were watching, she turned out all of the lights and, leaving all doors unlocked, went to bed. In bed, she mechanically read each word of every article of the journal she propped against her bent knees, but her mind retained nothing from the printed pages.

And now it was midnight. No noise escaped her. In the rafters overhead, Sam heard the scratching of some unknown tenant. Mice, maybe squirrels.

Tapping, tapping . . . as the wind hurled snow against the window.

The monotonous scraping of the tree branch against the bathroom window in tune with the wind.

The ticking of the grandfather clock.

Dare not move.

Dare not sleep.

Dare not think.

She caressed the .38 Special. He would come.

The adrenaline pumping through her body kept her awake. But as the hours crept by, sleep tried to overpower her.

She could not, would not, move.

He would come.

She waited for the sound of an opening door.

She waited for a creak on the stairs.

She waited.

Many times John came to mind, but each time she pushed him out. He would not approve.

She thought about picking up the phone and calling Derek. Just to say Happy New Year. If he jogged he might be getting up now. He didn't jog, he smoked. And knowing him, he was probably just getting back from a party. Probably with a model draped over his arm. She redirected her anger and forced Derek out of her mind.

The red digital numbers changed slowly.

He would come.

One thing she allowed herself to remember was Karen. Karen's bulging eyes that cried out to her.

Karen.

Sam felt nauseated as she thought of the nylon being forced around Karen's neck, choking out the air. She took a sharp breath, thinking of Karen's lungs collapsing.

Her hatred kept her awake.

She thought of the painful entry into Mrs. Taylor's dry, prolapsed vagina.

Sam played the scenario in her mind, over and over. Cold beads of sweat trickled down her face as she remembered his hazel eyes.

She waited.

As a milky-white streak of light filtered through the window, she had to acknowledge that which had nagged her for the last couple of hours: he wouldn't come. She had failed Karen.

She put the gun in the drawer of the nightstand and threw the covers over her head. A restful sleep did not come, nor did pleasant dreams. The pear-shaped figure, dressed in black, crept toward the bed. A stocking covered his pig face. He twisted the stocking over his knuckles as he inched forward.

Drenched in a pool of sweat, Sam sat up and screamed. It was only a dream. The clock was closing in on eight. Had he struck somewhere else? Would she be getting a call?

Sam yanked back the covers and went into the bathroom. She turned on the shower and stepped under the warm jets. The water beat down on her sense-numbed body. Her fatigue was overpowering. She couldn't be bothered with towel drying, and wrapped a blue terrycloth robe around her wet body. Perhaps a cup of coffee would get her going? No, she wanted sleep. She stepped back into her bedroom.

Sam froze.

Her heart pounded wildly as she stared at the pear-shaped, naked man framed in the doorway. The limbic system in her brain triggered fight instead of fright.

The gun . . . she had to reach the gun.

Her legs had already adopted the idea of their own accord. She propelled her body across the bed, but before her outstretched hand could reach the drawer, she felt the hand around her ankle.

She clawed at the bedsheets as her body jerked back.

With every ounce of strength she possessed, Sam lurched forward and pulled, the drawer and all its contents landing on the carpeted floor next to the bed.

The intruder saw, too. He let go and ran around the bed. But not before Sam rolled over and dropped to the floor.

She fumbled the gun, finally, frantically, getting it aimed at Fredrick Wilson when he was only inches away from her. So close, she could hear the pounding of his heart. So close, she could smell death.

She held the gun with both hands. "Step back."

It was her voice. "Step back."

He moved ever so slightly.

211

More than afraid, she was angry. "Step back before I pump you full of lead," she burst out hoarsely. She wanted him back. She was drowning in his dirt and slime. "Move."

He moved back another step.

"Move back, you motherfucker!" she screamed.

When he was at the foot of the bed, Sam lifted herself to its edge.

Taking a deep breath to calm herself, she picked up the phone and punched the bottom middle button, never taking her eyes from Frederick.

An eternity stood between the ringing and answering of the phone. Finally, the operator answered.

"Operator, connect me with the Sheridan County Sheriff's Office."

"Thank you for using AT and T." Sam couldn't help but smile.

The dispatcher came on the line. "Send your men to the Turner —"

He lunged at her.

She shot.

Frederick squealed like an animal in a slaughterhouse. He fell crushingly over her. His eyes looked questioningly and innocently at her as if asking why she did that.

She scrambled up and pushed the weight off of her and rolled him from the bed.

He groped at his groin.

Sam took hold of the phone's cord and pulled until the receiver was at her ear. "Make that an ambulance . . . to the Turner Ranch . . . Big Horn."

She tore the phone's cord from the wall jack and wrapped it around his thigh and hip in an attempt to close off the spurting artery. Her hands were covered with his blood and the cord kept slipping away. The man fell into unconsciousness, and it became another race against the clock.

Sam used the tail of her robe to wipe away the blood so she could see what she was doing. The femoral artery was the source of the squirting blood. Sam dug her fingers into the puckered hole and clasped the bleeder.

The bleeding slowed.

The absurdity of the situation did not escape her; all she had to do was let go. But she couldn't. Her fingers held tight to the artery. When her legs gave way, Sam sat cross-legged on the blood-soaked carpet. She didn't know what she would do if he regained consciousness. He had lost too much blood for that, she assured herself.

In time she heard the distant sirens. Her wait would soon be over.

His radial pulses were absent; carotid pulses were palpable, rapid, and weak. His breathing was rapid, shallow, and irregular. The grim reaper may steal him away after all.

"Upstairs," Sam yelled as she heard the commotion downstairs.

She pulled her robe together with her free hand as she heard footsteps on the staircase.

Hank arrived first, followed by the new deputy.

"Where's the ambulance?" she asked the dumbfounded men.

The sheriff cocked his head over his shoulder while the deputy snickered in embarrassment at the location of the wound.

They stood like statues.

"Will one of you fetch the dental floss out of the medicine cabinet in the bathroom?"

"Get it, Tom," the sheriff directed.

The deputy looked around.

"Through the closet." She jerked her head. "There."

He sauntered off through the closet.

"Could you hustle, Tom?" Sam yelled.

"Is this the one?" Tom asked, holding up a plastic box.

"Yeah, that's dental floss. Could you tear off a piece?"

Two members of the rescue team came in, one of them her friend from the YMCA weight room. She was always happy to have his help in the E.R., and today he was a godsend. "Am I glad to see you, Eric. He has a bleeder. Take that string and tie it above my fingers."

Eric took the string in his gloved hands and crouched down beside her. She stretched the vessel as he looped it. "Femoral?"

"Afraid so. You always wear surgical gloves?"

"Yeah, not that it helps . . . Adhesive tape rips a hole in them every time."

Sam nodded as she watched him tie the knot. "Double glove and you're too clumsy. Don't worry about this one. He doesn't have AIDS. I know, I've been studying him under my microscope for a very long time."

He looked at her blood-soaked hands. "Glad to hear it."

"Let's get him out of here. Stat," she said when the vessel was tied off.

As they carried him off on the gurney, Hank asked, "Who is he?"

"Frederick Wilson. The Holiday Murderer." She walked up to him and closed his jaw with her clean elbow. "It's New Year's Day, isn't it?"

18

Frederick Wilson, wearing the bright-orange issued jumpsuit, walked gingerly from his cell in the county jail to the visitors' room. After two months, he still suffered from the wound in his groin. His young, timid attorney sat waiting. After the customary greeting, the lawyer came to the point. "The county attorney is willing to plea-bargain. He'll not seek the death penalty if you plead guilty."

"But I didn't kill anyone."

The attorney glared at him. "Don't lie to me. I'm representing you. They have a strong case. Not to mention catching you red-handed. And if you want my advice . . . take the deal."

"But I'm innocent."

"I've seen the case they've got against you. Blood types match, hair samples the same. Caught you in the act." He shook his head. "The plea bargain is the best I can do for you."

"But my shop. . . ."

"You should've thought of that before."

His life was over, and he knew it. He would never be free again. Tears streamed down his face. "I don't want to die. Please don't let them kill me."

Sam took a seat in the back of the courtroom

next to Bob Wallace and silently watched the courtroom fill up. She usually charged a hundred dollars an hour for appearing in court. Today she would have paid twice that for the pleasure of seeing Karen's murderer arraigned.

The arraignment, which had been postponed owing to Frederick's hospitalization and recovery, was short, but by no stretch of the imagination, sweet. The defendant pleaded guilty to all six counts. Sam craned over heads to see Jeffrey. She could see only his back when he told the judge that the prosecution would not seek the death penalty.

Sam was on her feet when the judge announced that sentencing would be carried out three weeks from the day. He hit the gavel, closing the hearing.

"Why would Jeffrey do this?" she asked, looking down at Bob.

Bob wasn't listening. His rage had dissipated over the months. It had been somewhat of a concern to his friends. He had just been going through the motions since Karen's death. Sam would worry about him later; now she had to talk to Jeffrey.

She started up the aisle against the flow of traffic. Jeffrey went out the side door before she could reach him. She dug her nails into the bar. "How could you do this, Jeffrey?"

"Now calm down, Sam," Jeffrey said from his brown leather chair behind his desk.

"I'll calm down when you change it to five," Sam told him as she leaned across his desk.

"I can't." He pushed back in his chair, trying to put some distance between them.

She sat down, trying to control her irritation. Crossing her legs in a seemingly calm manner, as if they were sitting down to a little chat, she asked, "Why not?"

"For one thing, he admitted killing her. For another, there is no admissible evidence that he didn't."

Sam jumped up and pounded on the desk. "The blood types don't match, dammit!" Picking up the pictures she had earlier thrown on his desk, she added, "And look at her hair. Tell me she just had it done."

"She was in a freezer all week, from late Saturday night until five o'clock on Halloween morning. How would you expect her hair to look?"

Sam pursed her lips. "Well, the blood types don't match, for chrissake!"

"The official samples were lost. Your backup samples weren't sent according to protocol. It's inadmissible evidence."

Sam glared at him, speechless.

"Be reasonable, Sam. The town's settled down ... you're a hero. If we opened this can of worms, neither of us could get elected to animal control."

Sarcasm curled her lips. "The way I understood it, I'd be assured of a landslide victory as an animal controller."

Shaking his finger at her, he warned, "You'll be lucky if Frederick doesn't think to sue you."

She smiled sweetly. "Why? Ranchers castrate animals all the time." She paced the floor, looked out of the window to the street below, then returned to the seat across from him. "Jeffrey, you're going to let someone get away with murder, and I'm not going to let you do it."

"That's not fair. My hands are tied." He neatly stacked the files Sam had thrown on his desk, squared them, and held them out to her.

"Well, mine aren't." She got out of the chair and ripped the files from his hand. After storming across the room to the door, she stopped. "Jeffrey, I no longer consider you a friend."

Sam had been to see the judge, even humbled herself by going to the chief of police, as well as the county sheriff, all to no avail. She had thought about calling the press, but decided that would be a mistake. Besides hating that rag, she believed the murder was an accident, and wouldn't be repeated. No sense in starting an unnecessary panic.

There seemed only one option. She would have to find Pamela's killer.

As Sam sat in her cubbyhole, she realized how very little she knew about her former employee, except that her parents lived in Denver. She could call them, but what would they know about her private life? A friend in town would know more.

What had the girl in Medical Records said?

Sam had total recall of anything said to her. It would come back. *Keri had been too upset to work.*

Sam rushed down the stairs. Looking at the nameplates, she stopped in front of a young woman with frosted blond hair. "Keri, would you mind if I spoke with you for a few minutes?"

"No, not at all," she replied, not moving from her desk.

Sam looked around at the closeness of the desks. "May I buy you a cup of coffee?"

Keri looked around, then shrugged. "I guess it would be all right, Dr. Turner."

The woman knew her name. She was an observer; perhaps she would know something.

Sitting at the table in the cafeteria, Sam began, "I need to find out some personal information about Pamela."

"Pamela? Why?"

"I can't tell you, but I can say it's to help her."

Keri rolled the cup of coffee between her hands.

"Keri, did she ever talk to you about her personal life? Boyfriends?"

Keri bristled. "Oh, I see. You're not trying to help Pamela at all. You're trying to help your friend, Dr. Miller."

"Dr. Miller?"

Keri got up and ran from the room.

Sam sat staring at the cup of coffee. "Dr. Miller?"

Kenneth Miller bent over in his chair and brushed the dried barium from his trousers as he waited for Dr. Johnson to answer the phone. Mary wasn't keen on throwing the barium in with her regular wash.

What a morning! He had been awake most of the night listening to Mary walk the baby. Then he was greeted with back-to-back barium enemas, one of which he was wearing. Three CT's, two ultrasounds, ten chest X-rays, umpteen bones later, he finds this. Ken looked at the light box in front of him.

"What can I do for you, Ken?"

"Mr. Barber in ICU has a pulmonary embolism."

"Thanks," Johnson said as he hung up, no doubt in order to call ICU.

He dictated the written report, ripped the films from the light box, and put up the next set.

The intercom box squawked. "Dr. Miller, Dr. Turner wants to visit with you if you have a moment."

"Tell her I'll come over to the lab when I finish here. Fifteen minutes or so."

"Sam, you wanted to visit?"

She looked up from her microscope. He looked tired, but otherwise his usual happy self. But then, looks could be deceiving. He'd deceived Mary, hadn't he? "Yeah, I did." People were milling about. She got off her stool. "Let's talk in a less open forum."

"Sounds serious." He followed her into her office.

She closed the door. "Big-time serious."

"Shoot. Let's see if I can buck you up." He straddled the corner of her desk.

"I know about Pamela and you."

His smile fell away. "So?"

"Tell me about it."

"Why? What difference does it make now?" He jumped down and paced the floor like a tiger in a cage. "It's ancient history anyway."

"Not to me . . . I just found out." She grabbed his hand as he went by. "Come on."

He twisted away. "It doesn't concern you."

"But it concerns someone I care about . . . you." She waited for him to speak. She waited a long time. "All right. Where were you Halloween afternoon?"

"The day Pamela was murdered, you mean. I didn't kill her, if that's what this is about. They've already caught the Holiday Murderer. Remember?"

"Pamela wasn't killed by the same man as the others."

"What?" He stopped short and stared at her. "Halloween . . . ah . . . here, I guess."

"No. You checked out for home, but Mary told everyone at Big Bob's that night that you'd been at the hospital since early morn."

He nodded. "Right, I went home to eat because I had to work late. But no one was home, so I took a nap."

"Pretty flimsy, Ken."

"I didn't kill her, Sam. You've got to believe

that. She'd moved on by then, anyway."

"Oh?"

"She was plenty mad about the baby."

"Mary's and yours?"

He nodded. "I had her figured . . . I didn't understand. All she wanted was what I already had."

"And didn't appreciate."

"She wanted me to leave Mary and marry her. She wanted to have my baby."

"And you wanted her to be your baby."

He cringed at her tone. "I didn't kill her."

"I didn't think you did. You'd know better than to put her in the freezer."

"She was in the freezer?"

Sam nodded. "She wasn't killed on Halloween. Someone just wanted me to think she was."

"How did you know?"

Maybe she'd given him too much credit. "She was shriveled, for one." He shuddered. "Do you know who she was seeing?"

He shook his head too slowly. "Not really."

"But?"

"She used to spend a lot of time hanging around Larry's door."

Sam jumped up. "Larry!" It was delicious. She'd love to pin it on Larry. Especially after he set her up with that supplier. "Yes, now that makes sense. The X-ray supplier."

"The X-ray supplier?" Ken asked.

She looked up. "What?"

"You said, 'the X-ray supplier.' "

"Yes."

"What are you talking about, Sam?"

"That's kinky."

"What's kinky?"

"Nothing. I was just thinking. Larry and Pamela." Her mind was far away.

19

The journal on Sam's lap slipped to the bed as she thought about Larry. She ran the plan through her mind, playing each scenario. She jumped at the sound of the phone. It was after eleven. A coroner's case.

"Dr. Turner here."

The voice was muffled. "Get your nose out of other people's business. Stick to medicine; the life you save may be your own."

"Who is this?" More mad than scared, she yelled, "Who is this?"

Click.

"Who is this?" Rage built, keeping fear at bay. She threw the covers back, stepped over the bloodstain on the carpet, and headed downstairs.

Sam and Boomer paced between the kitchen and living room. "Boomer, Larry knows I'm onto him."

"Jean," Sam said as she plopped down in the chair beside her desk. She pointed toward Larry's office. "Larry's out?"

His secretary clicked off the typewriter and reached for a cigarette. "For a while, anyway. I'll tell him you're looking for him."

She shook her head. "You can handle it . . .

probably better then he could." Sam opened the new appointment book she'd spent the last hour creatively writing in. "The IRS is interested in my mileage." She flipped to the first marked page. "Let's see, on October thirty-first last year I had an appointment with Larry. What time was that?"

Jean flicked an old butt and ashes into the trash, then set her burning cigarette in the aluminum ashtray. "I'll have to go get last year's appointment book."

Sam watched her disappear into Larry's office, then leaned back in the chair and listened to the business-office girls on the other side of the big reception area. Someone was selling Tupperware. Maybe she should order something. She was always throwing out moldy containers.

"You said October thirty-first?" Jean returned with book in hand.

Sam jumped up to look into the book. "Uh-huh."

"No. Couldn't be. He was in Denver most of the day. Came back on the three-thirty plane."

Grabbing the book away, Sam looked at the page. A line was drawn down the center. *Back* was written on the three-thirty line, and *Tommy* beside five o'clock. She turned it back a day. He had caught the early-morning flight on the thirtieth.

It had to be Larry. She wanted it so bad she could taste it. Undaunted, Sam picked up the blood tray and walked down the hall; as she sauntered by the administrator's door, she stopped and backed up. "Oh, hi Larry."

Larry looked up.

"No, no, don't let me disturb you." She wandered in and sat down. "I'm just out rounding up a volunteer or two."

Larry laced his hands behind his shiny head and leaned back. "For what?"

"Oh, nothing. Got a couple of samples in the mail for a new HIV test. Just wondering how it works. Might be a little hard to find volunteers . . . might be afraid they'll find out they have AIDS." Sam laughed. "Oh, well, I'll just announce their names at the doctors' conference on Friday. Start a list of possible suspects."

Larry had his nose firmly in his work.

"Well, I'm not getting anything done this way." She got up and started for the door. "Oh! I'm sorry, Larry. Did you want to volunteer?" She went back to his desk and stuck her middle finger, sporting a dot Band-Aid, under his nose. "Doesn't hurt."

He shied away. "Well, I'm . . . Sure, why not?"

Sam grabbed his finger, wiped it down with alcohol, and punched it. She got great satisfaction in seeing him flinch. She jabbed the skinny glass tube against the bleeding finger a little too hard. He recoiled. She held his finger tight. "Now, now. Someone would think you had a very low threshold for pain."

Anger reddened his face to the color of the blood in the tube, but after the incident with the

X-ray salesman and Sam's revenge, the administrator knew better than to say anything. There'd
be time, later, he was sure.

The luster of the hundred-year-old mahogany
staircase was lost on Sam as she climbed to her
billing office on the second floor of the Cady
Building. "Type B. Dammit, Larry, why couldn't
you have been the one?" She looked around
when she got to the top of the stairs, making sure
no one heard her talking to herself.

"Good morning, Daisy," Sam said as she en-
tered the tiny, celery-green room.

Daisy quickly took her stocking feet off the
desk as she threw a paperback down.

"Another busy day, I see." Sam knew the work
was done for the day. Daisy was nothing if not ef-
ficient. Sam had stolen her from Larry. Fastest
typist Sam had ever come across. Smoke rolled
out of the machine when she used it.

"I'm afraid so." The middle-aged woman
slipped on her high heels before crossing to the
filing cabinet and pulling out the big, black corporate checkbook. "Got some checks for you to
sign."

Sam scratched her signature on the first three,
which Daisy had made out in her fine hand, and
then turned the page and scribbled her name on
three more. "How many overpayments did you
have this month, for petesake?"

"A bunch. They either pay too much, or not at
all."

"This one for taxes is larger than my pay-check," Sam said as she dutifully signed it.

Daisy nodded. "Your silent partner."

"Isn't this down?"

Looking to see which check she meant, Daisy said, "Yes, you've finally paid off Pamela's unemployment compensation."

"I would have kept her on if I'd known how expensive it is to fire someone." Without looking at Daisy, Sam casually asked, "Say, have you ever heard her name linked with anyone?"

"No." Daisy shook her head. "Except once my husband told me that his golfing buddy once walked in on a friend and her. They were naked in a hot tub. Apparently they both jumped for towels."

Sam wiped an imaginary hair off the checks. "Do you remember the hot tubber's name?"

"That was the best part. It was the judge, Judge Moot."

"Fat Stanley, eh?" Sam closed the checkbook. "Anything else?"

"I put some mail on your desk."

Sam turned to the desk in the corner. It was more a catchall than a desk, with boxes of supplies teetering on the edge. She took the pile of mail and, standing over the wastepaper basket, began filing. After throwing in one piece after the other, she stopped and looked at a brochure for a pathology conference in Hawaii. "Wonder if my silent partner from the IRS would come work his butt off so I could go to this conference."

"I think he'd just as soon you'd send him his check." Daisy slipped off her shoes and put her feet back on the desk and picked up her book.

"What's this?" Sam asked, holding up a real letter.

Daisy looked around. "It had 'personal' written on the front. . . . I didn't open it."

Sam ran her thumbnail under the flap. It was a note written on narrow-lined notebook paper. Her heart skipped a beat as she unfolded it and read, "I have the advantage. I know who you are."

She quickly returned it to the envelope before Daisy had a chance to see it. She looked at the postmark: local, with yesterday's date. "Did this come today?"

"Yes."

"Call me if I ever get another personal letter like this," Sam said as she headed for the door.

"Sure. Is something wrong?"

Sam shook her head. "Is your book any good?"

"A real tearjerker. The little girl has an incurable disease . . . just what, I'm not sure."

As she walked out, Sam said, "Sounds like they need a second opinion." She stuck her head back in the door. "Let me know if they find a miraculous cure."

The judge! Didn't you have any taste, Pamela?

Sam returned to the hospital to be greeted with the news that her father had been admitted. She ran up the back stairs to find him in a semiprivate room, the other bed unoccupied.

"Daddy, how are you feeling?" she asked as she looked at the frightened man. "I'm Samantha, your daughter."

"Water."

They had a pitcher beside the bed, it was probably all right, but she wasn't sure what tests he was scheduled for. "Daddy, let me go look at your chart, then I'll come back to give you water."

Taking the chart from the box at the nurses' station, Sam read Big Bob's notes. Her father had fallen out of bed the night before, and wasn't able to walk today. The tests all looked appropriate. Closing the chart, she decided to wait until after the CT scan was read before calling Sharon. She returned to her father's side and poured the water.

"Here, Daddy," she said, lifting him under his shoulders, "drink this."

The water from the straw rolled down his chin. She dried him with the sleeve of her blouse, then placed her finger over the end of the straw, took it out of the water, and stuck it in his mouth. "Swallow," she said, lifting her finger.

Eyes of a frightened child looked up at her as the water slid over his tongue, catching in his throat.

"Swallow, Daddy, swallow." Finally, she saw him work his throat. "Good." Again the half-filled straw went in his mouth, and again, she reminded him to swallow.

She turned to put the glass on the nightstand.

"Help . . . help."

Sam took his hand. "I know, Daddy. Your mind's caught in a maze and it confuses you, but I'm here for you."

"Help . . . help . . . help."

"I know, I know," she whispered in his ear.

"Help," the helpless man whispered.

"Daddy, it's not long now. Soon you'll be free and your mind will be clear again . . . I promise."

She sat on the edge of his bed, holding his hand as he continued to call for help. She smiled as she looked into his frightened, wild eyes. They bulged from his sockets; not so unlike Karen's and the other four victims'.

"Thank you for taking time out of your busy day to see me," Sam said as she took the offered chair in front of the judge.

"If you have some new evidence, you really should take it to the county attorney."

Sam looked at the big man dressed in a blue suit with a red tie. Lawyers — always concerned with images — dressed better than the doctors. "I think you're the one who needs to hear what I'm going to say."

He looped his thumbs into his vest pockets.

"I know that you and Miss Duncan were having an affair."

He stiffened, his hands gripping the armrests. "First of all, even if it were true, the same thing could be said about half the town."

The male half, Sam presumed.

"Being jealous of her lovers was like being jealous of the telephone book. Second, I know what you're thinking, but there was no trial. He pleaded guilty. . . . I'm just sentencing him according to the law." Stanley's eyes bored into hers. "Third, the sentence would be the same for five as six."

"But you're letting someone get away with murder."

"People get away with murder every day." Leaning toward her, he said, "You told me before that you thought it was an accident. Do you really think the man would kill again?"

Sam slowly shook her head.

"Is it really worth frightening the townspeople over?"

Sam rested her chin in her hand. "I don't know."

"If solid evidence ever turns up, the case can be reopened."

She didn't know that. Suddenly, she felt as helpless as her father. She started to waver, a victim of his persuasion. Perhaps she *was* chasing windmills. "You must have been a hell of a courtroom attorney."

He laughed. "There's one more thing I want you to remember. And this is my best advice . . . no charge." His tone became serious. "You're a woman in a predominantly male profession. Do you want to alienate your colleagues by sifting through their shit?"

She thought about how her feelings had

changed toward Ken. Perhaps he was right. Perhaps she was discovering more than she wanted to know about her friends. Sam got up and leaned over the desk to shake his hand. "Thank you for your time . . . and your advice. I'll think about what you've said."

Patting her hand, he said, "I'm sorry about that buffalo."

"Thank you."

As she got to the door, Sam turned around. "Your Honor, do you know who did it? Pamela, I mean."

He paused, measuring his words. "No. But I feel very sorry for the poor bastard. Don't push him over the edge . . . Doctor."

"I'm sorry I'm late, guys," Sam said to the cat and dog as she took off her trench coat. "I suppose you're both starving." Kitty rubbed up against her legs in reply, while Boomer wagged his tail. In the kitchen, Sam poured out their food. "Chow down, guys."

Then she made her call. "Sharon, it's Sam."

"Sam, nice to hear from you. How's Dad?"

"Well, that's why I'm calling. He's in the hospital." She went on quickly. "He's having motor trouble. Fell out of bed last night . . . can't walk today."

"Is he going to be all right?" Sharon asked, sounding half resigned and half worried sick.

"All right? He's not going to die this time . . . but no, he's never going to be all right again. At least not in this life."

"Shall I come out?" Sharon's voice sounded strained.

"No, but I would plan a trip before next Christmas."

"Is that when . . ."

"I think so. Unless he's lucky enough to catch pneumonia and die before then." Sam wouldn't tell her yet that after looking at his CT scan, she would be surprised if he ever walked again. Soon he'd have to be fed.

"I'll talk it over with Jack and see when I should come out."

"Come for yourself, not for Dad. He probably won't know you." Sam listened to the static; Sharon was probably fighting to hold back tears. "Is Jack around, Sharon? I have a legal problem I need to talk with someone about."

"Yes, the couch potato's just sitting here watching the boob tube. I'll put him on." Sam heard muffled sounds. "Take care of yourself, Samantha."

"You, too, Sharon."

"Hello, doll."

"Jack, I'm facing a moral dilemma. A man killed five women, but he has pleaded guilty to six. And I know he didn't kill one of them."

"Wait a minute. Is this a riddle?"

"No . . . unfortunately." She went on to tell him the story, and then added, "Oh, and we have fibers from his clothing. The other man left his clothing outside." She wouldn't tell him she knew this because she found Fredrick's overcoat and boots on her front porch. "We have fibers from a gray carpet. Hairs. But apparently they're all inadmissible because the lab lost them . . . or the police department here didn't send the first batch. I sent part of my duplicate set, but not by the book."

"Sam, I'm a corporate lawyer. I can't advise you, because I don't know. But if I were getting threatening letters and phone calls, I'd pull back."

"He's not going to hurt me. He's a victim himself. He just wants to scare me."

"You don't know that for certain. He *has* killed. And even if you discovered his identity, the prosecutor wouldn't touch him with a ten-foot pole if the evidence is inadmissible."

"But the judge said they could."

"Could . . . not would." He added, "Fall back and punt, kid."

"How eloquently stated," she teased. "Tell Sharon I said good-bye."

"I will, honey. Now stay out of trouble. Promise?"

"Now, how will you know if I've got my fingers crossed?"

He laughed. "You're a smart cookie, Samantha. Leave it alone."

"Good-bye, Jack. And thanks."

She sat staring at the phone for a minute. Boomer put his head in her lap. "Am I so wrong? Did they change the moral rules while I wasn't looking?"

20

Jake squinted to read the markings on the young buck silhouetted on the ridge. He made a mental note to tell Sam that Alfred was still among the living. How she had kept the critter alive was a mystery in itself. But nature's miracles were wondrously numerous.

Boomer and the new puppy Sam had given him were wrestling under his horse. The palomino whinnied and sidestepped; Jake reined him in. He glowered as Boomer took an obvious fall, allowing The Little One to crawl on top of him. The Little One was growing quickly; soon he would be as big as the father.

He reined the horse around the playful dogs wanting to reach home before night fell. This favored hour — just before dusk — held magic for Jake. The graceful deer began to make their move in their quest for water. No matter how many times he watched, Jake would never be jaded by such sights.

He felt, rather than heard, the dogs give chase, then he saw The Little One roll underfoot. He would be a nuisance for another season still. The horse reared, but regained his footing without incident. "The Little One, shoo." The pup scampered off toward the road, hightailing after the older dog. A richness overwhelmed Jake as he watched the big-pawed little fellow clumsily chase the graceful father.

The circle of nature was not broken. The young replace the old. His ancestors believed that, and even though the hoop of the Sioux Nation would be forever broken, he too believed. He thought of his people's old ways, when the buffalo could not be counted, when all people had enough food to fill their stomachs, when they lived in round dwellings, not the white man's square, unnatural ones. All before the circle was broken.

Hearing a crack, Jake reined in. He listened, but heard only the snorting of the horse. He turned the horse in the direction of the noise and spurred hard.

He saw everything at once. The speeding car, The Little One licking the fallen father, the blood as he closed in. Instinctively he gave chase, jumping the horse over the buck-and-rail fence across the road and flying through the pasture in an attempt to close off the car and noting the plate numbers.

Suddenly the car stopped and the driver got out, a look of panic on his face. Jake turned the horse as he saw the rifle. He heard the crack a fraction before he felt the burning sting.

He slid from the horse, feeling the sharp pain fade to a dull thudding, and then to a nameless bliss. Transcended beyond pain, he realized that the hoop had no end. Out of pain came peace.

Sam skidded to a stop as The Little One ran

into the headlights. She opened the door and coaxed him into the Jeep, and then wondered why she bothered when he left muddy paw prints all over.

"You're a mess, you know. What are you doing out here, anyway?"

She carried the heavy puppy to the house, intending to change clothes before taking him to Jake's place. Seeing Boomer on his side made the idea slip from her mind. The puppy slipped from her arms as she dropped down beside Boomer. She felt sticky blood, but could not see the entire wound in the darkness. She hurried to the door and switched on the porch light, all the time trying to convince herself that it wasn't true; Boomer hadn't really been shot.

Why would anyone do this?

Sam ran around the house and across the field to Jake's. His lights were off. Maybe he was already asleep. She pounded and yelled. Exasperated, she burst through the door. "Where are you, Jake?"

She ran to the stable. His palomino was missing. Why would he be riding in the dark? Why would anyone kill Boomer? He never chased cattle.

At the house she called the sheriff. It was then that she realized. Pamela's murderer killed Boomer. It was a warning. How ironic. She was just beginning to give in, to let it go. Now she was going to get him!

Sam started yelling at Hank before he was out

of his car. She knew she was being hysterical, but she didn't care. "He killed Boomer. He killed my dog."

"Who did?"

"The killer!" Why was Hank just standing there?

"The killer killed your dog. I understand."

"You don't understand at all! What are you going to do about it?"

"Well, Sam, I'd like to have a look."

Sam led him to the porch in time with her pounding heart. "Look at him!"

The sheriff squatted down and ran his finger over the wound. He stood up. "I'll call it in. We'll have the vet look."

Take her Boomer? "No! Leave him alone!" Her voiced sounded frantic even to herself.

"Sam, what do you want from me?"

She couldn't think. "I want you to go away and leave us alone!"

"All right. Call if you change your mind."

Sam dragged Boomer into the house and covered him with a blanket, then sat with The Little One in Jake's shack and waited for him to return.

She hadn't felt like this since John died. They had chosen Boomer together: John had picked him for his physical attributes; Sam liked the way the puppy nuzzled against her. She wanted him back. She wanted John back, too. Neither could come back.

As the hours passed, her sorrow turned to rage. Her rage allowed very little room for rational thinking, but what little she had was concentrated on worry for Jake. By time the sun carried a sliver of light to the east, Sam had changed into jeans and was astride her horse.

He hadn't slept a wink all night. *What should he do?*

It was the question he had asked himself all night. Would he ever stop having to cover his tracks? He'd only meant to kill the dog to scare Sam off. He hadn't meant to kill the old Indian. Another soul on his conscience. An eternity of hell couldn't be any worse than the hell he was living now.

He had to kill Sam. It was the only solution.

Sam rode the range, looking for Jake. She didn't get it. He didn't drink, so a binge was out. He had always been so reliable. Was he off on a vision quest on top of the mountain? He'd picked a great time for it, if that was what he'd done. But it was an outside chance.

It was late, and she needed to get to work. She showered and changed. At the front door, she uncovered Boomer to have a better look in the daylight.

Sam put her finger in the puckered hole. She would take the bullet out when she returned. The bastard might be able to get away with murdering Pamela, but she'd see that he served time for killing Boomer.

She saw Jake's saddled palomino as she turned

the bend, and she pulled the car into the barrow pit. Climbing over the buck-and-rail fence, Sam started across the field.

She barely felt the burrs catching and tearing her nylons as she ran.

Something had happened to Jake. But why was the horse in Guy's pasture? The need to find Jake was urgent. If he'd been out in the field all night, he would need medical attention. Or perhaps a coronary had already claimed his life. Sam slowed as she approached the horse to avoid spooking it, calling gently as she stole closer. Finally, she caught the double rein.

"Shh, it's all right." Sam pulled her skirt up thigh-length and hoisted herself into the saddle; if Jake was in the field finding him would be easier on horseback.

She heard the growling about the time she saw the gathering of hawks overhead. She headed toward the scavengers, then saw the pack of coyotes fighting over the body. Wave upon wave of hatred swept through her. She hollered and yelled, not only to scare them off. What she really wanted was to hit them, anything, anyone. The frustration of everything came back on her. The coyotes vanished into the bushes, where they would wait.

Sam gagged as she fell on her knees on the sticky blood-soiled ground beside him. Big chunks of flesh had been flayed, but he was alive. Barely. She looked closer. He had a bullet hole in his back, and had lost a great deal of blood. He needed to be transported immediately, but how could she summon help without leaving him to the scavengers? The hawks, hidden in the grass, lifted on clumsy wings as she screamed in frustration.

Against everything she'd ever been taught and on raw emotion, Sam struggled to raise him over her head and onto the horse. The palomino sidestepped, but as the helpless Jake slipped down, Sam gave a last-ditch push and balanced him. They headed toward Guy Walker's house.

Her Jeep was sitting in the drive when the sheriff dropped her off. A burr caught on the seat as she swung her legs around to get out. She ignored it. "Thanks, Hank," she said, closing the car door behind her. She watched as two of the deputies put Boomer in the back of the county's Bronco. Leaning over the dusty tailgate, she cuddled Boomer in her arms and whispered in his ear. "You take care of John," she wiped her eyes on soft hairs of his neck, "and I'll take care of The Little One."

Sam waited for the cars to pull away before she opened the front door, then she stripped off her burr-ridden nylons and threw them in the trash. She would decide later if the shoes were salvageable — not that she cared.

Between her depression and lack of sleep, she was just able to climb the stairs. She stood under the jets of the shower long after they'd turned cold, then slowly dressed in clean clothes.

Cars passed and honked at her as she drove to

town. She didn't care; nor did she care that it was a warm and sunny day.

Peter Nelson had Jake in the O.R. by time she got to the hospital. The fact that he was still hanging on was a miracle in itself. He was one tough old Indian. Sam walked through the halls of the hospital by rote, went straight to the lab, into her office, and closed the door. She sat down at her desk and cried until she fell asleep.

Derek lit a cigarette as he watched the Company jet turn tail. He had had his suitcase in hand and was walking out when Hank's phone call caught him. A couple of calls, a quick job of repacking, and he was in Sheridan instead of Rio.

The airport attendant ripped off her ear protectors, and her arm-shaded eyes followed the plane's progress. "That's one fancy piece of machinery." She looked Derek up and down. "You work for Texaco?"

He motioned with his cigarette to the plane positioning on the runway. "They have a plane like that?"

"No. Thought they might have gotten a new one. You with a movie studio? Scouting a location?"

"See a lot of scouts, do you?"

She waited until the plane lifted off before answering. "For Westerns, that kinda thing."

Both of them turned as the plane dropped a wing and circled. When it was out of sight, Derek picked up his suitcase and walked inside to the terminal's pay phone.

"Sheridan Memorial Hospital." The voice sounded harried.

"Dr. Turner's office, please."

"One moment."

Kate answered. She was the last person he wanted to talk to; he didn't need a long conversation with her at the moment.

"Dr. Turner, please."

After an uncomfortable moment, she said, "I don't think I should disturb her. Can I take a message?"

"No . . . thank you."

Derek fished through his pockets for another quarter and called for a cab. The penciled number graced the wall behind the phone.

"You didn't used to be a redhead." He took Kate's hand and kissed it.

"Like it?" She patted the lacquered hair with her free hand.

"It's stunning." He looked over at the closed door. "Is she in there?"

She bit a burgundy thumbnail.

It was enough of an answer. Derek walked to the door and knocked, walking in without invitation.

"Yes?" She didn't turn around to see who was intruding.

"Did you forget me?" he asked, dropping his suitcase to the floor. She wore a striped purple shirt with a brown plaid skirt. They clashed almost as much as Kate's hair and fingernails. And her hair was a tangled mess.

"Derek? Did I know you were coming?"

She looked worse from the front. Her face was swollen and blotched red. And puffy lids covered most of her red eyes. She looked as if she'd gone ten rounds. "Wrote a letter, guess I forgot to mail it."

He took out his handkerchief and wiped away her tears. "Do you want to tell me about it?"

"I pushed him over the edge. He shot them because of me."

"Shot who?"

"Jake and Boomer." She cried convulsively.

He pulled her from the chair and wrapped his arms around her. He rocked and soothed her, as one would an injured child. "Samantha, let's go home."

"I can't. I have to work. I have to check on Jake."

"You can't work today. Look at you."

She pulled away, wiping her nose on the back of her hand. "I have to go to the vet's . . . I have to get the slugs."

"Tomorrow, not today." He pressed the handkerchief into her hand. "Here, you keep this." Derek picked up her purse and his suitcase.

"My father's in the hospital. He needs me," she protested.

"Tomorrow. Today is for Samantha."

21

He waited until dark. Leaving the car well up the dirt road, he walked up the creek bank toward her house, all the time telling himself he had no choice. She would find him out and destroy him, unless he destroyed her first. The old Indian was in a coma and not expected to live. But she was still in his way.

This was the perfect time. She was too distraught to work. Others saw her distress. Who would question her suicide?

He pulled nervously at his gloves as he neared the house. He went around back to the laundry-room door. If the doggy door had been big enough for Boomer, it had to be big enough for him.

He looked through the smoke-gray plastic flap. The Mexican tiles felt hard and cold against his exposed forearms as he slid his shoulders through the hole. Beyond the dark room, he heard a voice — a man's voice. He leaned up against the wall, afraid to breathe. She wasn't alone. He should run. His legs were frozen in blocks of ice. Only his heart raced. Raced faster than the yelping of the puppy.

"Shhh. Don't go upstairs, you'll wake Samantha," he heard the man say.

He had to think. She was asleep, which was

good, but she wasn't alone. The voice was vaguely familiar. Was the sheriff protecting her? Before he could place it, he heard the front door open. The man was leaving; he could still do it.

"Here, dog, go outside . . . no, wait. You look like the type to run off. Do you own a collar or a leash? You're not much help."

The conversation with the puppy was stupid enough to be Hank's, but the hick twang wasn't there. Maybe a deputy? He slowly climbed the stairs, illuminated by a skylight. The full moon's rays shining through the window cast light upon the figure on the bed. He took the vial and syringe from his pocket as he walked slowly and silently toward it.

The puppy ran between Derek's legs and halfway up the stairs before Derek could catch him. "And where do you think —" Derek stopped as he heard a thud. "You woke her now, you little rascal," Derek scolded, and flipped the puppy's ears. "All right, go on," he added, putting the squirming animal down. "She's awake now anyway."

The puppy ran into the bedroom and started a ferocious round of barking.

Samantha screamed.

Derek raced in and turned on the light.

"What's going on?" She drew the covers around her.

Derek chased the puppy through the room into the bathroom, where he found him trying to jump up on the toilet seat. Above the toilet was an open window. Branches scratched across the screen behind the hissing cat.

He picked up the puppy. "I know the feeling." She was staring at them when they got back to the bedroom. "Sorry, Samantha. I let him come up . . . I thought you were awake."

She slipped on a wine-colored velvety robe and got out of bed. "That's all right. I was having a bad dream anyway."

What was the noise? Even the fat cat couldn't have made such a thud. Derek put the puppy down and went back into the bathroom. He stood still a moment, listening, then slowly inched his hand around the shower curtain. He ripped it back. The shower was empty.

"What's wrong?"

He dropped flat against the hard tile. The cat jumped down with a startled screech, landing on his back. She dug her claws in for traction and sprinted off with an angry howl. The timing was perfect. "You startled me," he said as he got up.

"Did she scratch you?"

He shook his head. Pure bravado.

"You fall on the floor every time someone startles you?"

"Just for beautiful women who have earned the reputation of aiming low." He put his arm around her shoulders and added, "I have some soup on the stove. Why don't we go down and have some."

Her eyes were focused on the carpet as they

walked through the bedroom. "Actually, I wasn't aiming at all. I'm not even sure I jerked the trigger."

"Pulled . . . pulled the trigger." He kissed her forehead as he nudged her ahead into the hall. He turned back and scanned the room before switching off the light. He felt trickling blood from the stinging wounds on his back. He wasn't fond of cats to begin with.

He hardly noticed the stiff wind gnawing at his back as he fumbled in his pants for the keys. He drove without lights until he neared the black-top.

Leaving the rutted dirt road didn't ease his shaking. He could still feel the burning pain where he had scraped his abdomen on the steel bed frame as he squeezed under.

His hand still shook like a leaf at the near disaster. Never again did he want to feel like this. He would wait until she was alone before he tried it again. The memory of sneaking down the stairs and crawling out while Sam and the man sat in the kitchen caused him to almost lose control of the car. If only it were over . . .

Derek sipped his soup, perfectly aware that he was the only one eating. "You don't like my cooking?"

She mumbled something and picked up her spoon. She made lazy figure-eights through the soup, but didn't eat.

"Are you ready to talk about it yet?"

She shrugged. "What's there to say? Frederick Wilson didn't kill Pamela, and I wanted to prove it. Now Boomer's dead and Jake's not far behind. I don't have a clue about Pamela. According to our illustrious judge, she knew every man in town."

He had checked Stanley Moots out. He was capable of this and Derek didn't want her having anything to do with him, but he didn't know how he could warn her. "I talked to him at the Christmas party and didn't like him much."

"I wish I'd listened to his advice."

"Which was?"

"Stay out of it."

"Good advice." Derek fumbled for a cigarette. "And it's not too late."

She nodded. "Except for Jake and Boomer."

"Jake may make it yet."

"I wish I were as optimistic."

He lit up and drew deeply on his Camel. It didn't give him much pleasure after he saw the look on her face.

"Did you know Jake has the Medal of Honor?"

Derek didn't know. It never occurred to him to check out the old Indian. He took a last drag and crushed out his cigarette.

Bob Wallace looked over the heads in the packed courtroom as Frederick Wilson stood.

Judge Moots took off his half-glasses and folded them carefully. "Do you have anything to

251

say to this court before sentence is pronounced?"

"No, Your Honor," the murderer said in a shallow voice.

"Frederick Carl Wilson, for the murder of Suzanna Lynn Fairchild, you are hereby sentenced to the Wyoming State Penitentiary for —"

Bob refused to listen. The death sentence was the only punishment good enough for the likes of him. An eye for an eye. The room whirled around him as he heard Karen's name and the sixth sentence of life imprisonment with no possibility of parole.

22

The predawn sky was white and wet and full of wrong.

"This is making me mighty uneasy." Derek threw down another bale of hay from the blue-tarp-covered stack and looked up again at whirling snowflakes. "Go back to the house."

"They're my buffalo." Samantha dragged one of the bales to the nearest of the three feeders. "Whoever said March comes in like a lion and out like a lamb never lived in Wyoming."

"Samantha, the roads are going to be slick. I don't want you hurrying to work."

"You don't want?" she asked snidely.

He didn't bother to answer. Mainly because he didn't know how.

They were standing in ankle-deep snow before the work was finished. Blinding snow blew in horizontal lines. The wind howled.

Her jeans pulled tight across her bottom as she lifted a leg to the stirrup. He was still staring long after she was on the horse's back. "Are you going to lift the puppy up?"

Derek looked down at the lively puppy, his wagging tail slinging snow on his wet and ruined dress pants. He lifted the fifty-pound beast over his shoulders and set him down just between the horn of the saddle and her belt buckle. The pup squirmed from head to toe.

She sank her fingers into the loose skin at the back of the puppy's neck and held on to him for dear life. "Give Rosie a slap."

He whipped the horse in the direction of the stable, then mounted the other horse and caught up in a matter of minutes.

The stinging snow drove like icy needles through his freezing skin as the thick squall became a curtain. Derek yelled over the gusting wind when he no longer saw her horse, but was unable to hear a reply. He saw a flash of the horse's tail and headed toward it, reaching over to grab her reins.

"I think we're going in a circle." She hunkered down over the shivering puppy, either to share her warmth or to keep him in place.

The horses plowed knee deep through the blowing snow. They stumbled over the white terrain from one drift to the next. She wanted to tell him something, but whatever it was was lost in the wind. She raised herself in the saddle, sending the puppy halfway under her. Reaching for the rein he held, she reeled it in, inch by inch, until the horses were brushing. "Give them their heads," she yelled.

It was as if she ripped the rein out of someone else's hand, for all the feeling the stump at the end of his arm had. He dropped the other rein and held on to the pommel.

His freed horse turned left and followed her horse at a gallop. Through the wall of falling snow he saw her horse stumble. The puppy fell. By the time he was sure Samantha was safely back on the racing horse, the dog was out of sight. He bent over the horse's neck to grab hold of the reins, but then changed his mind. Staying with Samantha was far more important than the survival of the puppy.

The horses found their way against the driving storm, stopping at the leeward side of the stable. Derek pulled the horses around the corner as Samantha caught the banging door. Inside, she rubbed her rawhide gloves over her frozen eyelashes as he led the animals into their stalls. Jake's palomino shied as Alanine bolted beside his stall. Derek jerked down on the reins with another person's hands. He should have looked for a pair of gloves. Jake had to have a pair.

Sam gave a tiny squeal and rubbed one eye with a frantic urgency. "The puppy fell off. I have to look for him."

"Are you crazy? We're lucky the horses found the way back."

She started for the door, still rubbing her eye. He grabbed her by the arm and swung her around. "We could have died out there."

The back of her hand worked at her eye.

"You can't go after the puppy. We can't even make it back to the house."

"I have to find Boomer's puppy. Don't you understand?" She pushed away from him.

He tightened his grip. "He'll find his way back."

She buried her head in his chest, her shoulders sagging. It only took a moment for her hand to go to her eye again.

"What's the matter with your eye?"

"Ice." She flinched as he held a numb finger to the irritated eye. "He'll die."

"Stand still." The culprit was an eyelash. He managed somehow to get it out. "There. He'll be just fine."

"He's all I have left."

All she had left of his father, he thought she was saying. "Rosie must like hearing that."

She tried to laugh. "I meant . . . I don't know what I meant."

He was afraid he did. "We aren't going to be able to stay here. We'll have to go to Jake's place and start a fire."

The wind caught the door as they started out. Derek put his body into it and pushed with all his strength. "Latch it," he yelled over the wind. She pushed the board down.

He took her hand as they felt their way through the whiteout to the shack. Pieces of skin tore from Derek's fingers at the touch of the frozen metal door handle. After shutting out the snow and galing wind, Derek leaned against the wall and caught his breath. "I will never again complain about New York's weather." He blew on his red hands as he watched Samantha flap her arms about her.

"April Fools!"

"We certainly are," Derek said on his way to

the potbellied stove. "We are going to find some matches, right?" He crumpled paper with tingling hands, then stacked the split wood.

"Jake surely has some." She looked around. "Ah-ha, by the stove." She got them for him.

He drew a tiny icicle out of her hair as she set the matches down. "Thank you, ma'am."

Samantha kept staring out the frosted window; it must have been a symbolic gesture. She couldn't possibly see anything other than the solid white mass. Derek looked around the tiny shack, wondering if Jake had any papers that might give a little of his military history. It didn't look promising.

"Samantha, get over here by the fire. Let's get you dried off." He hoped she understood that it was a command, not a suggestion.

She took one last longing look and came over, shivering. "It feels good, but it's still damn cold in here."

"It'll warm up." He hoped. He pulled the chair over to the fire. It was the only chair in the room. "Sit." He tugged at one boot. "I think we could make a fortune if we manufactured cowboy boots with zippers."

"Just like an easterner," she said, twisting to free her foot. "That would be sissified."

The boot flew off, sending him flat on his butt. "This is making me feel very macho, that's for sure." He motioned for her to lift her other foot. Taking this one off proved an easier task. Practice, he theorized. After the second boot stood beside the fire, Derek said, "Now the pants."

She dampened her lips.

"You want to stand on ceremony, or you want to be dry?"

She stood up and unzipped her jeans. He reached up and started to pull them down, catching her panties. "Just a minute," she said as she wiggled them up. "A gentleman would look the other way."

"A fool would look the other way." He noticed her eyes were slits. "I'll tell you what," he said as he tugged and jerked the soaking-wet jeans, "I'll turn away when you pull off *mine*. Sit down."

She plopped down as he struggled with one leg, then the other. Sam pulled down her T-shirt that had worked up as he peeled off her jeans and socks.

They changed places. Sam swung a leg over his and, with her back to him, pulled on the heel of the boot. After struggling a spell, she looked over her shoulder. "You could help, you know."

"I was. Did you want me to put my other —" The boot popped off. The other came off with the same degree of difficulty.

She whistled as he took off his pants. "Those are the second-best pair of legs I've ever seen," she said in a husky voice. "You didn't get those from John." The words were barely out of her mouth before she turned pensive.

He suspected she was thinking of his father's scrawny legs. As a kid he always tried to be at least a block ahead of the rest of the family when his father wore those god-awful plaid Bermuda shorts. He wondered if, like the down parka, Samantha had those old shorts stashed in a drawer somewhere. Knowing his father, he probably had them to the bitter end.

"I guess I won't be going to work today," Sam said, again tugging down her T-shirt.

"Don't think *anyone* will be at work today. Does this happen often?"

She shook her head as she paced back and forth, keeping her watch at the window. She was sobbing so softly, he wouldn't have known she was crying except for the quivering shoulders that gave her away.

Derek pulled her into his arms. "The puppy will be all right, you'll see," he said, stroking her wet and tangled hair.

"The Little One is all I have left."

He tucked a strand of hair behind her ear. "No, Samantha, you have me. You'll always have me." The words frightened him. It was as if he'd opened Pandora's box and everything he had wanted to keep safely locked away escaped. He wanted to cry with her. Instead he lifted her chin. "Come on, now. Don't cry . . . we're wet enough." Her sobs were punctuated with laughter.

Derek looked around with a sigh. It was too cold to stand around and the bed was the logical place to be, but he didn't know if he could trust himself. He sighed again. "Come on. Let's get under the covers." They crawled under the buffalo robe and curled up together. It was one of those awkward moments. If she felt it too, she gave no signs. She was probably too concerned over the puppy to even be aware. "You must have a warm heart, Samantha . . . your feet are freezing."

She pulled her feet away, and in time, he heard her even breathing. He held her close and wished he always could. He had never known such longing, or if he had, he'd forgotten the hollow feeling. He wished she were anyone other than his father's widow. Not that it bothered him so much, but it was pretty obvious that she still hadn't let go. And he was nothing more to her than a walking reminder. Many times he'd caught her studying his profile, or reacting to a gesture. He'd say something and she'd jump out of her skin as if her precious John had said it. He would never be his own man, only his father's shadow.

He was about to drop off when he heard scratching at the door. Hurriedly he opened it against the strong wind. The Little One strolled in as Derek fought to close the door. As a reward for being rescued from the cold, the puppy covered him in snow and sleet. Derek should have known the puppy would shake, and said so under his breath.

She was still asleep, but how she had managed with the puppy whimpering and carrying on was beyond him. He pulled, then pushed the big-pawed pup across the rough planks to the fire. It didn't take long for the puppy to realize that he liked the warmth, and soon he settled down beside it.

Derek stoked the fire before returning to Samantha's side.

As night fell, Sam stood by the window watching the snow. The howling blasts of wind whirled the snowflakes high in the air in circular patterns, before dropping them against the snow-covered ground. The ice crystals glazed the corners of the windows in kaleidoscope fashion. Would the snow ever stop? She had never known a spring blizzard like this.

"Dinner is served," Derek announced in his best butler imitation.

"I hope I'm dressed appropriately."

A stuffy English butler looked her up and down disapprovingly. "We will allow this one time, but please be attired in your long black gown the next time we go to the trouble of opening a can of chili."

She rather enjoyed his brand of humor. It suited him. John never teased her, not even at home. "That must be the imperial *we*. I don't remember having a hand in it."

"Whatever madam says," the butler said, leading her to an old Naugahyde chair with cotton stuffing coming out a split. She would replace it and everything else if Jake came out of the coma. He was a fighter, she gave him that. She sat in front of Jake's one bowl. Derek was apparently planning to eat out of the pan.

He settled on the foot of the bed and reached over the split-log table for some elk jerky. He remembered his calling and jumped to attention. "Madam?" He offered her the jerked meat.

She was hungry enough to take some, but it went against her sense of propriety to partake of the elk those two bastards from California killed on her land. "Maybe later."

"Madam doesn't know what she's missing. Next best thing to crackers."

"I'll eat my chili ungarnished this evening. I've been trying to cut back on my cracker consumption."

"Very good, madam." The mattress turned up on its edges when he sat down. He ripped off a piece of jerky with his teeth and grunted like a caveman. A versatile entertainer, this man.

"Good?"

"Fit for a dog." He threw, caveman style, the rest of the piece to the puppy.

"Thanks a heap. You're teaching The Little One to beg."

He stood up and bowed. "My apologies, madam."

"I'm not a psychiatrist, you understand, but my six-week psychiatric rotation as an intern makes me suspect a dual personality. Very bipolar, I might add."

"Moi?"

"Multiple personalities, I meant."

"How did The Little One get his name?"

She feigned horror at the real Derek. "Yuck. Bring back the caveman."

"Neanderthal, *please*," the butler said with fitting sobriety.

"I beg your pardon. Bring back the Neanderthal."

"Madam, that would be impossible. Nothing's left but dusty bones." He swiped at imaginary dust. If he had aimed a little lower he could have cleaned out the dust bunnies under the bed. Rustic and dirty was Jake's place. And only marginally warm.

"Then I'll tell you. Boomer and I had the pick of the litter. We decided to give a puppy to Jake. When Boomer and I brought him the puppy, I said, 'The little one's for you.' "

"Very good, madam."

"He's outgrowing his name, but until he tells me to call him something else, I guess it'll stay The Little One."

The night was white with glistening snow, and cold drafts penetrated the chinks in the log walls. Sam crawled under the buffalo robe after the chili was polished off and the few dishes were done. She didn't like the way Derek shook his head as he looked at the dwindling woodpile while stoking the fire. "It had better stop tomorrow," he said as he and the cold air rushed under the cover. She winced as sharp bristles scraped across her shoulders. "I certainly hope so. My back's raw from that beard of yours."

"Sorry. I didn't have the chance to shave this

morning." He grunted like the Neanderthal man or a Sumo wrestler and pinned her down. He rubbed his rough cheeks over hers. She giggled and cried for mercy until his lips stopped her.

A gentle hand stroked her hair. His tongue glided across her lips, stirring a long-forgotten feeling. She pulled him closer.

"Samantha, Samantha," he whispered. "Oh, Samantha." He brushed back her hair, and his warm lips moved with a tickling touch down the line of her neck.

All of her senses came alive under his touch. She closed her eyes, feeling her T-shirt crawl up under his fingers. She shuddered as a busy hand stroked the side of a breast. A small moan tore from her throat.

His hands and mouth roamed her hungrily, whispering muffled words, tasting the clues.

Her fingers burrowed into his shoulders.

"Samantha, Samantha." His lips trailed kisses down her trembling belly.

She came to her senses and pulled away. "No . . . don't." She scrambled over him, pulling down her shirt, and padded across the cold floor to the colder window. She stared with unseeing eyes into the whiteness.

He was behind her. His arms wrapped firmly around her.

She strained away from the tickling lips at her ear.

"Samantha, I love you. I can't help it."

She fought the feeling his closeness brought.

"Please don't . . . just . . . don't."

"Samantha, look at me." He lifted her chin, but she closed her eyes tight against her shame. How could she look into those eyes? John's eyes. "He's gone. My father was your past. I'm your future." He crushed her to him. "He's only a memory. I'm flesh and blood. Let him go, Samantha. Let him go."

She was so confused.

Derek woke to a calm morning. The snow glistened like a thousand diamonds under the bright blue sky. But the fire had gone out during the night, and it was cold. Freezing cold. He lit the stove and jumped back into the warm bed.

"Shit, you're cold!" Samantha shrieked as she recoiled. The Little One took that as an invitation and jumped up.

Derek pushed him off. "No!" He was at the very edge of the bed, but it was too small for them not to be touching. "No thanks is necessary for rekindling the fire."

She pulled him into her arms. It was not an unpleasant experience. "Thank you for building the fire. Tell me when you're warm."

"Hmmm." He rolled his hands over her back and whispered, "We have to hash this out."

"You're John's son. I'm his wife. That makes us —"

"Absolutely nothing . . . as they said in that movie we saw." He no longer whispered.

"The guy was a second cousin's roommate

or something. I'm —"

"My father's widow," he tone was sharper than he meant, "not his wife." His hands held her tight as she tried to flee. He rolled over on top of her and pinned her down. "If you want to be a relative, be my wife."

She searched his eyes. "What?"

"Marry me."

They made their silent trek to the house with only minor inconveniences. The puppy jumped through the deep snow with the kind of zest reserved for the very young. Next to the back door was a small white-tailed deer.

"Well, so the prodigal son doth return." She boxed its ears, and the deer butted up against her.

Derek stood in amazement.

The puppy sniffed the deer suspiciously.

Samantha opened the door and the deer walked right in.

Derek told himself he wouldn't ask. The house was cold. He started right in building fires. And told himself again not to ask. If she didn't think a deer in the house was unusual enough to give him an explanation, he wasn't going to ask.

After he had showered and changed, he found the deer stretched out in front of the fireplace with the cat curled up next to him. He wouldn't ask, but he did go after his camera. He had snapped off several shots by the time Samantha had cleaned up. She sat cross-legged beside the deer and stroked it, laughing as it turned and lifted a leg; it liked having its belly scratched. Derek took a couple more pictures.

"I found Alfred on the road, cowering up next to his mother's body. He was only a few days old at the time, and I wouldn't have given much for his chances. But as you can see . . ." Her voice trailed off. "A wise buck would visit again next hunting season."

"The cat seems to like him."

"You should have seen him with Boomer. They had some big times marking their territory. Alfred would rub the scent glands on his back legs as he urinated so the scent would be carried to the ground. Boomer would go along behind him, lifting his leg to remark it. They made quite a pair."

Derek caught her hand and pulled her to the couch. "We'd make quite a pair. Can't we even talk about it?"

She took back her hand. "Couldn't I just think about it for a little while?"

Frustration was his constant companion. He wanted to pack her up and take her away before anything else happened. But he couldn't without explaining, and explaining would be to lose her. And now he wanted her for himself. Duplicity had painted him into a corner.

23

The snowplows unclogged the main arteries of the town. More and more four-wheel outfits moved around, and on the third day following the spring storm, Sheridan was bustling.

On the night before his planned departure Derek smoothed Samantha's long blond tresses in his lap. He watched the colors of the flickering fire dance from orange to red, red to yellow, yellow to orange, with an occasional green or blue flash. The crackling fire would have warmed his heart, had it not been so heavy. Every fiber of his being yearned for her.

It wasn't a great plan, but it was the best he could come up with. Short of telling her the truth, that is. "Samantha, we need to talk about something."

Her body stiffened. "Derek, I need more time."

He stroked her cheek. "I know. This is about something else." Her face was unguarded for a split second. "I've been thinking about the best way to investigate the murders."

"I'm listening."

He ran a finger over the soft down on her arm. He liked the way it stood up. There wasn't much he didn't like about her except her persistence. "I have to go back to New York, but I could be back here in a week's time. Let me interview Pamela's friends. Maybe if they're approached as if it were part of a story on Frederick Wilson —"

She propped herself up on one hand. He had her full attention now. "You're going to help me? I thought you were against my trying to find the killer."

"I am, but you're going to anyway." He gathered her into his arms. "I just want to keep you safe."

"And Jake." She nuzzled against his neck.

Derek had already seen to Jake's safety. But what kind of a threat was a comatose man? The murderer wouldn't go after him again, Derek was certain. But just in case, he had a man there. He measured his words carefully. "The way I see it, the murderer knows you're looking for him. Otherwise he wouldn't have tried to scare you away with the note and killing Boomer."

"And he shot Jake to keep him from identifying him. So he's a local person." She wiggled free.

"Stay here. I like you close . . . you smell good." He kissed her ear. "And you taste good."

"Don't. You're tickling me."

He nibbled ever so lightly at her neck, making her squirm. "Maybe he's even someone you know. You've got to seem like you've given up on fingering him," he told her as he brushed a silky strand away from her eye. "Wait a week . . . until I can get back to help you."

"What's so important in New York that you

couldn't put it off a few days?"

He kissed the hollow of her throat and parted her robe. He lifted her breast, finally seeing the scar, a fine red line like a tiny tear at the edge of a rose petal.

"Did you hear the question?"

He kept his eyes on the scar as he lied. "I have a deadline on another story." He let her breasts slump as he looked up. "Saturday night I have a command appearance at my mother's birthday party." Her eyes burned through him like acid. "I'll be back on Sunday."

"Ignoring the party, which seems too trivial to even discuss, is the other story more important than finding a killer?"

He wouldn't tell her that his "interview" wasn't in New York but in El Salvador, with one of the world's most vicious killers. "It's all arranged. I have to be there. Your man isn't going anywhere, and as long as he thinks you're not searching for him, he won't kill again." He didn't add, "I hope."

Derek had gone back to New York, Alfred to the great outdoors. The Little One seemed bigger each day. Sam was busier than ever trying to catch up. Pamela's killer was never far from her mind, but she had promised Derek she wouldn't do or say anything until he came back.

She had skipped lunch the first two days of the week, but by Wednesday she was able to break away. Bob was dressed in clean green scrubs and eating alone. She knew what he was feeling, and her heart ached for him. She had had so many ups and downs after John died, and the last thing she wanted was to be around people trying to cheer her up. That, and those who tried to tell her they knew what she was going through.

"Waiting to catch a baby?" She put the tray down across from him.

He gave the chair in front of her a shove with his foot.

She'd had better invitations. She plopped down and looked at the bowl of salad and the saucer of squash and wished she'd gotten the bean soup.

Bob nodded. "I usually do my waiting in the wee hours of the night."

"Now, Bob, you know the saying, 'Conceived at night, born at night.' And we all know when most people find time to get laid."

Bob's eyes dulled.

She was being too cheery. "I'm sorry, Bob, I didn't mean . . . I know how much you must miss her."

"It's all right."

She covered his hand. "I know . . . I know."

"And Amy . . ."

"I know." She was batting a thousand. She was being all those people who tried to be nice after John's death. She slipped her hand away and picked up her fork.

"There's no justice."

Sam picked at her salad.

He sipped a spoonful of soup.

They ate in silence for an awkward time.

He reached for the salt.

She took it away from him. "Now, Bob. That's not good for you."

Bob laughed sardonically. "Listen to you." He pointed to the empty package of crackers. "They don't call those Saltines for nothing."

"These little *crackers?*" she asked with as much naïveté, as she could muster.

He used the salt and they fell into silence.

"I'm truly sorry about your Indian and Boomer," Bob said, finally.

"Thank you."

"How's he doing?"

Sam shrugged. "The longer the coma lasts, the worse it is."

He nodded apathetically.

She couldn't hold back any longer, and she wanted to say something that would help. "If it's any consolation, Frederick was sentenced to one murder he didn't commit. Guess that's not much comfort. Time doesn't bend. There's only so many years in a lifetime." Time, though, had a way of dragging on its belly, and she knew that's how it had to be for Bob these days.

"What are you talking about?"

"He didn't kill the one at Halloween."

A flicker of interest enlivened his flat eyes. "Then why was he tried for it?"

"Technically, he wasn't tried for anything." She dropped her fork in the squash hard enough to splatter yellow mush on her lab coat. "As a community service, our self-proclaimed protectors decided the town was better off not knowing that another killer is loose on our golden streets. Speaking of no justice!"

"Not that I care about Frederick Wilson," the name caught in his throat, "but why would they do that?"

"No evidence." She hoped her tone made her position crystal clear.

"Then how do you know *he* didn't kill her?"

She tore the other package of crackers with her teeth. "Technically, there's no evidence. There was plenty. Fibers, different blood type, but a screwup in the state crime lab made it all inadmissible. Another bungled job by those who service and protect."

"Are you serious?"

"No, Bob, I'm making all this up. The funniest part — not that any of it is funny — was that the bastard put her in the freezer until five o'clock Hallow—" Sam gasped for air.

"You're hyperventilating. What's wrong?"

"I know who the killer is." The room whirled; she couldn't breathe.

Bob felt for a pulse. He jumped up and snatched a paper sack off the next table.

One of the nurses turned around. "Hey, that's —"

"I'll bring it right back. Here, Sam, breathe into this."

Sam shook her head. "I'm going to be sick."

273

She grabbed the bag and ran.

Sam slumped in her office chair, her purse and keys still in hand. She'd heard the page from the bathroom. It was Dotty, the woman who had the room across the hall from her father. She'd called to tell Sam that they had tied her father to the bed. He *was* strapped in his bed when she arrived, yelling a whole list of vile words. She'd never heard so much as a "damn" pass his lips before. Sam had gotten him up, placed him in his wheelchair, wheeled him out to the television room, and parked him beside a green recliner. Before Sam left she wrote orders in his chart that he was not to be left restrained in bed during waking hours. She had overstepped her authority — nonexistent at the nursing home — but Big Bob would see the note and make it official. The time would come when he would have to be bedridden, but it hadn't come yet.

Sam pounded her fist on the desk. "Jeffrey, how could you have done this to me!"

Only one person could have known what time Pamela's body had been taken out of the freezer. Sam hadn't even known, not until she heard it from him. Anger had let it slip right by. Boomer would still be alive if she'd been able to check her emotions. And Jake wouldn't be in the shape he was in. Jeffrey! She hadn't even considered him.

He had been so crafty. How could she have missed it? Plea-bargaining with Wilson "for the good of the community." She wouldn't even be surprised if the missing evidence somehow got lost thanks to his doing.

Jeffrey knew the law. Why hadn't he gone to the police and explained that Pamela's death was accidental? It was quite apparent to her what had happened, even after he had toyed with the evidence. She would have backed him up.

She sort of understood why he didn't come forward. He would have been finished in this town. What jury would convict the criminal before them on his say-so when he himself went scot-free for killing another human being, even accidentally? Not to mention the impropriety. The sexual nature of it could cause quite a sensation. The scandal-hungry newspaper would have had a field day. And what if Frederick's mother had sent him a Halloween card and set him off? She would have liked seeing Jeffrey double-talk away two murders at the same time.

But no matter what the cost, he should have owned up. Legally, ethically, morally. His shooting Boomer and Jake had made him as guilty and as contemptible as the worst of criminals. And she would see him punished.

How would she go about it? She weighed her options. Run to the police, go to Moots. She didn't relish either, but favored Moots. Hank would have been her choice, but this wasn't in his jurisdiction. The one thing she knew, she had to present irrefutable evidence. Evidence so damaging that if Jeffrey tried to bribe the judge,

Stanley would have to refuse. The samples she'd taken from Pamela's body might be inadmissible in a court of law, or so Jeffrey would have her believe, but if she could convince the judge, he would start the ball rolling. She only hoped that good ol' Stanley would remember that he'd been suckered too. He was the one who sentenced Frederick Wilson. But she'd leave nothing to chance.

She could use hair, seminal fluid, blood, or skin tissue. Hair would be the easiest to get, but not so good in Jeffrey's case. He might try to weasel out by reminding Stanley that his hair falls out everywhere and maybe one of the police officers carried the hair on his uniform and accidentally dropped it on her body. Or say the real killer was framing him. Blood would be best, and maybe she could pull the Larry stunt on him. It would be a whole lot easier if he worked at the hospital. Maybe she could get him to come to the lab under some pretense. The trick was to do it without making him suspicious.

Christopher Newman sat at his office desk and looked out over the tops of the buildings to the Golden Gate Bridge. Today the cloudless blue sky offered a commanding view, one he'd never tired of.

He held up the slip of paper and read the message again as he waited for Sam to come to the phone. He had been worried sick about her ever since she picked up and moved to the wilds of

Wyoming, obviously to do penance for John's death.

It took a good five minutes before she came on the line.

"Sam, it's Chris."

"Thank you for returning my call, Chris." She sounded breathless. "Sorry to keep you waiting, been trying to jump-start a heart in the E.R."

"They still have E.R.'s in hospitals?"

"Ah, the good old days when I was just a pathologist." She took a deep breath. "Chris, I need your help."

"Name it. You know I'd give you the shirt off my back."

"You're not still wearing those starchy white ones, are you?"

He could see the pinched-up face she always made when she teased him. He missed her. "I'm afraid so."

"Then I'll settle for your influence. I need a rush job at a DNA lab."

"How rushed?"

"Overnight."

He laughed.

"A couple of days?"

"I don't have that kind of influence. Three weeks at the lab in Orange County is the best I can do."

"I can't wait three weeks."

She never did have much patience. "Remember Toshibana? The first-year resident when John . . . when you moved to Wyoming?"

"The kid from Sacramento."

"Right. He's at a lab in New Jersey. Want his number?"

"Please."

He looked it up and gave it to her.

"Thanks, Chris. I owe you one."

"Pay me back by coming home, Sam."

He thought he heard a sniffle over the usual long-distance static. "I am home, Chris."

"Come back to me, Sam. No E.R."

There was a long, static silence. "Guess what?" she asked too gaily. "John's son is doing an article on me."

"I can't believe it." And he couldn't. Those rotten kids sided with their brainwashing mother and wouldn't have a thing to do with their father or Sam. It hurt him as much as it had hurt John.

"And guess what else. He doesn't hate me. In fact, he says he loves me."

"What's not to love?" Apples don't fall far from the tree. "And how do you feel?"

"Confused." She sighed. "I don't have time in my life for another man anyway."

"Take some advice from an old man. I knew John better than any other man alive. He wouldn't have wanted you to live like you are. He would have wanted you to find someone else to love. And what better man than the son he so dearly loved?"

"You're not an old man." Her strained voice told him she was about to lose it.

"Don't try to change the subject," he said in a

scolding tone that he hoped would make her bicker instead of cry. "You heard what I said. Now you follow my advice, young lady."

"Pathologists don't give advice. They just tell other doctors what mistakes they made. And always when it's too late to do anything about it."

"I'm going to hang up. I don't have to listen to that crap on my nickel."

"Thanks for the number."

"You're welcome. And don't forget to heed my advice."

"Good-bye, Dr. Know-it-all."

"Good-bye, Love-of-my-life."

24

Sam held up a bottle of her favorite wine when Jeffrey came to the door. "Brought a peace offering to say I'm sorry for being so cranky." He opened the door wide and ushered her in. Her breath caught as he looked up and down the dark street.

The gray carpet loomed up at her. A rifle, no doubt, was hidden somewhere in the house. She focused her eyes on his red sweater as she handed over the bottle. "I left your number with my answering service for the call I'm expecting. You might as well offer me a drink while I wait."

He twisted the bottle to have a look at the label. "Johannesburg Riesling. Hmmm, Napa Valley." His smile seemed so innocent. "Your old stomping grounds."

"Just about. It's imported, if you live in France."

"We'll pretend we live in France." When he got to the penitentiary in Rawlings, he could pretend he lived in Sheridan. "Have a seat. I'll open it." He headed for the kitchen.

She sighed heavily when he left the room, but then, steeling herself, wandered out to the kitchen to keep an eye on the bottle. "How's your puppy?" she asked, leaning against the sink, trying to look casual. *Yes, Jeffrey, tell me all about the puppy whose father you killed.*

He glanced her way. "Just fine. He's out in the back. Want to see him?"

"Maybe later." She watched him search for a corkscrew. "Should I have brought one with a screw cap?"

He chuckled. "We'll manage." He seemed so much like her old Jeffrey that she had to constantly remind herself that the inner Jeffrey was a monster she didn't know at all.

They returned to the living room with the opened bottle and two stemmed glasses. She stood in front of his Dali print until he sat down, then she sat next to him. Close. Uncomfortably close.

Jeffrey rested an arm over the back of the couch as he saluted her glass. "To your health."

"And yours," she said, clicking glasses.

A couple of fortifying sips later, Sam inched closer. She teased the fine hairs on the back of his neck and tickled his ear with tiny wet bubbles. His after-shave had worn off and he didn't even smell like her old Jeffrey. "Don't be angry with me," she whispered.

Jeffrey's mask of respectability fell away. His mouth took hers with a harshness she hadn't expected, and his arms cut off her circulation. Her skin crawled under his angry touch. She tasted an oily film as his tongue forced its way into her mouth. Her temples throbbed with repulsion.

He trailed acid-scorching kisses down her neck. Sam could stand no more. She pulled away

281

and stood in front of him. She stepped out of her shoes and unbuttoned her blouse with tantalizing slowness. He flashed a grin. A Lewis Carroll cat couldn't show more teeth. She slipped the blouse from her shoulders and let it float to the floor. She hadn't worn a bra.

"God, you're beautiful," he said, reaching out with rattlesnake quickness.

She backed away. An obscure study on the hypnotic powers of belly dancers served her well as she swayed to unheard music. Her skirt fell in a circle around her feet. She tucked her thumbs into the hollows beside each hipbone and inched down her bikinis. "Here? Or in the bedroom?"

Jeffrey gnashed his teeth and yanked the rubber band from her hair. Her head jerked back from hungry fingers. He carried her to the bedroom and stretched her out on the king-size bed, pinning her hands above her head. She gasped as a scorpion's bite involved the tender incision above the nipple. "Your boobs are so . . . big," he said, giving the other a twisting pinch.

Sam flinched from pain and closed her eyes with shame. She tried to remember all the times with John. But everything was happening so quickly, and harshly; all so menacingly wrong. Jeffrey's heavy hand ran down her belly to the triangle of hair. He twisted a curl around his finger. Nausea overpowered her, and she tried to shrink from his poking fingers.

"No!" She scrambled up. She had to be the one in control. "You planning to make love to me in your clothes?" She hoped she sounded more sexy than frightened.

Jeffrey pulled his red sweater and yellow polo shirt over his head in one swift motion. He kicked his loafers under the bed, then plopped down next to her and pulled off his khaki pants and blue boxers together. His socks were off in a flash. His clothes lay in a heap in the otherwise spotless room. Sam didn't know he could move so fast. She wondered what someone with the apparent experience of Pamela thought of him. Was his position so prestigious that she was willing to put up with this?

He was losing his erection.

Disgusted and not altogether flattered, she slid down between his legs. She stroked his left thigh lightly, noticing the tortuous retraction of the left testis resulting from contraction of the dartos fascia. It was not the reflex she sought. She nipped and nibbled at his thighs, then slowly brought him into her mouth.

"Harder, Sam."

Her sentiments entirely. He gasped with delight as she clawed into his thighs. She didn't break skin, but the thought crossed her mind. Scratch him now and get the hell out. Sam felt him swell. When at last he had risen to the occasion, she gave the corona ridge a couple of cat licks and freed him.

"Sit on my dick."

How romantically put. She wanted him on top so she could get at his back, but she obliged.

Straddling him, she forced him deep inside her. He made love with his eyes open; she smiled and tried to look excited. She caught herself wincing from the dry chafing as she mechanically moved up and down. He didn't notice her discomfort. Causing pain seemed to be his strong suit.

Sam wasn't sure how long he would last. Seminal fluid was nice, but she wanted skin tissue and blood too. Overkill was her new motto. Stanley would appreciate it. She had to get under him. She rolled to the right. He took the cue and tumbled over with her. The perfect gentleman held tight to her buttocks as they maneuvered tangled limbs.

His rhythmic thrusting didn't cause her moans and little cries, but she hoped he thought so. His breath came in a succession of short gasps. As she felt him near his climax, she ripped through the skin on his back with great satisfaction. He screamed with delight as he exploded deep inside her, and then he fell against her as if dead.

Sam wiped beads of sweat from his forehead. "Darling," the word dripped vinegar down her throat, "I have to go."

Jeffrey made no effort to move off. "No, stay the night."

"My sister's ill and I'm going to see her." She wiggled out from under him. "I'll be gone for a few days, but I'll see you the moment I get back . . . I promise."

He pulled a pillow out from under crumpled covers and tucked it under his head. "All right

. . . but the moment you get back, call me."

"I'll do better than that, I'll deliver a kiss in person."

She turned and waved at the door. "Don't get up, I'll see myself out."

Sam stowed a small suitcase in her Jeep, then returned to the empty house. The Little One and Kitty were banished yesterday evening, journeying to the kennels. Guardedly she placed the old and new samples in the donor organ carrier.

After trying one more time to get Derek on the phone, she turned out the lights, locked the door, and hurried to the Jeep.

The blanket of darkness slowly slid away. By the time Sam parked at the airport the whole sky reflected dawn.

Keeping one eye glued to the parking lot, Sam inched her way along the line to the counter. The attendant looked at Sam's ticket. "Got a tight connection in Denver, I see. Running a bit late this morning to boot." She leaned over the counter at the suitcase. "Carry-on?"

Sam held up the organ carrier; it looked to be the size of a six-pack cooler. "They'll both fit under the seat."

"Sorry, only two pieces — your purse included."

She checked her bag all the way through to Newark. With her purse teetering on her shoulder, ticket in one hand and the cooler in the other, Sam paced back and forth in front of the windows facing the parking lot. Jeffrey was not stupid. He might have figured it out already. After the flight was called, everyone lined up for a carry-on search. Sheridan had a new X-ray machine, but it apparently belonged to the competitor.

At her turn, Sam opened the cooler for the attendant. The woman seemed concerned about the possibility of contamination to the other passengers and wanted to know what was in the vials.

"Seminal fluid. I suppose in the event of a crash, the vials could escape the cooler, sail through the cabin, and lodge in a woman's reproductive tract . . . causing pregnancy. But those astronomical chances are slimmer than the woman's chances of surviving the initial crash."

The lid slammed on the cooler. "I needed to check. Might have been some plague or something." She slid it to the other side of the counter. "Just go on through," she said, nodding to the metal detector.

Sam picked up the cooler and her purse. She stood just at the side of the metal detector in order to continue watching for Jeffrey while the rest of the passengers were screened. None of them looked to be carrying the plague.

The attendant opened the outside door and collected the tickets as the passengers filed out. Sam walked through the early-morning dew and climbed the stairs to the plane, all the time looking over her shoulder. She found row nine, seat B and sat down — her eyes on the terminal door. Not until the plane was high in the sky did Sam feel safe.

It had been a struggle to get up so early, and Jeffrey wondered why he bothered. He'd lain awake most of the night thinking of all the things Sam and he would do to each other when she returned.

At the restaurant's door, he exchanged four dollar bills for a breakfast ticket, then looked around the banquet room to see which of the elite were present. All of the businessmen in town belonged to Rotary, as did many of the attorneys and a few doctors.

Spying the younger Bob Wallace, Jeffrey sauntered off in the other direction. He would probably always feel guilty about the Frederick Wilson plea-bargaining.

"Jeffrey," the voice behind him called.

He turned around to see Ken. He wasn't smiling, for a change. "Ken, how are you?"

"Fine. What did Sam tell you?"

"What are you talking about?"

"Pamela's killer. Sam told Bob she knew who it was."

Jeffrey felt himself go numb. She'd come to him, all right, but not with accusations. That explained her sudden interest in him. He knew she would remember his slip. He had wanted to bite back those incriminating words about taking Pamela's body out of the freezer at five. She hadn't realized at the time, but obviously she remembered. He needed to find her.

It never failed. Daisy could sit all day without a call, but step out a minute and the phone rings off the hook. Juggling the mail and her purse, she fumbled to get the right key. She rushed to the phone, dropping everything to her desk.

"Dr. Turner's office," she answered breathlessly.

"Yes, this is Dr. Bradshaw from Campbell County Hospital. I need to get in contact with Dr. Turner."

"She's been called out of town," Daisy said, trying to catch her breath.

"It's very urgent. Perhaps you could give me a number where she could be reached."

"I don't have a number, but when she calls, I could give her a message."

"Could you tell me where she is?"

"New Orleans. Her sister lives in New Orleans."

"When do you expect her back?"

"Monday morning."

"I'll call back then, thank you."

Not much of an emergency if he can wait until Monday.

She gathered up the scattered mail.

He had called everyone connected with Sam. They all thought she was in New Orleans. He'd like to believe she was, but he knew better.

The last call was finally answered by a female airline attendant.

"Jeffrey Talbot, County Attorney. I'm afraid I'm in a bit of a fix. The coroner left town this morning, but neglected to sign off on a pending case. Maybe we can catch her as she gets off the plane. What time does she arrive?"

"What's the name?"

"Oh, I'm sorry . . . Samantha Turner."

He could hear the computer clicking in the background. "Yes, here it is. ETA three-oh-five."

"Good, we'll be able to call the airport. Oh, what's that flight number?"

She gave it and then said, "I remember her. She was taking some . . ." her voice broke, "some test tubes on the plane. We always have to make sure they're not a health hazard to the other passengers, kind of thing."

Test tubes. He could guess what they contained. "Which airport was that again?"

"Newark."

"Thank you for your help."

Mr. Nemesis was barely recognizable on the ten-year-old battered manila folder. He pulled it out of the filing cabinet. He read it through before copying down the Denver telephone number, which was current as of last summer, according to the notation. He carefully refiled the folder and put the number into his pocket.

He drove to the bank for a roll of quarters, then on to Safeway where he remembered seeing a pay phone. There he placed the call. "Answer it," he said under his breath.

"Hello," came the husky voice.

"Yes, my couch is frayed. I believe it needs reupholstering," he said, using the trick phrase. He waited with bated breath to see if it would work.

There was a long pause. "Perhaps we should meet." A command, he feared. He had hoped to send the money.

"I'm not in Denver, and I need your help by 3:05 EST today at Newark Airport."

"Too much paperwork to get anything done by then."

"Perhaps you could just look after someone until the paperwork is completed."

He was silent for a minute. "I can have an associate at the airport by then, but unless . . ."

"I can be in Denver by Saturday."

"All right. Meet me by the bronze bear on the west steps of the Natural History Museum at ten A.M. Saturday. You understand that it's *ten?*"

He understood what the ten meant. "Agreed, ten." He wiped beads of sweat from his forehead. He gave a description of Sam, as well as the flight number of her plane, before hanging up.

He would have to make smaller withdrawals out of several accounts so as not to call attention to himself. Ten thousand had to be reported, and he wanted no ties. He would drive to Denver Friday night and return Saturday night.

25

After twelve years as a customs official, he could pretty much tell which travelers would smuggle in dutiable items. Just this morning, he had spotted a middle-aged woman bringing in a full-length mink coat. The label was from Saks Fifth Avenue, but the coat was from France.

Another spurt of activity after the lull. He watched the passengers pick up their luggage. Looking at the predominantly dark skins, he knew there would be no furs in this group. This had to be the South American flight.

After processing the usual sort, he looked up to find a haggard, stubbly-whiskered man standing before him. He looked carefully at his passport. *Journalist.* He might have known.

He thumbed through the pages looking at the visas and stamps. Tunisia, Libya, Dahomey, Mauritania, Nepal, Afghanistan, Mauritius, were a few of the places this passport had taken him. Not the usual hot spots for tourism.

"Where's Mauritius?"

"It's an island in the Indian Ocean, famous for the dodo bird."

Satisfied, the customs agent handed the weathered passport back. "Welcome home."

Sam slammed down the pay phone. Derek still

wasn't home. She would have to get a message to him; otherwise, he'd fly to Sheridan on Sunday. And she wasn't going to be there. She'd all but crawled on her hands and knees getting them to promise to have her results by Monday. She hurried back to the cab and gave him Derek's address.

"Lady, that's in Manhattan."

"You don't know how to get there?"

"Yeah, sure, I know how to get there, but if you want me to take you there, you'll have to pay double. Have to come back empty." He was so cantankerous. He hadn't liked waiting at the lab, nor was he thrilled to search for a phone booth. Now this.

"No, I'll be coming back with you."

His smile was humorless.

Sam tried to take in the sights as they drove along. The highway was surrounded by so many bushes. No vast horizon to be seen here. Kiowas would be quick to pick up stakes. And the traffic! A big culture shock. She had lived in Wyoming too long. This was no different than California; she'd just forgotten.

The traffic allowed her to see the little microcosms of Manhattan culture, which changed every few blocks. She thought about dashing into the corner drugstore and buying a toothbrush while they inched along, but she'd have time after she checked into the hotel back in New Jersey. She wondered how so many people could live in such a confined space.

"Hey, lady. You going to get out or what?"

"This is it?" She looked at the return address on the crumpled letter. "This is it. And it seemed like just yesterday we started."

His eyes were flat.

She stuffed the envelope into her pocket and sprang for the building. The doorman quickly opened the glass door.

"I need to leave a message for Derek Turner. He hasn't been answering his phone."

He gave her a wink and a slanted smile. His voice had more Irish than she supposed was normal. "Well now, lass, let's see if I can raise him." He pointed to a hunter-green love seat sitting against a coral-and-green papered wall. It reminded her of the nursing home, except it smelled as fresh as it looked. "The chair's soft."

"Looks soft." She sat.

He took his time. She guessed he was listening to rings. Perhaps he was a marathon ring counter.

She got up and pointed to her cab. "His meter's running and his fuse is getting mighty short. Maybe I could leave a message?"

He cradled the phone and then ran his fingers through his thin white hair as he squinted at the driver. "Here, then, take this pad and pencil. A message for the lad."

She scribbled and handed back the message with a twenty-dollar bill. "Make sure he gets that by Saturday. And thanks for the kindness."

"I'll see to it, lass," he said with a big slanted

grin. "And thank *you*."

She ran down the steps and was opening the cab door when she felt the hand jerk her arm. She screamed.

"Samantha," Derek said, turning her around, "what are you doing here?"

"You scared the wits out of me." She had a closer look to make sure it *was* Derek. He looked awful. His clothes were rumpled and sweat-stained, his eyes were bloodshot, his hair was greasy, and he hadn't shaved in days. "I came to tell you not to come to Sheridan. I'm not there . . . I'm here."

"But why?" he asked in astonishment.

"Uh-uh." Watching the passersby, she said, "I'll tell you later . . . I'll call." She started to get into the cab.

Derek pulled her back. "I think not." He stuck his head into the cab, still holding tightly to her arm. "She's staying." He took out his wallet.

"But my bag's still at the airport," Sam protested as she pulled away.

"It's twice that, man," said the cabdriver.

Derek paid and sent him on his way.

"But my bag."

"Where is it?" He rubbed his temples as though he had a splitting headache.

"Newark. I'm not going back until Monday. I'll need my things." She noticed the suitcase at his feet.

"Is there really anything in it you need that you can't buy in New York?"

"No, I guess not." *Where have you been?* she wanted to ask.

"We'll call. They'll keep it locked up for you. We'll get it Monday."

Picking up his suitcase with one hand, and taking her by the arm, he led her up the stairs. "And if you're real nice to me, I'll loan you the shirt off my back. Give it to you if you get it bloody."

She looked at the sweat-stained shirt. "A bag lady wouldn't want *that* shirt."

The doorman winked at her. "See you found him."

"Made a new friend, I see," Derek said once they were on the elevator. He dropped his bag with a deadening thud. He was either quite put out with her, or very tired. Probably both. She trained her eyes on the numbers flashing in rapid succession; his were burning through her. She wasn't sure what she would tell him. "Here we are," Derek said as the doors opened.

"I've never known anyone who lived in the stratosphere," she said, taking in the long corridor. Sam was amazed at the apartment's spaciousness. Its gray walls matched the plush gray carpet and shutters. The furniture was chrome and black leather. A splash of color — mainly corals — loomed in the enlarged photos on the walls. His photos, she supposed.

"This is nice," she said, twirling around. So Jeffrey and Derek had something in common — gray carpet.

"I'm glad you approve . . . you paid for it."

The inheritance, he must have meant. "It was the only fair thing to do."

"Now, sit down. Tell me why you're here."

"All right, then you can tell me why you weren't," she countered as she flopped down on the black leather couch.

Derek straddled the chair's arm. "I was called out of town on an assignment."

"Jeffrey Talbot murdered Pamela."

He rubbed his forehead. "Go on."

"You don't seem surprised."

"I'm *very* surprised. But why are you here?"

"So I brought some specimens to a lab in New Jersey."

"Fatigue must be dulling my senses. New Jersey's a bit far from Wyoming."

"I have a friend here."

"So?" He looked so strung out.

"He can do it quicker."

"My journalist's mind needs a little more detail. You've told me the who: fill in the where, when, why, and how."

"Jeffrey told me . . . I've known for months . . . but it didn't register. If it had, Jake and Boomer would be alive."

Derek was beside her. "Samantha, don't do this to yourself."

"Jeffrey told me that she was in the freezer until five in the morning. As the examining pathologist, I didn't know that. The only way he could have known was if he had taken her out."

He leaned his head back.

Sam ran her hand over his muscular shoulder. "When did you sleep last?"

He drew her into his arms. "Is he in jail?"

"Well, actually, no." She pulled away.

"Finish the story."

"I needed evidence." She got up and paced the floor. "I have some samples from the murder victim. So I got some samples from Jeffrey and I brought them east to have them matched."

"You didn't go to the police, did you?"

"Well . . ."

He turned a bloodshot eye to her. "I see. You walked up to an alleged murderer and said, 'Do you mind if I take some blood? I think you may have killed someone and I want to check it out.'" Derek sat up and leaned forward. "Don't you know how dangerous that was?"

"I got the blood by scratching his back. He didn't know." Sam looked out the window to where a tiny boat floated down the Hudson River.

"You scratched his back and he didn't know?" His voice was no longer pleasant. It sounded like John's had that night she went into Chinatown. John never could get it through his thick head that their nurse, Kim, was too distraught after the call about the gang stabbing to go looking for her son alone.

She stepped around him and went down the hall looking the apartment over.

"Why do I get the idea you're purposely avoiding my question?" He reached around her and pulled a door closed.

She stuck her head into the bathroom.

He grabbed her and turned her around. "You had sex with him, didn't you?"

She didn't say anything. She didn't know what to say.

He hit the wall beside her viciously. It was dented, and his hand was reddening and swelling faster than a balloon. He wasn't even holding it.

Both hands were tan; they hadn't been last week. "You would have sex with a murderer," his sharp tone was frightening her, "and keep me at bay . . . the man who loves you?"

She turned her face to the wall. She was more afraid of him than she had been of Jeffrey.

He placed firm, but gentle, hands on her shoulders and turned her around. The hatred had left his face. "I'm sorry. I'm just so tired." He wiped her face with his good hand and kissed her cheek. "It must have been awful for you."

With that, she burst into tears.

"I know," he said, rocking her. "I know."

When he was pretty sure she wasn't coming out, Vito got out of the car and walked across the street to the corner phone booth.

He placed the call to say that he'd found the woman at the airport and was following her. She was a looker, all right, just like they said.

"Good. Just stay with her until I tell you otherwise," the Denver man instructed.

Walking back to the car, Vito remembered

how much he hated this waiting. But it was all just part of the job.

Sam tiptoed through the living room, where an exhausted Derek still slept, and slipped out the door. Wearing yesterday's clothes made her feel dirty, even though she had showered.

The Irish doorman hailed a cab for her. She asked to be taken to Bloomingdale's. She thought that's where the mermaid in *Splash* shopped. She hoped it was. Besides, it was the only name she could come up with. "Macy's."

The bearded driver looked through the rear-view mirror at her. "Macy's, lady?"

"No, Bloomingdale's. I just remembered that Macy's has the Thanksgiving parade."

He shrugged and turned his eyes back to the street's heavy traffic. After a few minutes he asked, "Where're you visiting from?"

Was it so obvious? "Wyoming."

He nodded. "Welcome to the U.S."

"Wyoming is in the United States."

He looked into the mirror. "It's in Canada."

She laced her fingers across her chest the way John did when he lectured. "No, it's not. It's between Montana and Colorado. Our population is over four hundred thousand. We have the very first national park . . . Yellowstone."

He nodded, then sighed a who-am-I-to-care sort of sigh before turning his attention back to the street.

As she was getting out in front of Bloomingdale's, he said, "Stay off the subway."

She gave him a thumbs-up sign as she slammed the door.

"And don't slam the door," he said under his breath.

Bloomingdale's wasn't all that special. It reminded her of the old Denver Dry, where her mother used to drag her every year to buy new school clothes. And that terribly long day when her parents bought furniture.

To amuse themselves, Sharon and she rode the escalator up and down, up and down, when the lace of her oxford shoe got caught. She shook for a week afterward remembering how humiliated she had been when they handed the shredded shoe back to her father. And Sharon, laughing the whole time.

Just as she was about to put her foot on the escalator, she backed away and headed for the elevators.

Jeffrey. Derek wasn't so sure. He had spent two days poring over Mister Perfect's file. Perfect school record all the way back to kindergarten, where he'd bitten a fellow student. Perfect traffic record — something *she* certainly didn't have — not so much as a parking violation. Perfect IRS returns, which he prepared himself. Credit rating perfect. No military info. Jeffrey's birthday was three hundred and twelve in the draft pool. He would reserve judgment until the lab tests were in.

Disappointment and worry unraveled Derek

as he realized Samantha wasn't in the apartment. He threw the pillow he had used onto the bed and picked up hers, lingering over the traces of her scent.

She had insisted on checking into a hotel, but he had dissuaded her by saying he would make up the hideaway in his study. In the end, he had fallen asleep on the couch. It was just as well, the study's walls were covered with candid shots of her. He didn't want her seeing them.

He looked at his watch. He should have placed the call yesterday, but it was inconvenient with company. Derek listened to the benign message and waited for the beep. "Scotty, had a great vacation . . . hunting was good. Birds migrated twenty miles inland from where you promised I'd find them. Expect they'll be that much farther in a week's time."

Derek was pacing the floor by noon, and by one o'clock, he was about ready to start looking for her. Finally, the buzzer sounded and the doorman sent her up.

"I was just going through the yellow pages looking up the addresses of the nearest theaters. Thought you'd gotten Saturday-matinee withdrawal."

A grin broke out on her face. "Today's Friday. Feeling better?"

Derek nodded as he took the packages. "Found Bloomingdale's, I see. How did you like our New York shopping? Did you get mugged more than twice?"

She narrowed her eyes. "The shopping was okay, but it has nothing on California shopping centers. Couldn't even find an Orange Julius."

"Did you buy an evening dress?"

"Only if jeans are now fashionable for evening apparel."

"Do you have that black gown of yours in your suitcase in Newark?"

"Yeah, Derek, take it with me everywhere. That and my bowling ball." She snapped her fingers. "I have to use your phone."

He led her to it. "It's a speakerphone, I'm afraid. Permanently broken," he lied. "There's another in the bedroom, if it's private."

"This is fine." She dialed.

"Dr. Turner's office," came the scratchy female voice.

"Anyone call, Daisy?"

Derek looked in the refrigerator, feigning disinterest.

"The usual — oh, and some doctor from Gillette. Bradshaw, I think he said. You have a noon meeting Tuesday for quality assurance and the nursing home called saying your father has a fever." Daisy told her.

"How high?" she asked, shaking the butts and ashes in the lung ashtray next to the phone.

"Didn't say, but not serious, just wanted you to know."

"What did the doctor want?"

"Didn't say. He'll call back Monday."

"When he calls, tell him it will be Tuesday.

Daisy, please take five dollars out of petty cash and take it to the bowling alley. Tell them to let my team know I'm not going to be there tonight."

"Okay."

"Ask the rent-a-doc if he can stay another day. If not, leave a message on my car at the airport and tell the lab that I'll be in late afternoon."

She turned to Derek. "How do I hang up?"

He switched it off, then took her by the hand. "Don't bother to take off your shoes. We're going shopping."

"Shopping's tiring. Let me at least shower and change into some new clothes."

He followed her down the hall. "Who's this doctor in Gillette? Someone I should be a wee bit jealous of?"

"I don't know a Bradshaw." She ran a flirting finger across his shirt. "I wouldn't be too jealous."

He sensed her hunger as they kissed. It matched his. A series of kisses followed. Fumbling with a button on her shirt was his undoing. His smarting and swollen hand wasn't as sly as it used to be. She broke off and backed away.

"Now why do I need a formal so badly?"

"To go to my mother's birthday party."

She glowered up at him. "Derek, I can't go to your mother's party. I'm the last person she wants to meet."

"True. You may be faced with difficult in-law problems, but they're just going to have to get used to you."

Sam put both hands on her hips. "Derek, in order to have in-law problems, a person needs to be married." Her tone was a mixture of teasing and seriousness. "And I don't remember saying yes."

"One day you will. I'll wear you down until you agree to marry me," he told her as he took her hands from her hips and placed them around his neck.

"You're truly an optimist," she said as he covered her lips with his.

26

"I was humiliated, utterly humiliated," Sam said as they reached the street. "Did you see the gleam in your mother's eyes when Donna made the condescending crack about how unfortunate it is that I pick up slang from all the low-class people I have to come in contact with?"

"It was Renee, and she said, 'to whom you are exposed.'"

Sam clenched her fists, cast her eyes upward, and shrieked.

He gave her the tiniest of shakes. "Now Samantha, settle down. Granted, they were a bit formal, but they *were* polite."

She groaned. "That's the problem. They bent over backwards being polite. It was worse than if they'd been nasty." She pulled away. "I felt like Cinderella with the two wicked stepsisters ripping off my gown as the wicked stepmother looked on."

"Just remember, in their eyes, *you're* the wicked stepmother," Derek said in a feeble attempt to make light of the unfortunate situation.

She wasn't amused. She lifted her skirts and ran out onto the wet pavement of the quiet street.

"What are you doing?"

"Hailing a cab."

He wasn't quite sure how to tell her that their chances were better if they walked to the corner where there was some serious traffic. Before he had a chance, he became abruptly aware of the headlights on the car gunning toward her. Derek raced between the parked cars and jerked her back just as the car zoomed by.

"What happened? That car almost hit me."

Deliberately. Only after the car was well out of sight did Derek free her. "This is New York. Hail your cabs from the curb."

She silently fumed over his mother's birthday party all the way home. Derek was preoccupied anyway, and thankful for the time to think. He was trying to formulate a plan.

Samantha changed her mind about talking as soon as they'd reached his apartment. "Look at this hem. It feels like lead." She picked up the bottom of the water-soaked skirt. "It's ruined."

"Sorry, next time I'll put my coat across the puddles," he said as he helped her out of her coat.

When the bathroom door slammed, Derek picked up the phone and dialed. The bathwater was running; he felt no need to keep his voice low while leaving his message. "Scotty, need to tie up some loose ends on a muddled DIA project. Meet me at the Statue of Liberty tomorrow morning. Treatment same as Jarvis in Geneva."

After hanging up, Derek looked out the window, memorizing the position of the parked cars on the block. Samantha closed the bedroom door about the time he poured a drink. He drained the glass before knocking at her door.

"Yes?"

"May I have my pillow," he called through the door, "or were you planning to slip it under my head again after I'm asleep?" He really should have bent his head to the problem and come up with an original line instead of using the same one as the night before.

"Come in."

He cracked the door. The light filtering from the hall showed her propped up against the headboard, clutching the covers to her bare chest like a schoolgirl in a nunnery. "I could loan you either a Giants or a Mets T-shirt. No 49er's, I'm afraid."

"I'm fine," she said, bunching up the sheet. "Thank you for saving me from that car tonight."

"So it's all right to take it?" He motioned to the pillow.

She bit her lower lip. "No. This is where it belongs . . . and so do you."

He didn't need a second invitation. He tugged at his bowtie as he walked slowly to the bed.

"Aren't you going to turn off the lights?"

The bed sagged under his weight. He leaned over and took off his shoes. Her hands worked nervously at the sheet as she watched him fold his pants over a chair, deposit his shorts and socks in a hamper, turn off the light in the hall, and draw the curtains back to let New York's artificial light shine in. He crawled under the

307

covers and put his head back on the pillow. She curled up beside him and waited.

And waited.

"Derek?"

"Yes?"

"Are you going to sleep?" she asked with a trace of cynicism.

"Trying to."

She nuzzled into his shoulder.

He let her wait.

"You don't want me now?"

"More than ever."

She sat up and looked down at him. "I don't get it."

"A smart woman like you?"

"Is this about Jeffrey? Are you waiting for my apology?"

"This has nothing to do with *Jeffrey.*"

She turned away, her hair flying as she buried her face in the other pillow. He was beginning to think he'd lost and was about to drop off when he finally heard her say, "John's dead."

"And where do I fit in?"

She turned over to face him. "At first every time I looked at you, I saw John. Every time you opened your mouth, I heard John. But now I see and hear only Derek. You're nothing alike. I'll love John always, but there's enough room in my heart for you. You once said John was my past and you are my future. Be my present, too."

He gathered her into his arms. "Every day for the rest of our lives."

27

The taxi ride to Battery Park took no time at all on the empty Sunday-morning streets. Sam didn't know why Derek had been so insistent on showing her the Statue of Liberty; she would have been content to spend the rest of the morning in bed. Even the afternoon. Definitely the evening.

In giddy delight they ran hand in hand to catch the ferry to Liberty Island. She hadn't caught her breath before the boat was away.

"Too bad."

"What's that, Samantha?"

"Too bad he didn't make it."

"Who's that?"

"The man you were staring at."

He brushed his lips against her temple. "He'll catch the next one. Come on. The aft rail isn't as crowded."

She always loved looking out over shimmering water and missed the ocean view she'd left behind in San Francisco, but it was even more special today; she didn't think she could ever be this happy again. Forget the water. She turned around in his arms and rose on her tiptoes to deliver a kiss. It was long and deliberate.

He broke away. "You're an addict."

She reached up and wiped a dew of perspiration from his brow. A muscle under his squinting eyes jumped. "You look tired."

"Guess I'm just one of those people who need more than twenty minutes of sleep a night."

Sam swallowed a grin and pointed to the Statue of Liberty. "Look, isn't she beautiful?" She wrapped her arms around him. "Isn't it all so beautiful?"

"And you thought we had only muggers."

After the ferry docked, they walked with the crowd under the long covered deck leading to the island. Derek seemed preoccupied as they continued down the sidewalk. He didn't even turn to see the back side of the Lady. "Look how straight she stands," Sam said, mostly to herself. "You can just imagine what it was like for an immigrant being welcomed by her."

He gave the statue a casual glance. "Yes, she's quite an impressive old gal."

It was early, and the line into the statue was short. She counted out loud as they climbed the 167 steps along the base wall. She wasn't sure what to make of his pensive mood. Perhaps he was having second thoughts about moving to Sheridan. Last night he'd said it didn't matter to him where he lived as long as she was there, but maybe touring New York City was changing his mind. He pushed her ahead of him when they reached the narrow spiral staircase inside the statue. Or maybe easterners just develop an edge when they're in a crowd.

Climbing the staircase was a slow proposition,

with many of the people ahead of them taking pictures out of the little windows in the crown. The harbor was even more fantastic at this height, she discovered when it was their turn to look out. She hurriedly looked, ever mindful of the people waiting their turn. "That's it?" she asked as they started down the other spiral steps.

"Looks like it."

"Haven't you been here before?"

"No."

"No?" She turned around and looked up at him. "A New Yorker who hasn't visited the Statue of Liberty? Isn't that disrespectful, or un-patriotic or something?"

"I think you'll find it more common than not," Derek said dryly.

She quickened her pace down the deep spiral staircase until she caught up with a man with a boy in tow. "Say, are you from New York?"

"Long Island," the boy answered.

"Is this your first trip to the Statue of Liberty?"

The boy said yes, but the man corrected him. "No, you've been here before, when you were four."

Sam turned her head around and looked up at Derek. "That's one."

She caught someone's eye who passed them going up. "Where are you from?"

"Seattle."

"Have a nice trip," Sam told him.

"Let's stop here and have a look." She pulled

Derek out onto the observatory deck. He unsnapped his camera case and posed her by the rail and clicked off a couple of pictures, embarrassing her. She left him changing rolls of film and continued walking around. There was a tight knot of Japanese tourists clustered on the narrow walkway on the side, and Sam slid around behind them.

They'd fanned out by the time Derek tried to get by. He was a foot taller than anyone in the group, and she watched in amusement as he tried to get them to understand that he wanted by. She hadn't known until then that he spoke some Japanese. Not that it did much good; instead of making a path, they closed ranks around him and each pointed to various landmarks, asking questions. She went on as he put on his tourist-guide cap.

"Oh, good, you did make it." The man stared nervously at Sam, startled at being addressed. "You just missed our ferry. I hope you didn't have to wait long."

He shook his head.

He seemed so uneasy. Easterners just weren't friendly like westerners. "Have you been to the Statue of Liberty before?"

He nodded.

Sam smiled and started off, feeling uncomfortable. She'd talked with several others before she saw Derek. He was turning in circles as if frantically looking for a lost child; that must be her. "There you are, Derek."

He reeled around. The storm cloud on his face was replaced by a relieved smile, then it turned stern. "You frightened me. Where were you?"

She shrugged. "Right here. There are a lot of first-time visitors from New York. I really find that very strange." She cocked her head. "Why were you frightened?"

"This is New York. People don't talk to strangers here." He took her hand.

"Everyone talked to me."

"Come on, let's take the elevator down," Derek said, leading her inside.

Both lines, one to the observatory deck and the other to climb to the crown, were the length of a football field by the time they emerged from the building after going through the Museum of Immigration in the basement.

"We came at the right time. Look at the lines," Sam said.

"Lunch? It's almost noon."

"Why not? A girl doesn't get a chance to eat at the Statue of Liberty every day."

They followed the sidewalk to the building housing the concession stand, rest rooms, and gift shop. Armed with hot dogs and a couple of Cokes, they sat at a reasonably clean table on the veranda.

Sam tore pieces off the bun and tossed them to the gathering birds. Derek looked out over the glistening water in the harbor, seeming preoccupied. Maybe he had decided that last night was a mistake. "Derek, what's wrong?"

He shook his head. "Nothing."

"You're not coming back to Sheridan with me, are you?"

"Oh I'm going to Sheridan, all right."

She breathed easier. "I thought you had changed your mind about me."

"I'm afraid it'll be the other way around." He reached across the table to take her hand. "Remember always that I love you."

"That sounds so . . . I don't know . . . terminal."

She was spouting nonsense. If only this Jeffrey business were behind her; it was making her edgy. She wanted to get back to a routine, one that included Derek. "You've made me the happiest woman in the world."

He squeezed her hand. "We should consider catching the next ferry."

"Yes, a Sunday-afternoon nap seems in order." He didn't even smile. She wished she could say something to pull him from the pit of depression he seemed to have fallen into. "Maybe I should use the rest room before we go." She started away, then turned back. He was reaching for his cigarettes. "And maybe pick up a trinket or two in the gift shop."

He nodded absently.

He had missed his chance on the observation deck. It would have been so easy to push her over the side when she stopped to ask him if he had ever been here before. He just didn't have a

314

chance to think, so surprised that she was talking to him and all. You don't see that very often. And he was taken aback when she said that about missing the ferry. It made him sad in a way. But it was business.

She was alone again. He wasn't foolish enough to do anything in front of her boyfriend, and was happy when she came back inside without him. Vito followed her to the isolated rest rooms, was just about to make his move when a young mother blocked his shot as she raced by with a little boy holding his crotch.

As his mama always said, what happens is meant to be. He would bide his time.

Watching her buy gifts, he realized that the few people in the shop were busily inspecting the merchandise. This was his opportunity.

Sam chastised herself for not making a shopping list. The lab techs, Kate, and Daisy were eight. She took nine Statue of Liberty canvas bags from the display shelf. She'd like to have one herself.

Who else? She rummaged through the Lady Liberty sweatshirts, picking out a large for Jake's nephew and a medium for her father. No, better make it a large, it will be easier to get it on him. If it's too hard, the nurses will leave it in the closet.

After placing her bounty on the corner of the counter, Sam grabbed a handful of sculptured pens. She would give them out to the detail men when they visited bearing trinkets inscribed with the name of their newest drug. She could almost see their faces now. Ol' what's-his-name from Minneapolis won't see the humor in it. He was so strange. It was like pulling teeth getting him to talk, and pulling fingernails getting him to go away.

The clerk was making a mess of the Visa form, and Sam was about to rip it out of her hands and fill it out herself when she felt a sharp burning pain between her shoulder blades. She'd been shot, she realized just as blackness engulfed her.

He watched her collapse. Someone raced to her side and broke her fall. Blood oozed around his fingers as he eased her body to the floor. "Call an ambulance," the man yelled.

Another man came out of the crowd and knelt beside the body. He checked her carotid artery, then took one of the sweatshirts heaped on the floor and covered her face.

His job was finished.

The morning's blue sky and blue water had become steel gray in the blustering afternoon. The symmetry wasn't lost on Derek. He stood at the water's edge while the two attendants pushed the gurney through the crowd and lifted it onto the official boat. The black body bag and the chorus of uniformed officials attracted more attention than the Lady. The crowd had no way of knowing that the black bag signified more than

Samantha's death; his dreams for tomorrow were in the bag as well.

He pitched his cigarette into the harbor and headed for the ferry.

28

The morning of the memorial service was warm, though windy. Derek hadn't realized until the moment Sharon stepped out of the limousine, her gray skirt swirling in the wind, that she and Samantha were twins. Identical twins. No wonder their father didn't know which one was taking him to the movies. Identical twins, except that Sharon wore makeup to the hilt and her hair was a sleek, collar-length style; Sharon was fashion-conscious. Judging from an outfit that would have made his mother envious, Derek suspected Sam's father was right about the husband being a successful lawyer. He'd have to be.

From the gasps of the mourners around him, he wasn't the only one who hadn't known. He watched her climb the concrete steps to the Presbyterian church, clinging desperately to a man's arm. The lawyer husband, no doubt.

"Did you know they were twins?"

Jeffrey shook his head.

"Her father made the point that they didn't have the same birth date. I thought it just the rattlings of a senile man."

"One was probably born before midnight and the other after."

"Presumably." Derek shook free a Camel.

"What time am I supposed to turn myself in?"

Derek drew deeply on the cigarette as he torched it. "The attorney general's office thought he was driving up. After lunch seems as good a time as any."

"Lunch." Jeffrey laughed emptily. "I'm sure I'll eat heartily."

"I can understand about Pamela, but the second was premeditated."

Jeffrey nodded. "It just snowballed, an avalanche."

Derek could have said the same thing about Samantha's memorial service, though he had found the copycat killer because of it. Daisy had put everything in motion. He simply asked her who told her of Samantha's death, and then it all came together. He took another drag, then pitched his cigarette. "Shall we join the other honorary pallbearers?"

The sanctuary was packed to capacity, just as it had been for Karen's funeral. Daisy had made the right decision in choosing the church over the mortuary chapel.

Derek took his place in the front pew between Jeffrey and Bob. He leaned back in order to see around Ken, who was on the other side of Bob, and stared across the aisle at Sharon. He would miss Samantha always. The music stopped, cuing the minister. The man rose and walked to the pulpit.

The man next to him probably agreed with the minister when he spoke of the better place where Samantha was called, but wished for nothingness after the grave, which was surely better than an eternity of punishment. Derek felt him claw at his collar, the stifling sanctuary and guilt choking him.

Derek hadn't heard what the minister said, but it caused Sharon to start crying uncontrollably. He watched the tears flow in a steady stream down her cheeks. She even cried like Samantha. And like Samantha, she didn't have a hanky.

Something made Sharon jump up and turn around. Derek heard the gasping noises erupt from the congregation, but he didn't look around to see what had caused the disruption, instead he looked at the man beside him. Color drained from his face.

Samantha was halfway down the aisle before Derek turned and caught sight of her dressed all in black. He'd never sensed her flair for the dramatic. The murmuring turned to silence, even as Sharon ran toward her. It was time for reckoning, not reunions, so Samantha pushed her aside with whispered words and continued down the aisle. She took off her veil and ran angry fingers through her hair. "You can't imagine how it felt to walk in here and find so many friends. But as you can see, to borrow from Mark Twain, 'The reports of my death have been greatly exaggerated.' "

Her eyes locked on Derek's. They had spoken over the phone, but he hadn't seen her since the incident at the Statue of Liberty; Sam had made it clear that she never wanted to see him again as long as she lived. But she did make him explain over and over how they had staged her death using a dartgun filled with a quick-acting tranquilizer. She never did quite believe that the car incident outside his mother's house was no accident. Nor did she believe, until Scotty took her to police headquarters and let her observe the interrogation, that the criminal Jeffrey had a personal vendetta against and on whom he kept an updated file, had really been hired to kill her. What Derek couldn't understand was why Samantha had been so irrationally upset that the packet of fake blood Scotty broke over her back when he took out the dart had left a stain on her blouse.

"But since you are all here, perhaps you would like to know why I was in New York." She bent over and gave Jeffrey an icy kiss. "I believe I promised to deliver that in person," she said in a careful monotone. "I would have been back earlier this week and saved you all this, especially you, Sharon, but things didn't work out like I had planned."

Samantha let the computer printout unfold like a runaway accordion. "This is a DNA fingerprinting." It collapsed on the floor when she let go. "As it turned out, we didn't need it. Jeffrey Talbot had all the answers."

She slapped her veil on Derek's lap as she looked steadily at Jeffrey. "Frederick Wilson didn't kill Pamela Duncan, did he, Jeffrey?"

"No."

"Who did, Jeffrey?"

Jeffrey sighed. "Bob Wallace, Junior."

Murmurs crescendoed to a symphonic pitch. Samantha held up her hand to silence the crowd. Derek restrained Bob as he started to panic; he could hear Betty Wallace's cries of denial from somewhere in the back.

"How do you know, Jeffrey?" Samantha went on.

"He came to me that next morning. He said it was an accident."

"It *was* an accident," Bob injected heatedly. "You knew how it happened. Nothing you liked better than telling us about your little escapades with Pamela."

"So I dated her. At least *I* wasn't married."

Derek questioned the wisdom of sitting between them. The church had grown very still. No one was about to miss a word.

"You're the prosecutor, Jeffrey. Why did you become an accessory, *Jeffrey?*"

"Accessory after the fact. I explained to Bob that the most he could have been charged with was involuntary manslaughter and that I'd see to it that he received a suspended sentence. But that wasn't good enough for Bob. He was concerned about what it would do to his practice, his standing in the community. His family was here. It would ruin them all. I could appreciate that. My career with the Denver D.A.'s office was stolen from me over something nowhere near as serious."

"We'd rather hear about Bob, if you'd be so kind, Jeffrey."

"Halloween was less than a week away." He shrugged. "It just seemed the perfect solution."

"Perfect? What about Karen? Did Frederick Wilson murder her?"

"No. Bob killed her, too. She'd figured it out and was going to turn Bob in."

"And you didn't do anything even then?"

"I was in too deep by then, as he," Jeffrey looked contemptuously over at Bob, "was so eager to remind me."

"And what of my little mishap in New York?"

"I knew nothing about it. Bob apparently broke into my office and stole a file I kept on a certain felon in Denver."

Bill marched up the aisle, Skip a step behind. "What's the meaning of all this, Sam? I'm the chief here."

"Well, chalk up another one to your sterling record, Mr. Chief of Police."

"I liked you better when you were dead," Bill mumbled.

Derek slipped out the door.

On the steps outside, he tapped out a cigarette. Scotty torched it with his Bic.

"It took you long enough." Derek exhaled. "Thought you were coming in last night. This charade has been out of control from the beginning."

"We came in a couple of hours ago, but she wanted to see who would come to her funeral.

Even made us take her out to her ranch so she could change."

"A touch of black humor." Derek smiled for the first time in days. "Somehow I knew it was her doing."

"She's," Scotty cleared his throat, "a little strong-willed."

"A little?" Derek tapped his cigarette, sending a trail of ashes to the ground. The knot in his stomach became a noose. His deception had hanged any chance he might have had with her.

"She hates cops, Derek."

"That's putting it mildly."

"And she was furious that you involved her sister."

Derek blew a cloud of smoke into the sky. "Her secretary involved the sister. I didn't have a thing to do with it."

"I tried to tell her that. Her reply was, 'He didn't stop her.' "

"What should I have said? 'Let's not bother to tell her that her sister's dead?' Why didn't she call her sister from New York if she was so concerned?"

Scotty shrugged. "Come on, the plane's waiting."

There wasn't any reason to stay. Jeffrey would explain it to the attorney general. Especially how he talked Frederick Wilson into plea-bargaining so there would be no trial. He couldn't afford to have it come out that Wilson was out of town visiting his mother at Christmas. The irony was that

Frederick hadn't cut Karen's hair at all. She'd cut it herself several days earlier.

He believed Jeffrey about going to Bob when the report on Jake's shooting crossed his desk. Bob lied, saying he didn't shoot him, that it must have been over poaching, and Jeffrey foolishly believed him. Perhaps he just needed to believe.

Derek shouldn't have allowed himself to get mixed up in any of this. He was sent to investigate the Fourth of July murder. The Defense Intelligence Agency was satisfied that Lisa Henderson was a random victim of Frederick Wilson, and that her murder had absolutely nothing to do with the treason case. He wished he'd left it at that.

He pitched his cigarette. It was over.

Epilogue

Sam sat on her patio listening to the sluggish flow of the late-summer creek. She picked up the magazine and looked at the pictures once more. He had lied even about that, saying the fall pictures had been ruined. She had read Derek's article so many times that she could recite it from memory. And the pictures were etched in her mind.

She had been surprised to get the copy of the magazine containing her story, assuming that the assignment was just part of the cover. Derek was some sort of a spy or something, here because of Lisa Henderson's death; pumping her for information, all the time pretending he was interested in her buffalo ranch. She had more respect for that imbecilic G-man who kept coming out from Washington. At least she finally understood why Lisa had no memorabilia.

Sam turned her attention back to the magazine. Sighing as she looked at Curly's pictures. She missed him. She bit her lip as she thought about all the useless killing that had surrounded her this past year. Boomer was gone. Karen — she should have picked up on the black stocking; it was different from the ones Fredrick had used. Pamela, the four other women, the Woods family. As Sam watched The Little One and

Jeffrey's pup sniffing around the buffalo, she decided she even missed Jeffrey. He was spending time behind bars. Not the kind of time Bob would be spending once his trial was over. She missed her Saturday movies; her father had withered away to skin and bones. The one person who would rejoice in death lingered helplessly on. The only glimmer of hope was in Jake's slow recovery. Jake's nephew, Emil, was helping out at the ranch, but he wasn't Jake.

She passed a hand over the slick paper to Derek's name, noting with disgust that her hand wasn't as steady as she would have liked.

The employees of G.K. Hall hope you have enjoyed this Large Print book. All our Large Print titles are designed for easy reading, and all our books are made to last. Other G.K. Hall books are available at your library, through selected bookstores, or directly from us.

For information about titles, please call:

(800) 257-5157

To share your comments, please write:

Publisher
G.K. Hall & Co.
P.O. Box 159
Thorndike, ME 04986